How I Came to Sparkle Again

ALSO BY KAYA McLAREN

Church of the Dog

On the Divinity of Second Chances

How I Came to Sparkle Again

A NOVEL

Kaya McLaren

ST. MARTIN'S PRESS NEW YORK

This is a work of fiction. All of the characters, organizations, and events portrayed in this novel are either products of the author's imagination or are used fictitiously.

Printed in the United States of America. For information, address St. Martin's Press, 175 Fifth Avenue, New York, N.Y. 10010.

www.stmartins.com

ISBN 978-1-250-01387-3 (hardcover)
ISBN 978-1-250-01703-1 (e-book)

First Edition: October 2012

10 9 8 7 6 5 4 3 2 1

To Jen, Randy, Ben, and Jody, for the best winter of my life

Acknowledgments

Thank you, Soul Sister Ranger Andee Hansen, for turning me onto tele skiing at a low point in my life and shouting, "Beautiful!" at me every time I fired off a decent turn. It brought me back to life.

I'd like to acknowledge Jen Reed, my soul sister and ski partner, and my ski brothers: Ben Whitting, Jody Wilson, and Randy Fox. They all took me under their wings, helped me ski better, and in doing so, cultivate some sparkly mojo. My friendships with them are what made me want to write a book about what good friends on snow can do for a person's spirit. Skiing Wolf Creek with them is the closest I've ever been to heaven. You guys gave me the best winter of my life.

Big thanks to John "Remy" Rimelspach at Crystal Mountain, for letting me hang out in his snow cat and listen to all his outrageous and hilarious stories. Let's remember that this book is a work of fiction and of course Remy would never do anything illegal or out of compliance with company policy. Remy would also like everyone to know that he is NOT a womanizer. I repeat: Remy is NOT a womanizer.

Thanks to my ski patrol sources: John Reed from Wolf Creek, and Elaine Marquez, Lisa Ponchlet, Alicia Sullivan, and Ron Lnenicka from Crystal Mountain. All of these people were incredibly generous with their time and patient with my questions.

Thanks Jan Covey, for being another ski culture and mountain life consultant and for taking me along to the Dirtbag Ball.

Thank you, Bobbi at Between the Covers in Telluride, Colorado, for helping me with the snow reports.

Thank you J. Wes Huesser II, attorney at law in the great state of Texas, for generously sharing your counsel on the legal aspects of the story. If I lived in Texas and had a dirtbag husband I needed to unload, I'd hire Wes to be my divorce attorney any day.

Thank you, Tess Haddon, for your expertise on OB/GYN nursing, for sharing your stories, and your heart. Thank you also, Sasha Hull Ormand, for nurse practitioner info. It needs to be said that nurses are earth angels.

So are EMS fire fighters. Thank you to those of them in my life who told me stories that just broke my heart: John Jensen Jr., Matt Laas, and Kent Huntington. Thanks to Kent's wife and my second cousin, Kathy Huntington, for more insight as well. Thank you, Mike Hamilton, for giving it a final read.

Thank you to Leanne Webster, for sharing your experiences with growing up LDS and breaking away from it. I need to add that one of my most cherished friends is Mormon and I have never felt judged by her. I was worried that this book would offend her and asked her about it, and she said, no, it wouldn't offend her because she's not like the mother in this book. It wasn't my intention to insult or offend; it was only my intention to illustrate how difficult relationships are when one person makes judgments about the worthiness of another person's soul.

Thanks to all the men in my life for their insight into the male psyche: my dad, my brother, Remy, and Randy Porch, Ben Witting, Travis Judd, Jordan Krug, Michael Kidder, Scott

Smith, and Mike Rolfs. Thanks for tolerating my uncomfortable questions, and trying your best to answer them.

Thanks, of course, to my agents at J.R.A, Meg Ruley and Christina Hogrebe, for their inspiration, counsel, laughter, and encouragement, and for making my dreams come true. Whenever I picture them, I always imagine them in really pretty fairy godmother costumes. They're sparkly like that.

Big thanks to Kendra Harpster and Elizabeth Day, for the time and talent they put into earlier drafts of this story. I love you both and deeply appreciate all you've done for me in my career.

Finally, thank you, thank you, thank you Jen Enderlin, for loving this book so much, for your passion and your clarity. You are a brilliant editor and I feel incredibly lucky to work with you.

How I Came to Sparkle Again

prologue

Austin, Texas

It was fair to say Jill Anthony's first day back at work had been a disaster—so much so, in fact, that her supervisor had sent her home early. She just wasn't ready to be back. Enough time had not passed.

She was still crying when, just four blocks from her house, her car died. *Perfect,* she thought. *Just perfect.* She shook her head in disbelief and then got out of the car. Usually she changed into street clothes before leaving work, but because she had left quickly today, she now found herself walking down the street in stork scrubs that looked a lot like pajamas. The combination of the scrubs and the crying left her feeling like quite a spectacle, exposed and vulnerable as she made her way home on foot through her affluent neighborhood.

She approached her big, beautiful Bavarian-style brick-and-timber house with relief, despite the fact that it recently had held so much grief and sadness. It was still her sanctuary.

She crossed the street and paused where the path to her house met the sidewalk. There, she opened her mailbox and pulled out a handful of envelopes. At the top of the stack was an envelope with handwriting on it—an actual personal letter! It was from her old best friend, Lisa, and postmarked Sparkle, Colorado.

Sparkle—it was home to her mother's brother, Howard, who had taken her in during a difficult time in her teen years. How long had it been since she'd been back for a visit? She tried to figure it out, but could figure out only that it had been well over a decade.

As Jill walked from the mailbox up the path toward the door, she counted down the eighteen steps she knew it took to get there. The embarrassing weepy walk in scrubs would be over in five steps, four steps, three, two, and one. She put her key in the lock, eager to get inside, turned it, and opened the door. She stepped in, shut the door behind her, and exhaled. It was over. She was home safe.

Then she heard them. Noises. It sounded as though two people had broken into her home and were having sex. Jill reached in her purse for her phone to call the police, but then she heard David's distinctive moans.

It couldn't be, she thought. It couldn't be David—her David, who had held her hand in the hospital during her complicated miscarriage just six weeks before. It couldn't be her David, who had said wedding vows to her and bought this house for the family they would have. It couldn't be.

A terrible doubt propelled her. She had to see. She had to see it for herself.

Creeping up the stairs with her phone, she rested her hand on her abdomen, still tender and loose even after six weeks. At the top of the stairs, she walked slowly and silently in her soft nurse's shoes past the closed door of the baby's room. They had found it easier to keep the door closed until they were ready to decide whether to adopt or change it back into a guest bedroom.

She walked a little farther, stopping right outside the bedroom door, then peeked around the corner of the open door and saw long dark hair falling down the back of a voluptuous woman who was straddling her husband in their bed. Jill pulled back in horror. It was true. How could it be true? Even as that new level of shock began to wash over her, disbelief still reigned. She noticed the cell phone still in her hand and knew that she would need a picture of this to help her through future moments of disbelief and denial. She peeked around the corner again. At least one of her husband's hands groped the woman's breasts as she bounced wildly on him.

"Fuck, yeah. Fuck, yeah!" he cried out.

Jill couldn't see his eyes, but she saw the very top of his head, his curly brown hair cut short and the places at his temples where his hairline had begun to recede dramatically.

She reached out with her phone and pressed a button, then pulled back to her place around the corner and looked at the picture she just took. It was undeniably real.

Slowly she began to absorb the parameters of her new reality. It stung her eyes and pierced her heart to its core. She tried to decide what to do, whether to confront him in the act, but she couldn't think over the loud voice in her head repeating over and over: *Run.*

As she clambered back down the stairs and opened the door, she made no effort to be quiet.

She walked the four blocks back to the Lexus, called a wrecker, and waited for it under a tree in a nearby yard.

When the wrecker finally arrived, the driver misinterpreted the horrified expression on her blotchy face and said, "It's going to be okay, ma'am. It's probably just your alternator. We can fix that. We can fix anything. So the real question remains whether every problem is worth fixing. The answer to that is no." Jill thought he bore a striking resemblance to Willie Nelson and contemplated how what he said applied to her marriage. Just as she was coming close to reaching a conclusion, the driver said, "The Lexus is a nice car. It's still worth a lot. When a car has that much value, it's always worth fixing."

She contemplated that too as he pulled into the shop. But maybe her marriage wasn't a Lexus. Maybe it was a Pinto—one of those cars famous for blowing up when rear-ended. As she waited for the mechanics to fix her car, she walked out the back door to the wrecking yard and through the aisles of totaled cars and pickups, vehicles that other people had decided weren't worth fixing. She felt just like them. She felt like that Buick with the driver's-side door so crushed that the driver was undoubtedly hurt, but from the look of the other side, the passenger likely skated through unscathed. She felt like the Saturn with the shattered windshield through which no one could see what lay ahead. It looked as if it had been sandwiched in a multicar pileup. Jill knew exactly how it felt to crash into one thing and then get smashed from behind. She studied the Saturn and wondered whether it would have been salvageable if it had only been rear-ended instead of sandwiched, and she wondered if the same was true about her marriage.

The late afternoon air turned a little cold around the edges, so Jill walked back to the waiting area. She sat in a vinyl chair, stared straight ahead, and waited. She thought ridiculous thoughts, like wondering whether all the food she bought for Thanksgiving would go to waste or whether David would try to make something out of it, and if so, whether he knew when to put the turkey in the refrigerator to defrost. She pictured herself running away from David with her frozen turkey, pecans, and cranberries.

Still, over the din of all these thoughts, one thought dominated: *Run*.

Run.

"Ma'am?" the man at the counter asked.

Jill looked up.

He was Hispanic, with soulful eyes, and he wore a crucifix around his neck. Jill noticed his wedding ring and wondered if he had ever cheated on his wife. Sure, he looked like an unlikely candidate, but she'd thought David was an unlikely candidate, too. How could anyone tell?

"You need a new alternator and I can't get one today. I'll have to do it first thing tomorrow morning. Can you call someone to pick you up?"

Run, she thought, *run*. But she just nodded and walked out.

So that is the verdict, she thought—salvageable, but not immediately.

When she reached the road, she looked both ways and wondered what to do. She was not going to call David, so she decided to walk west because it was late in the day and that's where the sun was. But she had no idea where she was going.

A quarter mile down the road, she walked by a used-car lot. A Mitsubishi Montero for two thousand dollars caught her eye. She could sleep in that car. She could drive away from here. She could just put it on her credit card. *Do it,* the voice inside her said. *Run.*

Figuring that she had twenty-four hours before David could report her as a missing person, she thought about where she could go. She could drive from Austin to the Gulf. She could go to Mexico. She ruled out visiting family right away. Even if her parents weren't on a Mormon mission in Africa, their home in Midland, Texas, would be the last place she would want to go.

Oh, her parents. Their response to her miscarriage had been an e-mail that read:

Dear Jill,

Your father and I are so sorry for your loss. Our hearts go out to you. The pain of losing a child is unbearable. We know, because it's what we felt when you told us you were leaving the Church. We lost you to the world, lost you from our eternal family, and that is a spiritual death. We hope you see this as an opportunity to return to the Lord's fold, and that you find comfort and hope in God's Plan of Salvation that will so graciously allow you to reunite with your child in the afterlife if only you live the Gospel principles. We pray for you to find your way back now that you know the pain of being separated from your child, now that you know the pain we feel being spiritually separated from you, much like the pain of damnation. Please don't inflict this pain on us or on yourself. We want to be with you and your child as a complete family for all eternity in the Celestial Kingdom. I cry myself to sleep every night just thinking about the possibility that your choices will prevent that when faith could have saved you. I know with every fiber of my being that the teachings of Joseph Smith are true. Please read the Book of Mormon again and

meditate on it. You too will know it in your heart to be true. Please soften your heart and return to Heavenly Father.
Love, Mom

They meant well. They did. But they never failed to make a bad situation worse.

Jill glanced down at her Chanel bag, a gift from David last Christmas, at the envelope from Lisa sticking out of it. She took it out and read it.

Hey Girl—
How goes it? I had a supremely delightful summer doing the Ranger thing at Glacier N.P. Made some nice turns on my birthday. Gotta figure any August first I'm making turns is pretty much better than any other August first. I met a tasty little morsel I call Ranger Mark. Of course it's doomed but it was a fun ride—literally. Great to be back in my own house—that is, if you can call it that with this crazy never-ending renovation going on and all the riffraff coming and going all the time. So what's the deal with you staying away so long? I miss you! Come back and visit! My guest room has no walls, but I've got a couch and a steady supply of carpenters that don't work on powder days. Level five eye candy. Just sayin'. I still can't believe that you, regional skiing medalist, moved back to freakin' Texas. What in the blue flaming hell? And by hell, of course I do mean Texas. Put down the butter-based foods and the hairspray and come home, girl. Sparkle misses you. You've got to miss it too. I mean, seriously, I know those hospital elevators are fast and everything, and sure, that might be fun for a while, but come on, it's no Southback or Horseshoe Bowl. You know you want to make some sweet turns with your old friend Lisa. You know you do. I know it's

hard for you to get time off, and I know your husband hates the cold and snow (how does anyone hate snow?), but ditch your job and your husband and just come home.
Love, Lisa

If there were signs, surely this was one.

Sparkle, Colorado

Cassie Jones sat up in bed to flip her pillow. Her tears had drenched the side she'd been lying on. The end of one of her long blond braids stuck to her cheek. She didn't cry during the day, but her tears often slipped out during sad dreams. Between her brows, worry lines furrowed much too deep for a ten-year-old's face. Instead of lying back down, she petted Socks, her gray cat, and then reached for her mom's fuzzy white bathrobe at the foot of her bed. She had given it to her mom for Christmas the year before. She wrapped it around herself and walked to her windowsill. The robe was much too large and dragged on the floor behind her.

On the windowsill sat a couple dozen heart-shaped rocks that she and her mother had found together throughout the years. She picked up the big blue one and held it close to her heart and closed her eyes for a moment. Then she exchanged the blue one for a white one with shiny black flecks. She turned it around and around, looking for the side that had looked like a heart when her mother had spotted it. It was the last one they found together. They had been sitting next to the river last spring, watching the high water rush by.

"Look at that," her mother had said. "Look at how bright the sparkles are today."

They'd watched the sunlight glisten on the tumbling water. Her mother was right. The sparkles did seem brighter than usual. Cassie had watched for a moment longer and then asked the question that she hadn't been able to get out of her head since March: "Mom, are you going to die?"

Her mother had taken a deep breath and let it out slowly. "Oh, Cassie, everyone dies."

Cassie had swallowed hard and blinked a few times when she'd looked in her mother's eyes and seen something that looked like an apology. *Maybe this is the answer mothers give when they simply don't know,* she had thought.

"Look," her mother had said, and leaned forward to pick up the white heart-shaped rock with the shiny black flecks. Cassie had smiled and put it in her pocket.

Now, back in her dark bedroom, Cassie put the rock on the windowsill. She returned to her bedside table and picked up her small flashlight, turned it on, and pointed it to three more heart-shaped rocks on her bureau. Each one she had found along the river as she'd walked near the low and lazy water of summer, talking to her mother as if she'd been right next to her, telling her how she missed her and trying to think of something to say that would make her mother feel okay about being in heaven. She didn't want her mother to worry in heaven.

In her own mind, Cassie had heard her mother say, *Look down,* each time. She was unsure if she was simply remembering her mother say it. But each time, she had squatted down, surprised and then not so surprised to find a heart shape among so many rocks. Each time, she'd closed her eyes and said, "Thanks, Mom."

She put down the flashlight, scooped up all three rocks just to feel their weight in her hands, and then decided to take them back to bed with her. Outside, snow fell, covering up all the heart-shaped rocks until at least April or May. She took off the robe and spread it with the outside facing up over her bottom sheet and pillow. Then, with the rocks still cupped in her hands, she crawled into bed on top of the robe, where she could almost imagine she was snuggled up on her mother's lap.

"Sometimes you just endure," she had heard her father say on the phone a couple of months ago. She guessed he was talking to her grandmother, his mother. It had become Cassie's mantra. *Sometimes you just wait for the night to be over and endure.*

Heartbreak settled in Jill's chest. It felt like so many things. Panic. Heaviness. A giant hole. Constriction. It felt like all of these things at once. It felt like being shot, like lying on the ground while life leaked out of her. She could hardly breathe.

Her wheels hummed on the highway. The heater cranked full blast, but still her car seemed cold. A dusting of powder snow blew across the pavement in waves.

Above her, the stars shone much more brightly than they did in the lower elevations. The heavens seemed so much vaster.

She tried breathing in for four counts, breathing in all the stars, all the expansiveness, all the possibilities, and then breathing out for four counts. In and out, in and out, mile after mile. It took all her concentration just to breathe.

Sometimes she cried. Sometimes she was simply in shock.

She wanted to pull over, lie down in the frigid prairie, and die.

In the hospital, every day she saw people whose lives seemed to have taken an irreparable turn. Some, against all odds, bounced back, slowly rebuilding. And she saw others whose prognosis was hopeless, who somehow kept fighting anyway. What was it, she wondered, that made some people give up and others fight harder? Where was her fight? She was out. She was out of will.

Still, she had the good sense to stall a little longer before deciding to lie in a cold field and wait for her ruined life to be over. She turned her thoughts to Uncle Howard and Lisa, instead, and kept on driving. They loved her, and they had saved her before. Surely they could again—as long as she could get herself to Sparkle. She kept telling herself that—that if she could only get to Sparkle before this heartbreak killed her, she would be okay. Uncle Howard and Lisa would make sure she was okay.

chapter one

• • •

SNOW REPORT FOR NOVEMBER 17

Current temperature: 29F, high of 33F at 3 P.M., low of 22F at 4 A.M.
Clear skies, winds out of the southwest at 10 mph.
25" mid-mountain, 33" at the summit. 1" new in the last 24 hours. 6" of new in the last 48.

Cassie and her babysitter, Nancy, sat silently at the table eating Lean Cuisine cheese cannelloni frozen dinners. Nancy's breathing bothered Cassie, even though she knew Nancy couldn't help having sinus problems. Cassie just didn't want to listen to it. It reminded her of her mother's last two weeks, when her breathing had become so difficult. To make it worse, Nancy was sitting at her mother's place at the table.

Cassie looked up at Nancy, wishing she weren't there—not in her mother's place at the table or in her mother's place as her caregiver.

"Do you need something, Cassie?" Nancy asked.

"Don't sit there anymore," Cassie said.

Nancy looked startled and slowly stood. "Where would you like me to sit?" she asked gently.

Cassie looked at her father's place at the table. "There," she said. "He's the one you're replacing."

She looked back down at her cheese cannelloni while Nancy moved. The mere smell of it made her stomach turn. Of all the frozen dinners, it was the least offensive, but it was offensive nonetheless. She'd never eaten out of cardboard during the ten years of her life that her mother was alive, and she feared that if she kept eating Lean Cuisine, she would become as weak and fat as Nancy. She stared at her food and wondered if any of it really mattered.

All of her Olympic dreams were going down the tubes anyway. She hadn't even joined ski team this year. When she skied, she felt sad now, so deeply sad that she just wanted lie down in the snow and fall asleep.

She looked down at her dinner again and wanted to throw it, but she couldn't rally enough will even for that. She simply said, "I hate this crap," got up, walked up the stairs to her room, and locked herself inside.

From her room, Cassie could hear the sound of Nancy's regular evening routine—the lid of the stainless-steel garbage can opening and closing as she threw away the cardboard trays, the spring in the dishwasher door creaking as she opened it to put in the forks, the sound of running water and the microwave beeping two and a half minutes later. Finally, Cassie heard the questions and buzzers on *Jeopardy!* and occasionally Nancy's voice when she shouted out the few answers that she knew. As usual, the TV stayed on for the duration of the night, and the noise, combined with Nancy's snoring, drowned out the sound of Cassie's sobs during or after her nightmares.

Mike Jones wanted to believe that Kate's soul was eternal, but he wasn't sure if a person could believe in that without believing in God. Believing in God wasn't so easy. Five hours ago, he was on a call for a woman who drove off a steep embankment and miraculously was okay. She gave full credit to God. And now he was here, at this accident, a head-on collision between a semitruck and a family in a minivan. Both parents and one child were dead. The other child appeared to have a punctured lung and probably internal bleeding. She was barely hanging on. With a dying little girl in the back of his aid car who would wake up without her family if she made it at all, he couldn't help wondering where God was this time.

It made no sense to him, this idea that some people got God and some people didn't. There were those who had told him that we could not know the intention behind God's plan for us—that we had to trust that we were in good hands and that maybe as our lives unfolded, we would see how something was for the best. And then there were the others who believed everything was a test, that God tried to protect us from the bad things, but sometimes Satan won and that Satan tried to do things to diminish our faith in God. Mike glanced back as he drove on and listened to John and Ben continuing to work to stabilize the girl. He did not see how the outcome of this accident would ever be for the best. And he did not see Satan, either. He saw only misfortune—human error and misfortune. It brought him the most peace to simply believe that people were imperfect, and life was imperfect, and sometimes bad things just happened. And if you were lucky, emergency services would show up in time to give you a second chance at life.

He thought about all the times he'd saved someone's life and the person had attributed this miracle to God. Part of him was always tempted to make a joke of it, something like *No, that was my hand stopping the bleeding* or *No, God didn't send me; the trucker with the cell phone did.* Why, he wondered, was it so hard to see humankind as capable of creating miracles? Miracles were just second chances if you really thought about it—second chances when all hope was lost.

But maybe he had it all wrong. Maybe there was more to it than that.

Eight months ago, the day before he'd found out about Kate's cancer, he went on a call that he thought about from time to time. A man had lost control of his car on the ice going down a long hill and plowed right into the back of another car. The front of his car was crushed, and his foot was caught on the gas pedal somehow. He said he saw flames creep out of the hood of the car and thought he was a goner. Then he noticed two identical tall, Nordic-looking men, one on the side of the road to his right and the other walking over to his door. Flames were now licking into the car around the edges of the fire wall. The twin on the side of the road disappeared, while the other opened his door, freed his foot, lifted him out of the car, and set him down on the side of the road. When a state patrol officer arrived shortly after, the man told him about the twins, wanting to thank the one who saved his life. The officer told him there was no one else at the scene besides the people in the car in front of him, and no one in the car in front had seen anybody. As Mike had driven him to the hospital to be checked, the man tried to understand how no one else could have seen them. He wondered out loud if they were angels.

The next day when Kate's doctor told Mike and her about the cancer, he wondered whether the man in the car accident and his angel story were sent to him to give him faith, faith that something would protect and strengthen his wife throughout her battle, that something would lovingly take her home when she died. He wanted to believe it. He did. But as time had gone on and he and his daughter, Cassie, witnessed unbearable and seemingly unending suffering, he couldn't help wondering about the God that would not grant a miracle then. He saw no divinity in all that suffering. He saw no divinity in God taking his daughter's mother. He saw no divinity in any of it. But he did see divinity in the outpouring of support for his family from the community.

So at the end of the day, here was what Mike was able to believe in: people. It was people and their kindness that made him feel blessed. It was people who were the heroes, and people who were generous, and people who comforted one another.

And he believed in nature, in survival instincts, in the way living things will cling to every last shred of life and fight for it. He believed in a cell's ability to multiply and repair even the most heinous injuries. He believed in life.

And just as he thought that, the girl in the back of the aid car flatlined despite all their efforts. And while he was glad she wouldn't be waking up in severe pain in the hospital without her parents and her brother, he was not glad she was dead. He wondered again where God was now, but truly he did not want to hear anyone make up a story to try to explain. He did not want to hear any more explanations, anyone else grasping to make sense of things that didn't make sense. He wished more people would just admit they didn't know.

He was glad that it wouldn't be up to him to notify the family's relatives. It had been only four months since Kate died, and he found it extremely difficult to deal with other people's grief while he dealt with his own. And even though he did not believe in God, he hoped the mourners did. He hoped they had some story they told themselves that would comfort them and would get them through such a huge loss, a story that would help them get out of bed in the morning when the weight of their loss would pin them down.

John and Ben were quiet in the back. What they all knew well was this: Life was fragile. And sometimes it was unspeakably sad.

Two blocks down the street from Mike and Cassie's house, Lisa Carlucci pretended to be asleep as Cody quietly dressed next to the bed. She didn't take it personally that he was sneaking out. She understood. She'd done it herself. And truthfully, she was relieved. She didn't want to have to look at him in the light of day and see how much this hadn't meant to him. It was bad enough to have seen it in the dark. She wasn't mad at him, though. She had chosen this situation knowing full well what it was and what it wasn't.

She felt discomfort in her core, a feeling that was hard to name, but something like anger and something like emptiness. She waited to hear Cody descend the stairs, no doubt bristling with fear that he would wake her every time a stair squeaked. She actually smiled just thinking of his inner terror. She listened to the front door open and then close. Only then did she open her eyes. She was thankful that he shut the door quietly because she didn't want any of the guys next door to look out and see him leave. For that same reason, she was also thankful he had arrived on foot and left the same way.

A shaft of light fell through a crack in the curtains and landed on a bronze crucifix near her door. It had been her great-grandfather's.

She hadn't gone to confession in years, but suddenly she believed it might feel good. She thought about what she would say and realized it wasn't the actual sex she felt was the great sin. It was the fact that she had lost faith. She had lost faith that God had a better plan for her when it came to love, and as a result, she had settled. She needed to repent for treating her body as if it were a cheap motel instead of a temple.

She crawled out of bed, paused near the door, made the sign of the cross, kissed her hand and gently touched the crucifix, and said a prayer pledging a faith forgotten, pledging change. She walked to the bathroom and paused to look at herself in the full-length mirror. She wrapped her arms around herself and said aloud, "What am I doing? This isn't a Holiday Inn." Although she was sleepy and wanted to return to her warm bed, she didn't like smelling like Cody and sex. So instead of going back to bed, she took a hot shower.

She emerged from the shower wondering what God's better plan might look like, because truthfully, she didn't want to get married. Women who got married got screwed. She saw it all the time. It wasn't just that she wanted the freedom to pull the cord when it got bad without having to go through an expensive divorce and possibly losing her house. She never wanted to be that dependent in the first place. And if she had to wait for marriage to have sex with integrity, she would never have sex again. That wasn't going to work, either. There had to be a way to have a healthy sex life, integrity, and maybe even love, and remain a sovereign person.

Lisa returned to her bed and contemplated her musky sheets but decided it was too big a task to change them in the middle of the night. Instead, she put on flannel pajamas to protect her clean body. But before she crawled back in, she sat for a moment on the edge of her bed and peeked out the window at the trailer next door, hoping to verify that all of her buddies had been asleep and hadn't seen Cody leave.

The Kennel was their name for this trailer and all its crazy additions built on. It got its name from its one-to-one human-to-dog ratio. Hans had a candle lit in his window. So did Tom, which was how they let one another and any other potential visitors know that they were "entertaining."

When she was in seventh grade and Tom was in eighth, his friend had approached her between classes and said, "Tom wants to know if you want to go with him."

"Go with him where?" she'd asked.

"You know, just go with him. Be his girlfriend," his friend had explained.

Lisa had shrugged. "I guess that would be all right," she'd said, somewhat indifferent.

But later that night, she imagined him holding her hand, imagined slow dancing with him at the next school dance, and even kissed her pillow, imagining it was him. By the next morning, she was downright mad for him. She took extra time doing her hair. She picked out her clothes carefully. And, pleased with the fruits of her efforts, she went to school feeling excited. She had attracted an older boyfriend—a really cool older boyfriend.

She casually walked to her locker, keeping her eye out for him, a little disappointed that he hadn't waited for her somewhere nearby. She thought he would hold her hand as he walked her to homeroom. That, near as she could figure, was what going together involved. Finally she gave up, took her books for her first two classes and her folder out of her locker, and started walking. When she had almost reached her class, she saw Tom holding Deanna Smith's hand. He even gave her a little peck on the lips before they parted. Deanna went into the classroom next to Lisa's. Tom looked up and for a split second noticed Lisa. She saw fear and shame wash over him as he quickly walked in the other direction, avoiding her.

He avoided her for the next three years, until he was a junior and she was a sophomore. He asked her to watch him in the basketball game and then go to the dance with him afterward. And she told him to suck it. Of course that, not what happened in junior high, was what Tom told people when asked how long he and Lisa had been friends. When Tom told the story, it was funny, and he always ended it by saying, "And that was the beginning of a long and beautiful friendship, my only real friendship with a woman, because it was the only one I was powerless to screw up." Lisa, however, didn't tell either story. She pretended she didn't remember.

On Lisa's nightstand sat two photographs in frames, facedown. One was of her parents, and the other was of her grandparents. She always turned them over when she had a guy over. Now she reached over and carefully set them back up. As she looked into her mother's eyes, she wondered whether being a wife had been worth it overall. She wondered what her mother might have given up to take that path, what other dreams she might have had, wondered how she reconciled staying with a man who had been unfaithful, wondered whether he still was. And then she wondered how her mother might have fared from a life like hers, from a lifetime of being unloved in that particular way, a lifetime of agreeing to be disrespected by men with intimacy issues who would never ask her to sacrifice her freedom, a lifetime of bad choices and freedom. Was it really freedom? On one hand, yes. If she felt like going somewhere, she went somewhere. If she felt like eating ice cream for dinner, she ate ice cream for dinner. If she felt like buying new ski boots, she bought new ski boots. She didn't have to run anything by anyone. She loved that. But there was another way in which it didn't feel so free.

She looked at her grandmother's face and wondered how

sad it would make her to know that not only was she no one's wife, she dated men who wouldn't even call her their girlfriend, men she didn't want to call her boyfriend. Maybe friends with benefits. But did they even qualify as friends? Not really. Fuck buddies. She nodded slightly. Yep, that's what she was. That was her title. Fuck buddy. Free—overall, yes. But respectable? No, not really. She felt shame looking at her grandparents' faces knowing they had wanted more than this for her. They had wanted her to be valued and to think enough of herself to demand that.

"It was the price of freedom," she whispered to the photograph. "Don't judge me," knowing full well it wasn't her grandparents who were judging her. The scent of Cody haunted her and inflamed her shame. She got out of bed, stripped off the sheets, and walked down the hall to the linen closet for new ones.

chapter two

• • •

SNOW REPORT FOR NOVEMBER 18

Current temperature: 28F, high of 34F at 3 P.M., low of 20F at 4 A.M.
Clear skies, winds out of the southwest at 15 mph.
35" at the base, 51" at the summit. 0" new in the last 24 hours.
1" of new in the last 48.

Jill drove through the night and into the morning. The vast prairie finally gave way to the rise of the Rockies. The white bark of the mostly bare aspens glowed in the low November sun. As the road slipped between two large mountains, Jill finally felt safe, as if she had been running from something and had just ducked around a corner.

She ascended higher and higher until she was among the snow-covered peaks, finally making it to the turnoff for the town of Sparkle. A mountain everyone called Big Daddy separated the little town from the main highway, and as she drove around it, she looked for tracks down the waterfall area. There were three sets down an impossibly steep and narrow chute. *Crazy,* she thought.

She crept higher on the windy road, all the way to the sign welcoming her to Sparkle, elevation 8,896 feet, population

1,284. Behind the historic little mining town towered Sparkle Mountain, covered in snow and striped with ski runs. People that looked like little dots traversed down.

Even though technically Midland was her hometown and Austin was her home, she found herself thinking, *I'm home. I made it home.* She inhaled deeply and exhaled slowly.

To her left, two women, one in a fur coat and the other in large fur boots, walked into an art gallery. They were clearly guests at the historic lodge near the base of the mountain. Just beyond them, a man wearing ski pants patched with duct tape walked into the drugstore. He was a local. She smiled in spite of her circumstances, having forgotten how comical the polarity of Sparkle could be.

She crept past the three blocks of brick buildings in the historic downtown to see what had changed and what had stayed the same. There were several new cafés and bakeries. Woodall's Hardware, Dick's Barber Shop, and the Gold Pan Bar were still there. The brick downtown gave way to another two blocks of businesses in colorful old mining houses before Main Street became residential.

She drove past the little red house that Uncle Howard had rented for them during the two years that she had lived with him here. She had been so frail and thin when she'd first showed up. Uncle Howard had convinced her mom that if Jill moved to Sparkle, she would get interested in skiing and be motivated to eat. The truth was, he understood she needed to be away from her parents in order to feel good enough. Now, here she was again.

After she went off to college, Uncle Howard had moved back into his studio apartment under the lodge at the top of Sparkle Mountain. He was like a hermit or a sage up there, but one who measured the new snow, read the thermometer and wind gauge, made judgments about avalanche danger, and called it all in to be part of the day's snow report. A short walk away from his apartment was a door that led to the generator room under the lift shack at the top of the Summit Chair, and inside were several shelves of carefully selected books, a table, and two chairs. Uncle Howard was both famous and notorious for this library. She wondered what he would pluck off his shelf and expect her to read this time. He prescribed books for people the way doctors prescribed medicine, and his equivalent of all-purpose aspirin was *Siddhartha*.

Jill needed sleep. There was no place for her to sleep in his studio and no place to sleep in his library, so she continued on to Lisa's house. At least Lisa had a couch to offer.

She turned up the next block and stopped in front of the yellow Victorian where Lisa had grown up. Her father had been the head chef and manager of the fancy Italian restaurant at the Sparkle Lodge, but after he died a couple years ago, Lisa's mother moved to Florida and sold the house to her. It hadn't changed much, though the aspens in the yard had grown significantly. Next door, the old trailer Lisa always found to be such an eyesore looked to be in even greater disrepair, with even more additions built onto it, and an even greater number of vehicles parked in the front yard.

Before she got out of the car, Jill took her phone out of her purse and opened it. A long list of missed calls from David popped up. Jill's twenty-four hours of not being a missing person were surely almost up, but she still didn't want to talk to him. He had sent texts as well. She read the last one:

> I'm calling the police now. The bank called to report some unusual credit card activity, so I canceled them. Someone used your card to buy a car! I'm so worried that you were

mugged and abducted or killed. Please, Jill, if you get this message, please let me know you're alive.

She wasn't sure what to do. She figured if the police were going to be involved, she'd better set the record straight. She hit reply and texted, "The Lexus died. It's in the shop. They should have called you yesterday. I bought the car with our credit card. I wasn't mugged. I'm alive. I just needed to leave."

She looked through her purse and found $48.43 in cash. She took her now worthless cards out of her wallet. There was no way to get replacements. Replacements could be sent only to her billing address. She wasn't sure how she was going to work this problem. She would figure something out. For now, she called her supervisor at work and asked that her last paycheck be sent to Lisa's in Colorado. It would have only three-quarters of a day's worth of wages on it, but every penny counted now.

She took a big breath, stepped out of her car, and walked up the little sidewalk to Lisa's porch. The sun had melted the sidewalk, thank goodness, because she had no boots—just her nurse's shoes. A little clothesline stretched between two porch posts, and on it hung an unlikely combination of ugly gray wool socks and lacy thongs, all black except for one, which was magenta. She hesitated for a moment and peeked through the window in Lisa's door. Walls were missing. Clothes were strewn all over furniture. It was dark. She wasn't sure if Lisa was still sleeping or if she had already left for the day. She knocked quietly.

Lisa woke up and for a moment wondered if Cody had returned, if he realized he wanted something more, if he had an epiphany about intimacy and his feelings for her. Immediately, she realized that was stupid girl thinking.

She got out of bed, descended the stairs, and approached the door. Slowly she began to recognize the face through her window. It was Jill. A small smile started on Lisa's face and then turned to concern as she looked more closely. She opened the door.

Jill smiled uncomfortably. "Hey, girl," she said as she held up Lisa's letter. "I just drove out of hell."

"You look like shit," Lisa said tenderly, and gave her a big hug. She kept one arm around Jill and guided her in. "You came to the right place. I know just what you need."

Lisa guided Jill past the gutted walls, explaining, "Yeah, I kind of ran out of money before the remodel was finished. Pardon the ugly chaos."

Together, they walked into the kitchen. Since Jill had seen it last, Lisa had painted the ceiling turquoise and the walls yellow. A few pots of Christmas cactus with bright red buds ready to bloom sat on top of the cupboards.

Jill sat on a stool at the counter while Lisa reached in the fridge and brought out some celery stalks, which she washed, cut, and put on a little plate in front of Jill.

"So, what's up, girl?" Lisa asked. She could guess; she'd never had a good feeling about David. "I mean, you're dressed a little oddly for a trip to Colorado."

"I . . . um . . . lost the baby six weeks ago."

"Oh," Lisa said, feeling the air leak out of her. "Oh, Jilly." She crossed the kitchen to hug her old friend. "Oh, Jilly, I'm so, so sorry," she said without letting go.

"And then yesterday, I found this," she continued, and pulled out her camera phone. Lisa looked at the display. "You remember David. I don't know who that is."

Lisa studied the picture and then looked back at Jill. In an attempt to hide the full level of her disgust, she simply shook her head and put the kettle on for tea. "So what did you do?"

"I just snuck off. I couldn't deal with it. I couldn't deal with explanations or apologies. That wasn't something he could explain. That wasn't something he could just apologize for." Jill took another deep breath. "I've been thinking maybe the best thing for both of us is to just let go and let each other start a new life."

Lisa remembered overhearing her grandmother telling her mom that men were weak animals when it came to resisting temptation and that indiscretions must be forgiven—they were not uncommon. At the time, her mother had been sobbing. Although Lisa couldn't remember exactly how old she was, she was old enough to vow never to sign on for that kind of suffering by getting married.

She walked behind Jill, put her arms around her, and said, "I love you."

Jill put her hands on Lisa's arms and shut her eyes. "Please help me," she whispered. "I don't know what to do now."

"Of course, Jilly Bean," Lisa assured her, and rocked her in her arms.

Jill opened her eyes and noticed a faded newspaper picture on the wall of the two of them, arms up, facing each other, jumping victoriously after some race their senior year, jubilant. "I can't imagine ever feeling like that girl again," she said, and pointed to it.

"No," Lisa said. "But you won't always feel this bad, either. The good times don't last and the bad times don't last."

"You've been hanging out with Uncle Howard," Jill said.

Lisa laughed a little. "Hey, listen, I've got to go teach the next generation of Olympians how not to fall down. We'll figure out your life when I get home from work. Take a nap. You need sleep. Don't worry. It's going to be okay."

Jill followed Lisa back into the living room, where she pulled out the ancient hide-a-bed and then climbed the now exposed staircase to the linen closet for bedding. They made the bed together, and Jill crawled in. Lisa kissed her on the forehead.

"Thanks, Lisa," Jill said.

"Everything's going to be okay," Lisa assured her again, and then walked out the door.

When Jill woke from her nap, she found her uncle Howard sitting in the rocking chair on Lisa's porch. She opened the door and he stood. "I heard you were back," he said.

Jill looked up at him, at his gentle face, at the red Norwegian sweater he had been wearing for the last twenty years, and at the hat with the pom-pom on top that he'd picked up in Whistler sometime in the mid 1980s. His ever-present backpack sat at his feet. Aside from looking a little older, he hadn't changed at all, and something about looking at him made Jill feel she'd made it to safety. She burst into tears.

"Hey," he said as he put his arms around her. "Hey, now. It's going to be okay. You're here now."

Jill tried to tell him that she had lost the baby and that her husband was cheating on her, but all the sounds that came out of her were indecipherable.

"I know," Uncle Howard said. "Lisa told me the story. I'm sorry." He hugged her a little longer, until her sobs quieted, and then said, "Let's go inside. I have something to make you strong."

They walked into Lisa's house and sat at the counter. Uncle Howard opened his backpack and took out a package of wild Alaskan smoked salmon. "To give you strength, determination, the ability to make it past any obstacle, and to affirm your homing device," he said.

Uncle Howard believed that people ingested the energy from food as well as the nutrients. He had been a world-class mountain climber in the 1970s and had come across many cultures in his travels. Their belief systems had all blended into Uncle Howard's unique set of truths.

Next, he pulled out some Jarlsberg cheese. "From Norway," he explained. "Norwegians are unstoppable. I suspect this cheese is their secret to health and longevity." Finally, he pulled out a whole-grain baguette. "Made here, in Sparkle, by Mari Wallace, yoga teacher extraordinaire. May it fill you with her sense of peace and her playful spirit." He took a little cutting board out of his backpack as well as a pocketknife and began to slice the cheese.

They tore off pieces of bread and fish and assembled them with the cheese slices. As Jill ate hers, she thought of all of Uncle Howard's good wishes. "Thank you," she said.

"Are you drinking enough water?" Uncle Howard asked.

Jill shook her head.

"That's the best way to get the energy and the strength of Sparkle back into you." He stood, found a glass, and poured some tap water for Jill. "Plus, you can't think clearly if you're dehydrated."

Jill smiled and drank the water.

"More?" he asked.

"No, thanks." Guilt washed over her. "I'm sorry I didn't come to visit all these years. It just was so hard to step out of daily life . . . my work, David's work, building a life there in Austin. I never wanted to go to my parents' house for Christmas, so on those rare years I didn't have to work that day, we always went back east to visit his. I feel bad that I didn't assert with him just how much you meant to me, how you were the dad I wished I had. But you know, I didn't really want to bring him here. Isn't that funny? I just knew he didn't belong here. And it felt disloyal to go anywhere without him. I realize now that was stupid."

"You know, Jill, the beauty of the uncle-niece relationship is overlooked in our cultural paradigm." With Uncle Howard, she often had to ignore his words and just look at his expression to understand what he was trying to say. He was trying to say he forgave her. "And, you know, it's not like I ever made it to Austin. I don't know where all those years went."

"You sent me a nice postcard from time to time, though. I always meant to answer, but it seemed I was always in a rush to work or to the store or to home. I feel bad about that." She had kept all of his cards, each with a brief philosophical message written on it.

He smiled sweetly. "Hear from my sister lately?"

"Mom wrote a few weeks ago to tell me she knows how it feels to lose a child because when I left the Church it was a spiritual death to her and that she cries herself to sleep every night because I won't be with them in heaven."

He winced. "The good old Mormon Church, bringing comfort to the masses. I'm sorry," he said, shaking his head. "It wasn't easy, you know, for us growing up. Your grandpa was a raging alcoholic. Your mom found that church because she wanted to spare you our experience. If you can, see her in the light of compassion. See her for her good intentions, for her resolve not to repeat the pattern. If that doesn't work, see her for the bruised little girl she was. Just don't for a minute let any part of you question your worth in God's eyes."

"It's hard, you know, not to wonder what I did to deserve this," Jill said.

"You didn't do anything, Jill. You're a good person. Don't question that. Clear it. If you can, just believe that relationship served its purpose for a time, and then you outgrew it, so the universe helped move you out of there so you could authentically live the next chapter of your life."

Jill knew she was supposed to be comforted, but the prospect of starting a brand-new chapter of her life terrified her. "Oh, my God, Uncle Howard, what am I going to do now?"

"Well, you're going to stay here. You're going to get strong. And then, when your mind is as empty as your glass, you'll know what to do."

Jill nodded, ate her last two bites, and wondered what the odds were of her mind ever being empty enough for Uncle Howard's level of clarity.

Uncle Howard packed up the rest of his food, his cutting board, and his pocketknife, looked at his watch, and said, "I have to get back up on the mountain to get ready for the storm that's coming in tonight. But I'm just a phone call away if you need anything."

Jill saw him to the door and gave him a hug. "I love you, Uncle Howard," she said. "You're my rock."

"I love you, too. I'll find you tomorrow," he replied.

Lisa remembered making Jill toasted cheese sandwiches back in the day, not long after she first arrived in Sparkle years ago. Jill was the skinniest girl Lisa had ever seen, and not in a good way at all. After four months and a hundred toasted cheese sandwiches, Jill started to look somewhat normal, and being Italian, Lisa found that satisfying. Now, they resumed their old spots, Jill on the stool at the counter and Lisa in the kitchen slicing cheese. It was comforting.

"So I was thinking," Lisa began, but a knock on the back door interrupted them, and without waiting for Lisa to answer, Eric and Hans stormed through the kitchen to the living room.

"Don't mind us," said Eric, the shorter of the two. He was by no means short—only in comparison with Hans, who was nearly six feet eight. Both had brown hair and mischievous smiles.

Hans went straight for the DVD player. "For my birthday, Eric got me some tasty new snow porn."

"It's possible Hans was under the influence last night and wondered what would come on TV if he put a Kraft Single in our DVD player," Eric explained.

Hans corrected him. "No, dude. That was you. You thought it would reveal the secrets of plastic."

"Eric, Hans, meet Jill," Lisa said. "Jill, these are my trashy neighbors—"

"Hey! I resemble that!" Eric interrupted. Then he extended a hand to Jill and said, "Pleased to meet you," in his most charming way.

"That's Slick Eric, and the birthday boy is Hans."

They flashed Jill sexy smiles.

"You actually used to babysit Hans," Lisa said. "Remember the Sorenson kid?"

"Oh, yeah," Jill replied, and smiled.

"My penis has grown since then," Hans said.

"Super," Jill replied.

"Eric is the head honcho of the cat crew. Hans drives cat,

too. They groom slopes all night, but sometimes ski with us in the morning before they go home to get their beauty sleep. They live in the ugly trailer next door and got into this habit last year when they didn't have their own TV," Lisa explained.

"Not true," Eric said. "We had a TV. We just liked yours better."

"Size matters," added Hans.

"Why aren't you at work?" Lisa asked them.

"Big storm predicted, so we're all pulling the late-late shift," Eric said.

"Big storm . . .' " Hans said with a big smile, and rubbed his hands together.

Then Hans and Eric turned and walked into the living room. From the kitchen, Jill and Lisa could hear the music from their movie.

Lisa took out two cans of Health Valley soup and poured them into a pan. "Sorry. It's not Campbell's like we used to eat. Your uncle Howard caught me buying Campbell's and made me switch brands," she said. "Something about angry chickens."

"Yeah, you can't be eating angry, conventionally raised chickens." Jill laughed. "What were you thinking?"

Just as Lisa put the sandwich on a plate in front of Jill, Jill's phone beeped once. Jill picked it up and checked the text message. "Listen to this: 'Jill, I don't understand why you left. I see from Visa that you've purchased gasoline from here to Colorado. Please come home, Jill. Talk to me.' "

"Oh, poor David," Lisa said, dripping with sarcasm. "He doesn't understand why you left."

Jill hit a few buttons and said, "There. I just sent him the picture. That should help clear it up for him. Hey, what's your

P.O. box? I'm going to ask him to send me a box of my stuff and some money."

"One thirty-eight. Tell him to be generous."

"I smell melted cheese!" Hans called out from the other room.

"Woman, where's my supper?" Eric shouted.

"Eat shit, you guys!" Lisa shouted back. Although she shouted it in jest, her chest felt lighter, as if a pressure valve had just released some of the anger she was feeling toward Jill's husband. She turned her attention back toward Jill. "So, I've been thinking about some of your choices," she said as she poured the soup into two bowls.

"I need to work. The bank notified David of unusual account activity, so, thinking my wallet had been stolen by the person who must have kidnapped me, he canceled the card and changed our account information. I've got a little less than fifty dollars to live on while that gets straightened out, if it does."

"So, how about a winter working on the mountain? Ski patrol?"

"You have to walk on water to get that job," Jill said.

"Usually," Lisa replied. "But a spot just opened up."

"Well, my body still feels weak from everything it's been through. I couldn't do the skiing part for a while, but I'm definitely capable of wrapping knees and handing out bags of ice."

Lisa walked over to the kitchen window and looked out. "Tom, the patrol director, lives with Slick Eric and Hans over there in the Kennel. . . ."

"The Kennel?"

"One-to-one human-to-dog ratio," Lisa explained. "Promise me you'll never go there." She could just imagine Tom or Eric smelling Jill's weakness and preying on it.

"Twist my arm," Jill replied.

"You remember Tom? He was a senior when we were juniors? Blond hair . . . sort of looked like Shaggy on *Scooby-Doo* . . . ?"

Jill nodded. "Oh, yeah, we looked for his tongue once when he thought he bit it off during a big wipeout, remember?"

"Oh, yeah." Lisa laughed and poured herself a glass of water.

Just then, Hans walked into the kitchen on his way to the bathroom.

Lisa blocked the doorway. "Oh no, you don't, sprinkler system. Go pee all over your own bathroom floor," she said.

"Um, I don't know what you're talking about," Hans replied.

"Seriously, the small lake you left in there last time—the lake so large I needed swim fins to cross it? Never again, pal. Go piss at your own house."

Hans walked out the back door.

Lisa picked up the phone and dialed. "Tom Cat. Lisa. Do you copy? We've got a twenty-six in my kitchen. Over." Then she hung up. "Watch this," she said.

Lisa and Jill both looked out the window as Tom bolted out of the trailer in flip-flops, long underwear, a parka, and a hat, followed by Stout, his German shepherd, and ran to Lisa's back door, which she opened so he could run in without breaking stride.

Jill sat on a stool rubbing her neck, which had been bothering her since she woke up on the pullout couch. Lisa greeted him by saying, "Twenty-six seconds. Excellent. Hence the name." Then she turned to Jill. "Twenty-six is code for hot chick."

Tom faked an expression of disbelief and looked at Jill.

"She's lying. It's code for neck injury. Good call, Lisa. It's always good to be on the safe side. Clearly she needs help." He moved behind Jill and began to massage her neck.

Good God, Lisa thought. *He wastes no time.*

Stout turned circles on the mat next to the back door, lay down, and began to snore loudly. "Thomas, this is Jill, Howard's niece. Remember her? She helped you look for your tongue that time you thought you bit it off. She raced with me."

"Oh yeah!" He turned Jill's stool gently to look at her. "I remember you!"

Lisa continued, "Well, you remember she used to be a pretty decent skier. She hasn't skied in years—long story—and she recently had surgery, but she is a nurse. Could you stick her in the first-aid room? If she was there, the rest of you could get in extra turns. . . ."

Tom appeared to consider Lisa's proposal and finally spoke. "Sure. I'm down a man. Travis is still in intensive care."

Lisa explained, "He was doing some avalanche control work at the top of Super Bowl. He was ski cutting—you know, where they ski across the slope to start a slide? And anyway, he went down with it. Jason was with him, right?"

"Yeah, Jason dug him out while I got the sled, and then we got him down to the base where he could be airlifted. There was still some hangfire, so it was too sketchy to airlift him from the site."

Jill looked confused.

"Hangfire is snow that's left in place at the top of the slide path," Lisa explained.

"Very unstable," Tom added.

"Any updates on him?" Lisa asked.

"Just that he's stable now," Tom answered. He turned to Jill and said, "Yeah, he didn't get completely buried. His skis popped off. But he got slammed into a rock. Broken ribs, punctured lung, compound fracture of his femur, fractured pelvis. So sure, you're hired. Meet me at the FAR—the first-aid room—tomorrow at one."

"Thanks," Jill said.

Tom turned to Lisa. "Hey, are we all on for the usual Thanksgiving plan? Same time, same place?"

"We want turkey!" Eric shouted from the next room.

"Turkey!" Hans chimed in, too.

"Same time, same place," Lisa answered.

"How's your neck now?" Tom asked Jill.

"Better," Jill admitted.

But Lisa was cautious. "Jill, whatever you do, do not look directly into the snake charmers' eyes. Tom, Hans, and Slick Eric have long philosophical discussions about who went home with the biggest boobs at the bar the night before."

"Lisa," Tom said with offense, "honestly, these vicious lies really hurt." For a moment, Jill believed him.

"Oh?" Lisa began. "Vicious lies?" She opened the door to the broom closet. On the inside of the door hung game boards for Candy Land and Chutes and Ladders that had been there ever since Lisa could remember. "Look, Jill, Exhibit A of our arrested development. We've been playing this game for how long now?" she asked Tom.

"Since I moved in about fifteen years ago," Tom answered. He turned to Jill and explained further, "I was running low on funds and Lisa took pity on me and was feeding me. The trade-off was that I had to listen to her stories about all these guys who had a better shot at her than me. I was having trouble keeping all of Lisa's suitors straight, so she dug her childhood games out of a closet to accommodate my inclination toward being more of a visual learner."

"Shall we catch up, Tom Cat? Here is Ranger Mark." She pointed to a picture of Ranger Mark's face that she had cut out of a photograph, peeled it off the board, moved him to the final destination of Candy Land, and stuck him back on the board with gummy tack. "Mark got a whole lot of shugga in Candy Land this summer. Mmm! And Medium Dan called yesterday. Move one." She pinched another face off the starting point on the board and moved him to the first spot.

"Medium Dan?" Tom asked.

"Yeah. Remember how I dated Big Dan and Little Danny? So this one is just Medium Dan. Don't ever let him know I call him that." Then she moved a face back to the starting line and off to the side. "This is Good Randy. He blabbed to all his friends about sleeping with me last spring. He's out. And Bad Randy massaged my shoulders in the hot pool last week. He has very nice hands. Move ahead one. And here's you. You haven't even got off the starting line." She left Cody at the starting line, thinking it best to just keep that a secret.

She knew how to play the part. She knew how to make light of it all, how to make it sound as if her love life was full of fabulous possibilities. But it wasn't. Every single man on her Candy Land board was limited in some very basic ways.

Tom walked over to the closet door next. Tom never took photographs of any of the women in his life. It led women to believe they were way more important or more permanent than they really were, he said. So rather than cutouts of actual people (with the exception of Lisa), his Chutes and Ladders game was covered with faces cut out of magazines that represented real women in his life. Usually, the real woman and the celebrity had the same first name, but occasionally he picked a celebrity that resembled the real woman. He had also cut out a bed from a Sleep Country advertisement and affixed it to his finish line. Twenty-five or thirty faces were stuck on or below the bed. Several waited at the starting line. His board spoke volumes about the quantity of women in his life and his complete lack of ability to have any kind of true intimacy. Lisa hoped Jill saw it for the damning piece of evidence it was.

As Tom unstuck a face and walked her up a ladder, he said, "Jen wants me to meet her family." He picked up another face and walked her up a ladder, too. "Jan wants to know where we're going with—you know—*us,*" he said with exaggerated hand motions gesturing back and forth, imitating Jan. "Angie told me I was lookin' good." He moved a picture of Angelina Jolie forward one. "Sarah's ape ex-boyfriend threatened to kick my ass if he saw me within a quarter-mile radius of her." He moved another picture up a ladder. "And a girl with big boobs I met at the bar slept with me last night." He moved one of the starting-line Pamela Andersons to his bed and stuck a cutout picture of a beer next to her. "Linda. Or Tracy. Stacy. No, Tracy. It was Tracy, I'm pretty sure."

"Good God, Tom Cat," Lisa said, "you're such a mimbo. Hey, I'm sure Jill will be able to help you identify any unusual genital rashes you may develop this year, too. Bonus."

Jill shook her head and rubbed her eyes. "No."

Lisa shut the closet door, happy not to look at her game board anymore. A part of her wanted to rip it off the door violently and throw it across the room or, better yet, out the back door, but the bigger part of her didn't want that kind of attention, didn't want to explain. Maybe she would just quietly take her game board down at some point.

"All right," Tom said. "I'm out. Jill, it was a pleasure. See you at the FAR tomorrow at one. I'll orient you."

"Take her out for some turns tomorrow!" Eric shouted from

the other room. "National Weather Service says ten inches possible tonight!"

Lisa's face lit up. "Yeah!" she shouted.

Tom turned to Lisa and said, "Lisa baby, I've got your ten inches tonight."

"Noted," she said, and rolled her eyes.

"Well, my offer stands," Tom said. "All right, everybody, I'm out." Stout woke up when Tom opened the door and trotted behind Tom as he jogged back to the trailer.

"Hey, girl, thanks for lining me up with a job like that," Jill said. "I mean, I know I can't stay in Sparkle and hide forever, but it feels so good to stay here and hide for a while,"

"Mm," Lisa replied, watching Tom and thinking of the candle lit in his window last night. What was that feeling in her gut? Contempt? Jealousy? It couldn't be jealousy. She would never want to be that girl. And "girl" was undoubtedly the operative word. Finally she snapped out of it and said, "This is going to be the best winter you've had since you were twenty."

chapter three

• • •

SNOW REPORT FOR NOVEMBER 22

Current temperature: 28, high of 31F at 3 P.M., low of 22F at 4 A.M.
Clear skies, winds out of the southwest at 15 mph with gusts of up to 20 mph.
28" mid-mountain, 35" at the summit. 0" new in the last 24 hours.
4" of new in the last 48.

The day before Thanksgiving, Cassie and Mr. Nelson sat in silence across his desk from each other in the counseling office at her school. His blond hair was graying, and he looked tired. His body was turned sideways, and he had one leg crossed over the other. One elbow rested on the table for a moment as he took his glasses off, rubbed his eyebrows, and put them back on. Cassie didn't think he was particularly smart, but she did think he was big-hearted. Some kids said he was an alcoholic, which made Cassie wonder if he simply didn't know what to say to her, or whether he was wishing he had a drink.

"So, Cassie, your teacher asked me to talk to you about this." He pushed a paper across the desk to her.

Cassie didn't touch the paper or even look at it. She knew what it was. It was her Thanksgiving essay. The topic was, of course, "What I Am Thankful For." Across the top, she had written the heading with her name and date, and then the title, as Mrs. Campbell asked them to for all of their assignments. Under the title, she had simply written, "ARE YOU KIDDING ME?" in capital letters, underlined twice.

Mr. Nelson looked at her and waited for her to say something.

Cassie hoped he wouldn't back her into a corner. She liked him and didn't want to unleash all of her anger, but she was prepared to. *He can't make me apologize,* she thought. *He can't make me do anything.*

"How about your dad? Are you thankful for your dad?" Mr. Nelson asked.

Should I have to be thankful for my dad? Cassie wondered. She looked sour and said nothing.

"How about your health? Aren't you thankful for that?" Mr. Nelson asked again.

She didn't really care. Now that she didn't have enough will to race, her health didn't really matter to her anymore. *God, don't let him talk about all the kids less fortunate than me,* she thought. *I don't care. I've got my own problems.*

Mr. Nelson changed his approach and reached for a picture of his father and him in hip waders and fishing vests, both holding up large trout. He handed it to her. "That is my dad. He died two years ago. I miss him like crazy. Whenever I catch a big fish, I wish he was there to see it."

Cassie looked at the picture and softened. Then she looked up at the sadness in Mr. Nelson's eyes and handed it back.

He looked at it again and smiled a heartbroken smile. "When we were together, I felt peaceful, like he just understood everything."

Cassie listened sympathetically, but still, she did not speak.

She couldn't find the words even if she wanted to. She looked at the other pictures behind his desk—family, dogs, and more fish.

"Well, listen. It's normal to be angry after a loss, and if you ever want to talk, I'm here. In the meantime, try to remember that your teacher cares about you and so does everybody else. We might not always know what to do or say to support you while you're hurting this much, but we care, and we want to help." Mr. Nelson looked sad.

Cassie took that as her cue to leave.

The clock said 2:57, so she didn't go back to class. Instead, she went directly to the lobby of the school and waited with the kindergartners, who were always dismissed a little before the bell so they could find their parents or get the front seats on the bus without all the chaos. They filed by Cassie, holding little paper turkeys made from tracing their hands on brown construction paper. Cassie imagined the kids giving their mothers the turkeys and their mothers fussing over them and enthusiastically hanging them on the refrigerator or in a window. *You have no idea how lucky you are,* Cassie wanted to tell each of them, but she didn't. She quietly walked out the door and headed home.

When she got there, the house was silent. Socks trotted partway down the stairs to greet her. Cassie tiptoed up the stairs to the door of her parents' bedroom. Her dad was sleeping, as he often did after a twenty-four-hour shift with a lot of calls. On the floor by his bed was a basket of laundry. Cassie recognized a few items of her mother's in the basket. He did that. He put some of Kate's old clothes in the laundry when he did a load. She didn't know why.

Cassie went to her own room, crawled into her unmade bed, and clung to her mom's bathrobe. Socks jumped up on the bed and joined her. Cassie closed her eyes and felt the fuzzy fabric on her cheek, breathed in her mother, and let herself fall asleep. Sometimes, she found, it was just easier not to be awake.

Cassie and Mike woke in the early evening and watched a sitcom neither of them particularly liked while Mike fried up pork chops and potatoes and warmed some peas in a pan on the stove. Sometimes it was nice just to have noise in the house without the pressure of talking all the time. Mike knew he should talk to her about the phone call he got from her teacher today, but in his gut, he thought it best to give her space. Holidays had indeed intensified the fact that everything had changed.

They sat for a bit, eating their dinners and watching the stupid sitcom with the canned laughter, and from time to time he'd look over at her to see if she was okay, but she didn't look back. He wondered how to really tell the difference between when someone just needed space and when you were actually losing them. When they were done, he took their plates to the kitchen and cleaned up, while she went upstairs and took a bath. And when she was out, he kissed her good night and tucked her in. It was a routine they could both do on autopilot.

He retired to his own bed but didn't stay there long. Missing Kate was bad enough, but missing her where they had expressed tenderness and passion, where they had lain entwined . . . it was unbearable.

So he got out of the too-empty and too-cold bed and went downstairs to stoke the fire. In the wood box was junk mail they had always burned, but now it meant something different. Credit card companies were still sending Kate offers. He burned them. Publishers Clearing House announced she may have won a million dollars. He burned that, too. Catalogs kept coming in her name. He wondered what he would do with her mail next summer when it was too hot to burn it. Maybe he'd build a fire pit so he could burn it outside. Or maybe he'd fill out her credit card applications and list her address as heaven and see if they got the point.

He went to the kitchen, poured himself some Scotch, and sipped it while he read a self-help book about grief. The only thing the book really seemed to accomplish was giving him the sense that he wasn't the only one experiencing this hideous level of despair. He wasn't the only one hanging on mostly for his child. He wasn't the only one who could no longer imagine ever being okay again. He wasn't the only one with regrets.

They should have gone to visit her parents after they had moved. He should have made that happen. He should have taken time off from work and taken her places. She had always wanted to learn to windsurf. He should have taken her to the symphony. She loved Vivaldi. She said his music sounded like snow. When he listened to her Vivaldi CDs now, he could hear it. Why hadn't he been able to hear it before? Why had he been so quick to dismiss something that had meant so much to her? He knew. It was because he'd thought he had time. He'd thought he had so much time. In fact, he'd thought he had so incredibly much time that if he budged on what he wanted or liked, it could mean a lifetime of misery. A lifetime of expensive vacations. A lifetime of Vivaldi. Stupid.

chapter four

. . .

SNOW REPORT FOR NOVEMBER 23

Current temperature: 29F, high of 33F at 3 P.M., low of 22F at 4 A.M.
Snow showers off and on, winds out of the southwest at 10 mph.
31" mid-mountain, 37" at the summit. 6" new in the last 24 hours.
12" of new in the last 48.

When Cassie woke up on Thanksgiving morning, she couldn't tolerate spending her first Thanksgiving without her mother with Nancy. Her father had already left for another twenty-four-hour shift. He couldn't help it, she knew that.

Nancy also had to work her day job on the holiday, though, so after Cassie got dressed and ate a bowl of cereal, Nancy brought her to work. The first stop was the home of a very large man who had partial paralysis from a stroke. His wife was too small and weak to be of much help. Nancy came over daily to help him get in and out of the bathtub, where his wife bathed him.

Cassie knew this would be her moment. Everything was in her locker at the lodge. She sneaked out the back door of the man's house and tore off toward the resort. She figured she had about ten minutes before Nancy had the man in the tub, and even if Nancy emerged from the bathroom to check on her and discovered she was gone, she wouldn't be able to look for her until the man's bath was over. Even then, she wouldn't be able to spend much time at it because other elderly people were counting on her. Cassie believed she had it made but wanted to be on the chairlift before word got out.

At her locker, she put on her extra layers, boots, ski pass, transceiver, and helmet. The clock said 9:37. She grabbed her skis and poles and rushed outside to the nearest chair. Scooter was working at the base of it. His face was pierced in several places, so Cassie thought he would probably respect her need to rebel. She stepped into her bindings and slid up to the loading line.

"Hey, Cassie. How's tricks?" Scooter asked. He tried to sound as casual as he was with everyone else, but Cassie heard it. She heard the tenderness and pity slip through. No one treated her the same since her mother died. She hated that. But she also would have hated it if they had treated her as if nothing happened.

"Hey, Scooter," she said. "You didn't see me."

"I didn't?" he asked.

"I escaped the babysitter," she confessed. "Please don't let them make me go back."

He smiled approvingly. "I'm glad you have your priorities in order on a powder day like this. It's good to see you on the mountain again, kid. I don't see you up here much anymore."

Cassie winced, but the chair whisked her away before she had to respond. As she rode the chair, she closed her eyes and imagined her mother sitting next to her. "Hi, Mom," she said quietly so that the people on the chair in front of her wouldn't hear her talking to herself. "I'm sorry for scaring Nancy, but I just needed to ski with you today."

At the top of the chair, she didn't know what to do. She had intended to ski the Southback, where she could be alone with her mother, but now she felt deflated, as if there were lead in her chest where her heart used to be. She looked toward the Southback but skied over to the top of a tree run instead. Her dad had forbidden her to ski trees alone, but no one would see her in there, and it would dump her near the racing shack, where she could hide, since she had now lost her urge to ski. She pushed off the little lip, dropped, and turned. She snaked her way through the trees, but not in the way she usually attacked it. Her reflexes felt entirely too slow and her body off balance. Her heart just wasn't in it. She fell, fortunately not in a tree well, and just stayed there for a long time, feeling defeated and hopeless. She looked up at the blue sky that peeked through between the treetops and wondered if her mother could see her now. She thought that if she could, it would make her sad, so Cassie got up and pretended to be all right.

At the end of the tree run, her feet hit the cat track below. She felt relieved to be out of the trees and coasted over to the top of Victory, the racing run. She traversed all the way over to the racing shack, where the flags and poles for the course were kept, found the key on a nail under the eve, unlocked the padlock, and went inside. She took the lock with her so that no one would see it unlocked and lock her inside. She hoped no one would notice the missing lock at all.

Inside, under the poles and flags and netting, were a little bench and a stool where the timekeeper sat and looked out the window on cold and windy race days. On the bench was a copy of *Siddhartha*. She flipped through it, but many words were unfamiliar, and soon the meaning was lost. She only got something about a river laughing. She rested her head on the counter and imagined her mother's hand on her back. Then she closed her eyes and surrendered again to the feeling that life would be more manageable if she was not awake.

Mike was still thinking about it, about the woman who was about the same age as Kate had been, who had driven off a cliff while drunk and who looked as if she were going to make it. He wanted to know why that more or less nonfunctional person got to live when his wife did not. He wanted someone to explain that to him. Instead of saying it out loud, he drove the engine back to the station in silence.

Ben and John talked about turkey and stuffing in the backseat, while Pete, his lieutenant, who rode in the passenger seat, wrote down information for the report.

Mike backed the engine into the driveway of the station, and everyone got out. He had just finished waxing it for the Thanksgiving parade before the call for the woman came in. Now it had a film of sand and silt on it. He quickly went about washing it again. They still had ten minutes to make it to the parade.

As he finished, Ben brought him a ham-and-cheese sandwich.

Ten minutes later, they all hopped back in and drove downtown to the parade lineup. The organizers told him where to park, and they waited there for what seemed like forever while the rest of the parade lined up behind them. Since Sparkle had just one engine, they were always in front, right after the veterans who carried the flag, just in case they needed to take off for a call.

While they waited, Mike noticed John's wife, Becky, approaching. She held their new baby in her arms, picked up one of his little hands, and made him wave to John. John got out and went to them. Mike waved. Becky was like a sister-in-law to him, and their baby was like his nephew. That's the way it was. The brotherhood truly was a family. Becky and John reminded him of the years Kate brought Cassie to the station when he was on a shift so that he could sit back in one of the recliners and let Cassie sleep on his chest. Those were good days.

He looked for Cassie with Nancy but didn't see her.

He checked his cell phone and found a message from an unfamiliar number. He listened. It was Nancy in a panic. Cassie had run off.

Nightmare after nightmare flashed before him of all the calls he had gone on involving dead or injured kids who had done something stupid. Just two days before, he had responded to a call for a kid who had held on to the bumper of a UPS truck so he could snowboard behind it through town. He hit some gravel and went down, but his arm got caught in the bumper and he was dragged for about two blocks. Stupid kid. He had to have surgery, but thank God, people on the street had screamed at the driver to stop before the kid was killed.

Here's what Mike knew about kids: They did stupid stuff. Pretty much all of them. Often it was the ones no one ever suspected would do something stupid who did the most stupid things. In addition to playing in traffic, kids dove in shallow water, played with fire, broke into abandoned and structurally unstable houses, jumped off and out of things and climbed things that no one should ever climb, and drove drunk. If you were lucky, they just got hurt. If you were really lucky, they just got stuck and scared. Several times a year, though, he saw families that weren't lucky.

And he didn't know what he would do if something happened to Cassie. He honestly didn't know.

"My daughter's run off," Mike said to Pete.

Pete frowned. "Do you need to go? We can handle the parade."

The guys had already covered for him so much in the last year. They'd covered for him when he had to take Kate in for chemo. They'd covered for him when he stayed home for her final days. They'd covered for him for a few days after she died so he could be with his daughter and just hold her while she grieved. And they'd covered his nights for months so he could be home for Cassie. He shook his head. "There's nothing I could do right now anyway. If it gets dark and she hasn't shown up, I don't know." He bit his lip, irritated. "See what you're missing out on, Ben?"

Ben was the one bachelor at the station. "Looks like fun," he said.

Pete chuckled. "Ah, it turns out okay. There are lots of moments when you think it won't, but it does. And then one day you get to be a grandpa and watch your kids get theirs. Very satisfying."

Mike couldn't picture Cassie getting married and making him a grandpa. He could picture her rappelling out of helicopters. He could picture her trekking in the Himalayas. He could picture her doing impossibly high jumps and stunts on skis in the half-pipe in the X Games. He could picture her kayaking down treacherous rivers. But he could not picture her walking down the aisle. He could not picture her pregnant. But if he was wrong, or even if he was right, Kate was going to miss it all. She wouldn't get to hold her grandchild. She wouldn't get to watch Cassie in the X Games. She was going to miss it all, whatever "it" turned out to be.

"Want me to call Barb and have her put the word out?" Pete asked. Barb, his wife, had an ability to mobilize a lot of people in five minutes or less. She rallied volunteers to pass levies, to bring safety education to the schools, and to raise money for burn victims. Whenever anyone needed anything, Barb was there.

Mike sighed. "Nah. It's her first Thanksgiving without her mom. Maybe she just needs a little space. Let's wait awhile and see if she shows up on her own."

Pete patted Mike on the shoulder. "I'm sure she's fine."

"Yeah," Mike said, "but she might not be after I find her."

Pete and Ben heard it for the empty threat it was.

At the end of the day, Jill counted the number of people who had come through the first-aid room–fifty-two. Thanksgiving was every bit as busy as she remembered it being. Right around closing time, an aid car showed up to whisk a man with heart problems to the hospital. Tom and Jason had just brought him down on a sled two minutes ago.

"Hey, Mike," Tom said to one of the paramedics, and handed him a copy of his notes and the EKG tape while he and another paramedic loaded the man onto their stretcher.

"Thanks," Mike said. "Hey, Cassie ran away this morning and no one's seen her since. I suspect she's here. It's getting late. Will you keep an eye out? I'll let you know if she shows up."

Tom picked up his radio. "I'm on it."

"And if you know anyone who could use extra work, Cassie's sitter quit because of this. Can't blame her," Mike added as he rushed to wheel the patient out the door and into the aid car.

Tom radioed to everyone to look out for Cassie.

Cassie startled awake when Howard opened the door. After he saw her sleeping next to his copy of *Siddhartha,* he turned his head a little so his headlamp wouldn't shine directly in her eyes and blind her. He picked up his radio, and said, "I found her."

That's when Cassie realized she was in big trouble. She stood up. "I guess I fell asleep," she said.

Uncle Howard nodded as if it were no big deal. "Well, come on, kid. People are looking for you."

Cassie picked up the skis she had leaned against the wall in the corner. She stepped out of the shack, locked the door behind her, hung the key back on the nail, and put on her skis. Uncle Howard stepped into his skis as well. Cassie waited for him to scold her or judge her, but he didn't seem to want to. He just looked off toward town and waited, and maybe because he didn't ask for it, Cassie felt she should offer him an explanation. "I just wanted to spend Thanksgiving with my mom," she said, barely louder than a whisper.

"Of course you did," Uncle Howard said. He paused for a moment. "Maybe there are some leftovers at the fire station," he said. "We'll go see. Ready?"

Cassie nodded. She knew that what awaited her at the fire station was anger—not leftovers.

Howard skied slowly in front with his headlamp and Cassie followed right behind. When they reached the bottom, they carried their skis back to Cassie's house and then walked to town.

At some point, Cassie broke the silence and asked, "If heaven is in the sky, why do people walk through a tunnel to the light instead of going up an elevator?" Howard had an ease for talking about these topics matter-of-factly that other adults did not.

Cassie also had the sense or maybe the hope that Howard knew some things other people didn't.

He scratched his chin with his free hand. He was a blocky man with a face that was both stoic and peaceful. "Good question," he said. "What do you think?"

"I don't know," Cassie replied.

"There are people who think the dimension of heaven isn't up in the sky, but just a few feet above this dimension," Howard offered.

"How would that work?" Cassie asked.

He shrugged. "There's no such thing as a solid. Everything is in a state of movement."

Cassie gave him a skeptical look and let it drop.

They walked in silence through downtown Sparkle, Cassie's anxiety about facing her father building.

At the station, the guys were only beginning to get to their dinner. They had been called out on several kitchen fires that day, most of which involved giant vats of oil that overflowed when people dropped their turkeys in and then ignited. The din of conversation quieted when Howard and Cassie entered. Cassie felt all their eyes on her accusingly, as if they all wanted to scold her but had to wait for her own father to do it first.

She picked out her dad's tired blue eyes. He stood up and shook Howard's hand. "Thank you," he said. "Please join us." He did not look directly at Cassie. "Come on, Cassie," he said, and walked out of the station.

Outside, he leaned his back against the wall and looked up at the sky.

"I'm sorry, Dad," Cassie said.

He took a big breath. "I just kept thinking, What if I lost you, too?"

"Dad, I'm sorry," she said again.

"Nancy was a wreck," he added.

Cassie was silent.

"She quit," he said.

Cassie was happy about that but had the good sense not to show it.

"I'm really mad, Cassie."

She looked at the deicer crystals on the wet sidewalk and squirmed under his gaze. "Sometimes when I'm on the mountain, I feel like Mom is with me," she said quietly.

Mike rubbed his forehead with both hands. "You've put me in a tough spot. I can't have this. I need to know you're safe, and I need a babysitter to do that. You're only ten years old. After this story circulates through town, no one is going to want to be your babysitter. You're a liability to them. If we can't solve this, I'm going to have to send you to Phoenix to live with Grandma and Grandpa."

Cassie's eyes bulged with disbelief.

"I have to know that you're safe," he said unapologetically.

And both their hearts sank as they walked back into the fire hall, each of them wondering what they would do without the other. They ate silently, as the others around them laughed and chatted, and when it was over, Pete's wife, Barb, brought Cassie to their house.

"Are you staying here for the whole winter?" Eric asked as he drove Jill to the top of the mountain in the groomer.

"I think so. Right now I'm just taking it day by day."

"You're not going to sleep on a couch all winter, though, are you?" he asked.

"I don't know. I'm just not thinking that far ahead yet," she replied.

"Well, look, think about this. Travis is out for the winter. If we don't get another housemate to replace him, we'll have to cut back on our consumption, and no one wants that. We've never had a lady housemate before, but I don't think Tom or Hans would object. Cheap rent—think about it."

"Lisa made me promise never to go in there," Jill said with a smile.

He laughed. "We know you're in a tight spot, so you can pay rent after you get your first paycheck. Just think about it."

"Okay," she agreed.

He dropped her off at the summit and continued on to groom more of the mountain.

She walked over to Tom, who was gathering wood for a fire. "Lisa's got the food and is on her way up with Hans." He rubbed his hands together excitedly. "It won't be long now!"

"Hey, did that little girl turn up?" Jill asked.

"Yeah, Howard found her sleeping in the racing shack. Do you remember Kate?" Tom asked.

"Kate?"

"Kate Paulson," Tom said.

"Yeah," Jill answered. "I used to race with her. She was fast."

"She died last summer," Tom said. "Breast cancer. Spread to her lungs. Her daughter, Cassie, has been breaking downhill records since she was five. We've all been waiting for the day she's old enough to dominate international competitions, but this year she's not racing at all. I used to see her all over the mountain all the time, but I haven't seen her once since her mom died."

"Oh," Jill said, and shook her head. Then she frowned, thinking. "I heard her dad say he needs a sitter. If it works with my schedule, I'd be interested."

"I know he works twenty-four-hour shifts. I'll get more info for you, or you could track him down yourself."

"David cut off my access to our funds, so extra cash would be welcome."

But it was more than that. Jill had no child. This child had no mother. They needed each other. In principle, it sounded great. A lot of things sounded great in principle, though. Kate Paulson had been one of those people she just hadn't liked, and near as she could tell, Kate hadn't really liked her. There had never been any aggression or hostility. It was the little things, like moments when she and Lisa were laughing at something and Kate hadn't laughed. Sometimes it seemed Kate looked at them as if she thought they were stupid, but maybe that was all in Jill's imagination. Maybe she truly didn't understand why something was funny. Maybe she had misunderstood why they were laughing and thought they were laughing at her. At this point in her life, she could think of a multitude of reasons. Kate surprised her once, though. Jill had forgotten her lunch, and Kate had given her an apple. It seemed funny to remember such a little thing, but sometimes little things are big things, like when you're hungry.

Tom crumpled and twisted some newspapers and wedged pieces of them in the woodpile. Jill joined in and helped. Then he lit the papers, and they stood back as fresh sap crackled and sparked.

Hans and Lisa pulled up shortly after. Over her parka, Lisa wore a silly vintage apron, pink with ruffles and an embroidered pocket. Jill and Tom walked over to help carry two Dutch ovens, a huge kettle containing a ten-pound turkey and a lot of Crisco, a few smaller pots and pans containing the rest of the food, and some lawn chairs. Then Hans drove away to groom for a little longer while Lisa cooked.

"When we're all done frying the turkey, we make the best grease bombs ever. They look just like miniature A-bombs," Tom said.

"I put all this work into the food, and all they care about are the grease bombs," Lisa muttered.

"Not true," Tom said. "We love them equally."

Jill held the kettle while Lisa rubbed dish soap on the outside of it so the soot wouldn't stick and then set it on the fire to boil.

Jill considered just how different this Thanksgiving was from the one she had envisioned, the one where she was nine months pregnant, and together she and David prepared their last Thanksgiving dinner where it would be just the two of them. It was sad. Uncle Howard had taught her at a young age that attachment led to suffering, and she tried for a moment to forget about everything she had hoped today would be and instead recognize that it was actually pretty fun. As long as she didn't compare it with what she thought it was supposed to be, she could see that it was actually a great Thanksgiving. But attachment is strong and usually needs to be grieved, so the moments where she could let it go and enjoy the day for what it was were fleeting.

"You're quiet," Lisa said.

"Just trying to absorb it all, you know—how my life is taking this radical turn. Even this moment is so different from what I thought it would be."

Tom asked, "What if your husband showed up here with a few dozen roses and said how deeply sorry he was and that he made a mistake? Could you forgive him?"

"If you were in my shoes, could you forgive him?" Jill asked.

"No way," Lisa said. "My people kill people instead of forgiving them."

"That's scary," Tom said.

"Don't you forget it," Lisa replied.

Tom turned to Jill and asked, "What if he told you he still loves you? Would you believe him?"

"I just keep thinking the way I feel now . . . is this how it feels to be loved?" Jill replied.

"Hell, no. Let's kill him," Lisa said as she poured Girls Are Meaner Gewürztraminer from Wines of the San Juan.

"If he said he loved me, at this point I wouldn't even know what he meant," Jill answered.

Tom said, "People mean different things when they say, 'I love you.' They shouldn't, but they do."

"Right," Jill agreed. "Like in this case, I would believe 'I love you' meant 'I'm attached to you,' or maybe 'Please don't take half of everything.'"

Lisa said, "Tom, you probably tell a hundred girls a year that you love them. What do *you* mean when you say it?"

"Well, Little Miss Presumptuous, I, in fact, do not tell a hundred women—"

"Girls," Lisa interrupted. "They're girls."

"Young women," Tom corrected himself, "that I love them. There is luv, l-u-v, and there is love, l-o-v-e. There's a big difference between 'luv ya' and 'I love you.' Luv just means you feel happy when you're with them."

"I call that love," Lisa said. "That expansive feeling . . . that's love to me. When I tell someone I love them, I don't really mean that I love *them*. I mean I feel expansive in their presence."

Tom shook his head. "No, l-o-v-e love is when you would give someone a kidney," he said definitively. "That's why if David tells you he loves you, Jill, you tell him your kidneys are failing and you need a kidney. If he offers his, he loves you. If he doesn't, you're right—he just wants to restore order to his life."

"Wait," Lisa said. "So you're saying there is just one kind of love—kidney love?"

"Yes," Tom replied.

"I don't buy it," Lisa argued. "I think there are lots of different kinds and levels of love. There's expansive love. There's I'd-loan-you-money love. There's I'd-take-good-care-of-you-while-you're-sick love—"

"Lisa," Tom stopped her, "all of those are like cents that add up to a dollar, but it still takes a hundred cents to make a dollar. All those steps are significant and made of the same stuff, just like all pennies are money and all dollars are money, but just like you need a hundred cents to have a dollar, you need the willingness to give up a kidney to have love."

Lisa studied Tom for a minute, and Tom could see the question written all over her face. *Would you give up a kidney for me?*

"Yes, I would give you a kidney, Lisa. We've been friends for a long time," he answered.

The look on Lisa's face shifted. She was obviously wondering if she would give up a kidney for Tom.

Jill decided to save her. "So, Lisa, how long does this take?" she asked.

"Nine minutes per pound, so theoretically, ninety minutes after the oil reaches three hundred and fifty degrees. I always let it go a little longer in case it wasn't that hot. I don't want anyone getting sick."

"Oh," Jill said, wary of the turkey already.

"Hey, is Jason coming up tonight?"

"No," Tom answered. "He never does anything anymore. Sometimes we hang out a little at work, but that's about it." He turned to Jill. "You met Jason for a moment today. He helped me bring that heart patient down."

"Jason was Tom's partner in crime until he got married and broke up with Tom," Lisa explained to Jill.

"Broke up, Lisa?" Tom said. "Come on, that's a little harsh."

"Okay, they weren't sexual, just inseparable. We used to call them Tason or Jom. You know, sort of like Benifer," Lisa said. "Yep, it sucks when all your friends grow up and leave you behind."

"Well, they haven't all grown up and left me behind. You're here. Eric and Hans are coming," Tom replied, and cracked another beer.

Jill didn't comment, but she mulled over the idea of maturity. She felt so far beyond mature. She felt old. Old and used up. She looked at Tom, playful and full of vitality, and she wondered what was so great about being grown up.

A while later, Eric and Hans joined Tom, Lisa, and Jill in lawn chairs around the fire. Tom lifted the turkey out of the pot with a large hook, set it on a large platter, and carved it. Lisa removed the pots of potatoes and mashed them manually with a potato masher. Jill took the green beans off the fire and began to make a plate for everyone. The Dutch oven containing apple cobbler had already begun to smell good, even though it had been set on the fire only a few minutes ago.

Tom handed out forks. When he handed one to Lisa, she said, "Thanks, baby. I needed a good fork."

"Oh, Lisa, you know I've been dying to give you a good fork for a long time," he joked back.

"Ten bucks says they'll be sleeping together by April," Eric whispered to Jill as he handed her a napkin.

Jill smiled, shook her head, and extended her hand to shake on it. She sipped her wine, looked at the stars, and wondered who she would be today if she had never left this place. Would she be like Lisa? Would she be who she was today, only unbroken? Would she be married to a faithful husband and have a healthy child?

"Nice job, you guys," Hans said as he took his first bite. "Cajun! I love Cajun!"

"Just like Mom used to make," Tom added.

"I love crunchy skin," Eric said. "I know it's theoretically gross because it's skin, but I really love it."

Lisa smiled. "I know how to please my men."

Jill picked at her dinner to make it look as though she were eating it, but she didn't have much appetite. Inadequacy curled in her stomach like sour milk. She choked down a few spoonfuls of potatoes and a bite of turkey.

When people had finished, Lisa opened the Dutch oven and spooned steaming apple cobbler onto everyone's plates, and Tom handed them out.

Something about the smell of apple cobbler comforted Jill. She closed her eyes and inhaled deeply. It smelled like home. But when she opened her eyes again and looked up at Lisa's friends, she felt disoriented. It struck her as odd that this mountaintop used to feel like home so long ago, and now she felt like such a foreigner.

Then Tom asked everyone to stand way back as he dumped a can of snow into the hot turkey grease with his long stick, making a huge mushroom cloud of fire. In it, Jill saw this moment of her life. Her old life had been the boiling oil. The other woman was the snow that had propelled her to Sparkle with the same explosive force. For the five seconds the massive cloud of fire burned, Jill was awestruck and felt equally awestruck that she had left David and come here. But when the flash of fire was over, the sky dark and empty again and the turkey grease cool and watery, Jill wondered, *What now?*

chapter five

. . .

SNOW REPORT FOR NOVEMBER 24

Current temperature: 26F, high of 30F at 2:30 P.M., low of 19F at 4:30 A.M.

Partly cloudy with occasional snow showers, winds out of the southwest at 5 mph.

33" mid-mountain, 40" at the summit. 3" new in the last 24 hours. 5" of new in the last 48.

Lisa," Jill called out, "Eric invited me to move into Travis's room in the Kennel. I think it's a very practical solution to my housing situation."

"You're kidding, right?" Lisa shouted back from the kitchen, and then walked into the living room.

"Well, you know, you're in the middle of this remodel and . . . I feel like I need a door I can close while I'm going through this . . . you know, low time. I feel like I need a place to make my own for a little bit."

Lisa shook her head. "The mere idea of this makes my skin crawl, but if you're going to go look at it, I'm going with you," she said.

Although the Kennel was mostly a single-wide mobile home, a sturdy roof had been built over it and a long, narrow addition had been built along one side. It was not pretty. They entered through something like a shed on one end of the addition. Inside, a mountain of skis stood next to the door along with a few shovels, some firewood, and a barbecue. Tom met them there.

"Come here, Bud," Tom said, and the yellow Lab walked over to him. "This is Hans' dog, Bud Light."

"I think anyone who names their dog after beer needs to go to AA," Lisa said.

Tom replied, "I gave Stout his name because he was stout. You make me sound like such a loser, Lisa."

Lisa turned to Jill and advised, "If you ever start thinking that any of them are developmentally more mature than a high school boy, just remember they named their dogs after beer."

The house reeked of stale pot smoke. It reminded Jill of lemon furniture polish and skunk. But surprisingly, the kitchen was clean. Above the table hung a Piston Bully calendar with pictures of snowcats.

Tom led the way down the hall. He stopped at what used to be the back door but was now a door that led to a very short hallway into the addition. There was one room on each side. Tom gestured to one. "Eric's room."

"Remember, stay out of there," Lisa said.

Tom replied, "At some point, she might need a little meaningless rebound sex, Lisa. It's not your place to judge that."

Lisa looked at Jill. "I'll buy you a vibrator."

Jill blushed.

Inside, Eric's bed was raised high enough for some boxes and a dog bed to fit underneath. On the dog bed slept an old chocolate Lab, gray around his nose and chin.

"That's Ale," Tom said.

Near the dog was a little refrigerator that doubled as a step up to the bed.

Tom's room was on the other side. For a place that apparently saw so much action, there was nothing particularly remarkable about it.

They passed the bathroom, which, like the kitchen, was surprisingly clean but, unlike the kitchen, smelled like good-smelling men. On top of the toilet sat a little basket of potpourri. Lisa looked at it and made a face. "Okay, which one of you is gay?" she asked.

"You were throwing it out and we wanted our bathroom to smell good," Tom said.

"You're kidding, right?" Lisa asked.

"Why would I kid? We're all crazy about the way you smell. We would walk to the ends of the earth just to smell you. This stuff kind of smells like you, don't you think?"

Lisa sniffed the basket. "I think it smells like ass and that's why I threw it out."

Tom sniffed it and made a turned-on face.

At the end of the hall, Tom said, "Jason's old room. Hans lives there now." Lisa patted Tom's shoulder to comfort him. He clearly still missed the days when Jason lived there.

Jill looked in. Hans's bedroom looked like the aftermath of an explosion, with clothes strewn everywhere.

And to the right was Travis's room. It was hopelessly ugly. There was nothing that could be done with dark fake wood paneling or the burnt-orange shag carpet, which undoubtedly housed a microbiological world Jill shuddered to consider. Travis had also hung a large mirror over his old, stained, and visibly sunken bed.

Lisa said, "Oh, Jilly Bean, no. No woman should live like this. There's got to be something else in Sparkle."

Tom said, "Lisa, look, she's got a mirror here that you and I only dream about."

"Jesus, Tom," Lisa said. "Don't you think that's a little insensitive given her circumstances?"

"Oh, I'm sorry," he said, and seemed to really mean it.

"It's all right," Jill said. She looked around the room. "Hey, it's cheap, functional, and close to you," she said to Lisa.

"Man, I wish my remodel was done. It won't be much longer. I'll have you out of here in two months."

"Carpenters don't work on powder days," Tom reminded her.

"I'll have you out of here in six months," Lisa corrected herself. "In the meantime, you can borrow sheets and blankets." She looked at the mattress and made a face. "I've got a space heater, too."

"Thanks," Jill said, and followed Lisa back to her place.

They returned to the Kennel an hour later with three Hefty bags full of things Jill needed and Lisa could spare. Lisa helped her make the bed, and Jill was so tired, she crawled right in.

Lisa sat on the other side and then lay down, too.

"Jilly?" Lisa rolled over to face her. "Do you want to talk about anything that happened? I mean, I don't want to pry, but I care, and I'm here if you want to talk."

Jill's eyes began to water, but she held the tears back. She shook her head gently. "Thanks."

"It's okay to cry in front of me, you know. You're the only one who thinks you're supposed to look like you're fine all the time. But I think it's normal to have messy, loud, sloppy feelings."

Jill pursed her lips and nodded.

"Well, I'm here," she said, and Jill nodded again.

When Lisa got up and went home, Jill stared at herself in the mirror on the ceiling. What she saw was a discarded woman in her mid-thirties on a nasty, stained mattress in a dumpy trailer.

She remembered the day David said he had a surprise for her. He'd blindfolded her, guided her to the car, and helped her get in. He was so excited. It felt to Jill that he made a hundred turns before they arrived. She wasn't sure if he was doing it on purpose so she couldn't guess where they were or if reaching their destination was really that involved.

Finally he stopped, came around to her side of the car, opened her door, and took her hand. She felt her feet leave the pavement and sink into lush grass with each of her tentative little steps. Then he asked, "Ready?" and took off the blindfold.

She stood in front of the brick house they had toured the week before. Of all the houses they had seen, it had been Jill's favorite.

"We got it!" David said. She jumped into his arms and he swung her around.

For years they were happy in that little house. When she thought of that house, she thought of the tiny bathroom and how they were always practically on top of each other when they brushed their teeth. She liked the way the small house necessitated closeness like that. They took their showers together nearly every morning. He always washed her hair for her, which she loved. And afterward, while he shaved, she stood behind him and dried her hair with one hand and let the other rest on his hip or back. She just liked touching him. Jill missed that house from the moment they moved out of it and into their German fairy-tale house. She missed the walls that had kept them close to each other.

Back in the Kennel, Jill looked at herself in the mirror and wondered what David saw or didn't see all those nights they slept together. She couldn't imagine going through the rest of her life unloved, but she couldn't imagine dating and then starting a new relationship from the beginning, either. What was the point? If David discarded her, everyone else would, too. If after all this time he didn't see her as worth keeping, who else would?

In the middle of the night, she woke from a dream where her baby was lost in the hospital and she searched frantically for him, to no avail. Although she was lucid, panic still coursed through her veins. She got out of bed, thinking a walk would be the only way to calm down and clear herself of its energy.

She wandered toward the center of town. Next to city hall was the fire station where an aid car was backing in. Jill walked across the street and waited for the driver to get out.

"Mike, right?" she said.

"Yeah?" he answered.

"I'm Jill. I was working with Tom on the mountain yesterday when you picked up the heart attack patient."

"Oh, right. Sorry. I was focused on that."

Jill realized that meant she was entirely unnoticeable. Men noticed stunningly beautiful women no matter what was going on. He hadn't noticed her. No wonder David found a new woman. It stung, but she recovered and addressed the task at hand. "I heard you needed a sitter."

"Very badly," he said. "Are you new in town? You don't look familiar to me."

"I lived here a long time ago with my uncle Howard," she answered. "You know Howard. He found your daughter. . . ."

"Howard's a good man," Mike said.

"Yeah, he is. Lisa was my best friend. I've been staying with her, you know, in the yellow Victorian? She works at the ski school. . . ."

"Right. I know Lisa."

"Well, if you need references, you can ask either of them about me. I've got to confess, though, that tonight I moved into the Kennel, but please don't hold that against me. I assure you that I don't share their lifestyle."

Mike laughed. "The Kennel? Wow."

"No, really. I was a nurse back in Austin. I make healthy choices." She wondered if she was starting to sound desperate. She felt desperate, although it wasn't really about the job as much as it was about being good enough. She wanted him to see that she was good enough.

Mike laughed a little more. "Oh, no worries. Tom's a great guy. I don't really know the others. Well, okay, here's the deal. I'm on for twenty-four, off for forty-eight, starting at eight A.M. There's a futon in our home office you can sleep on. On weekdays Cassie's at school until three. She's ten, so she'd be okay until you could get there. On weekends . . . well, I could probably just turn her loose on the mountain. She *is* ten. But it would be nice to know she could come to you if she had a problem or something."

"Sure," Jill said.

"I paid Nancy fifty bucks a shift. Ten shifts in a month, five hundred bucks a month. I know it's not a huge sum, but it's what I can afford."

"Five hundred bucks would help me a lot."

"Okay, then, you're on for Monday. I'm at 210 Aspen Street. It's a blue-purple Victorian. My daughter picked the color."

His daughter picked the color. Cute. She smiled.

"Okay, it's periwinkle. I live in a periwinkle house. I have trouble saying it because it sounds like a magic word used by fairy godmothers."

Jill laughed, pretended to use a magic wand, and said, "Periwinkle. Yeah, you're right. It totally does. All right, well, I'll be at your periwinkle house on Monday after work. Is there anything else I should know? Allergies? Anything like that?"

"No allergies, but she hates frozen dinners." He paused to take a breath. It was so hard to say. "I don't know if Tom told you that she lost her mom last July. . . ."

"Yeah," Jill said. "I knew Kate."

"You knew Kate?"

Jill nodded. "We raced together. I didn't know her that well." It was nicer than saying she hadn't liked her. And it was true. In reality, she hadn't known Kate that well. "She was much better than me. I think I felt intimidated by that."

Mike laughed. "For what it's worth, I never beat her down the mountain either." He smiled for a moment, remembering how hard he tried. "Well, Cassie has nightmares pretty often. Just—" His voice broke. "Just go hug her . . . you know, until she falls back to sleep."

Jill could see tears in his eyes. She nodded sympathetically. "Of course."

"It's hard. You know. I wish I could be there all the time," he said.

"Yeah, that would be hard."

"Jill? Thanks. I was worried that no one would take the job after hearing how she took off and that I'd have to ship her off to my parents in Arizona."

"Well, if she takes off, she'll likely go to the mountain, right? I've got connections up there. I think we'll be okay."

He smiled. "Okay. Well, thanks."

They shook hands, and she walked away.

She turned around and caught him looking at her and gave him a little wave.

Back at the Kennel, she tried to sleep but found herself obsessing about David and about forgiveness. *It takes a strong person to forgive,* she thought, and she did not feel strong. She felt shattered. *Could I? Could I?* she asked herself over and over. *Could*

I ever go back? What if he does it again? How could I ever trust him? How could it ever be okay again?

At four in the morning, she heard the front door open and close as Hans and Eric returned from their shift. She heard one of the guys go into the bathroom, piss loudly, flush, and not wash his hands. Suddenly she imagined the fecal contamination all over the house. She was going to need the big guns, Lysol, to live there. As she struggled to rectify the conflict between which she disliked most—germs or the hospital smell of Lysol—she fell back into a dreamless sleep.

At six-thirty, Tom woke her.

She went into the bathroom that smelled like limes and men but which she now knew was full of germs, shut the door, and sat on the toilet. New droplets covered the sides of the cabinet next to it. She noticed shiny little dots on the floor. The roll of toilet paper had been sprinkled, too. Nasty. She unwound the toilet paper until it looked dry and ripped some to use. Then she rewound the gross toilet paper over the roll since it obviously didn't bother anyone else and made a mental note to buy her own toilet paper to carry to and from her room. When she was done, she looked for evidence that anyone ever cleaned with a cleanser that contained bleach, found some Ajax under the sink, and felt a little better. She was going to need a lot of it. She skipped the shower, got dressed, and joined Tom in the kitchen.

He silently handed Jill a plate of scrambled eggs.

"Thanks," she said, surprised.

"No problem," he answered.

They watched Stout sit on the carpet and walk himself forward with his front paws. "His ass itches," Tom explained.

"Does he have worms?" Jill asked, imagining not just bacteria but parasite eggs in the carpet.

"Nah, I worm him. Sometimes your ass just itches, you know?"

Jill made another mental note to never touch the floor.

Tom poured coffee into his travel cup and then they put on their boots and walked to the mountain. It all seemed so surreal. Two months ago, she had a normal life, and now she had an unfaithful husband and a rental room in a trailer with men who peed all over everything and dogs that dragged their butts all over everything else, and she had a job working on ski patrol in the ski patrol first-aid room and another job taking care of Kate's daughter—Kate, whom she'd never really liked that much but couldn't quite believe was gone. None of it seemed real—none of it.

chapter six

• • •

SNOW REPORT FOR NOVEMBER 28

Current temperature: 27F, high of 29F at 2 P.M., low of 25F at 2 A.M.
Increasing clouds with occasional snow flurries. Winds out of the south at 20 mph with gusts up to 25 mph.
34" mid-mountain, 42" at the summit. 1" new in the last 24 hours.
1" of new in the last 48.

Just as Mike had warned her, Cassie had a night terror in the early hours of the morning. Jill bolted out of the guest futon in the office and across the hall to her room, sat on the edge of her bed, and rubbed her back. Cassie kept her back turned to Jill as she wept and sputtered. And Jill stayed until Cassie cried herself back to sleep.

The evening had not gone well. Jill had knocked, and Cassie had opened the door. Jill introduced herself and then went to the kitchen, where she surveyed the contents of the refrigerator and cupboards and began to make a stir-fry. "I heard you hate frozen dinners," Jill said. "Me too."

"I hate pretty much everything," Cassie replied.

Jill knew that was intended to sting, and instead of reacting, she simply replied, "Bummer." She wondered what she had gotten herself into. After a long, awkward pause, she tried again. "How was your day?"

"Look, don't try to be my mom, okay?" Cassie sneered.

Fortunately, Jill was putting the bag of frozen broccoli spears back into the freezer, so Cassie could not see the expression on her face. She took a breath and tried to choose her words and tone of voice carefully. "Perhaps you can make me a list of the things your mother used to do and then highlight the things on that list that you think are my job description so I can really understand where the line is between being a nice person and trying to be your mom, because I didn't think I was trying to be your mom. I just thought I was being a nice person."

With that, Cassie got up and went to her room.

Jill finished dinner, ate a few bites, and then made Cassie a plate. She put the leftovers away, cleaned up, and then got ready for bed. All around the house hung pictures of Kate, Mike, and Cassie. Jill paused for curious glimpses of their past—arms around each other in all kinds of scenic places, big smiles. She didn't remember Kate smiling that much in high school and wondered who she had grown up to be.

Then she brushed her teeth and crawled into the bricklike futon bed in Mike's office.

The next morning, Cassie pretended like nothing had happened—not the rudeness and not the nightmare. She said good morning and ate her Cheerios in silence.

Jill noticed that the plate from Cassie's dinner sat in the sink and was glad she had eaten it at some point in the night. She put it in the dishwasher.

Cassie rinsed her bowl and put it in the dishwasher before Jill shut it. Then she put her school books in her bike messenger bag and headed for the door with a casual, "See you later."

Mike came home just as Cassie was walking out the door, kissed her, and wished her a good day.

"How did it go?" Mike asked Jill.

Jill hesitated, trying to choose her words carefully.

"That good, huh?"

"Nothing big. She was a little hostile last night, but seemed civil enough this morning. She had a nightmare last night, but did go back to sleep."

Mike rubbed his forehead. "Well, thanks for being patient with her until she comes around."

Jill shrugged as if to say, *We're all doing the best we can, aren't we?* and then said, "I hope you'll be patient with me, too. I can see she's going to test my boundaries and she might not like me for a while while she figures it out. We might have some tense moments before we hit our stride. I hope you won't jump to the conclusion that it's not working out. Sometimes it just takes some time."

"Right," Mike said, nodding skeptically.

Jill picked up her bag and put on her coat.

"See you next time," Mike said as he walked her to the door and closed it behind her.

Jill walked to the mountain under heavy clouds. An occasional tiny flake kissed her face. She liked her new commute. It was by far better than traffic in Austin.

By midmorning, there was only one person in the FAR, so Tom came down from the Pneumonia Shack, the oldest and draftiest mountaintop patrol shack that was his domain most of the time, and told Jill to take a ski break, pick an easy run, and look for tourists in distress. Lisa had loaned Jill her rock skis for the rest of winter since she used them only at the beginning and end of the season, when the snow was thin and she didn't want to trash her newer skis by scraping them on rocks.

As Jill rode the chair, snow began to fall, lightly at first, but as she neared the top, it thickened. When her feet hit the ramp, she stood and slid down. She hit a little bump, lost her balance, and recovered. She realized that she was locking her knees and that to stay balanced, she'd have to bend them. She'd have to soften.

She started down Meander, an easy run that had been a favorite warm-up in the past, and glided over and down hills and slopes that felt like old friends, places she had known as intimately as she had known parts of David's body. She kept her knees bent and absorbed the shock of whatever came her way without losing her balance. She was surprised how easily her body remembered what to do. If only it were that easy to absorb shock and stay balanced in the rest of her life.

She reached an unexpected fork in the trail and couldn't remember which way to go. This place she had known so well, this place that felt like an old friend, suddenly felt foreign and cold. She went left and had no idea where she was. Her legs began to burn and tremble. It wasn't the run she remembered, and her own weak legs felt just as foreign. What little confidence she'd had was gone. She stopped and rested and tried to recall this run from her memory, but nothing looked familiar because she couldn't see anything. There was almost no visibility.

Eventually, she figured that all roads led to the base, and even if she ended up on a black diamond run, somewhere deep inside her was a girl who knew how to ski it. She took it slow and tried not to worry about what might lie ahead. Instead, she tried to keep her mind simply on the sensation of floating in new snow. And she realized that was also likely the answer for this particular moment in her life—have faith in herself, take it slow, and try not to worry about what might lie ahead.

Mike really could understand why Cassie might have felt uncomfortable with all the sitters. It had nothing to do with them. Sometimes it just felt as though their mere presence painted over the little things Kate left behind, like when they put something back, but not quite back to the place Kate would have put it. Just little things like that. Little things that shouldn't have mattered, but for some reason, they just did.

Uncomfortable with the stillness in the house now, he busied himself with chores. He pulled clothes from the laundry hamper and dropped them into one of two piles on the floor: darks and whites. He set the dial on the washing machine, and as the water began to fill the basin, he poured in a little bleach and detergent. In went the whites.

"This is not what I was born to do," Kate had said to him one day last February, before they knew she was sick—at least before he knew she was sick. He wondered now if she had found the lump by then, if she had known something was wrong. Mike had just come home from a shift, and Kate was folding laundry on the bed. "I know we agreed that I would stay home to raise our daughter and you would work, but I feel like everyone's slave, and I hate it. It is a waste of my life."

"Are you saying you want to get a job?" Mike had asked.

"I don't know," Kate answered.

"Are you saying you'd like Cassie and me to pull more of our own weight?"

"I guess so. Yes," she said.

"We can do that. I'm happy to do that. Kate, I really hope

you don't feel like you've wasted your life raising Cassie. She is who she is because of you. And she's bright and happy and confident, she does well in school, and she's one hell of a skier. That's all you, Kate," Mike said.

Her shoulders slumped. "Thanks," she said, more like a resignation.

Mike felt crushed watching her deflate like that. He wondered if he'd done this to her, if it wasn't any different from catching butterflies and keeping them in a jar, where they inevitably died just like the caterpillars, grasshoppers, and ladybugs he'd caught before that. Everything dies in captivity. He knew that.

He looked around at his house, at the washer and dryer. He had never thought of this as captivity before. He had put so much effort into making it nice. But then, he had put a lot of effort into making those jars nice, too—adding leaves and grass, a stone, and maybe some water, and then punching holes in the lid. He thought about Kate, bored and lonely in this house, doing chores. After that conversation, he and Cassie did all the laundry. He made an effort to help out more in other ways, too, and to show his appreciation as well.

But as he thought about it after Kate died, it haunted him. Kate's life was short, and Kate's life was over, and she had spent the last part of it feeling that she had wasted it. She left unsatisfied. He would do anything to give it back to her, even if she chose not to spend it with him again.

But maybe that was just a moment. We all have our moments like that, he thought. *We all have moments when we look at the sacrifices we made instead of all we gained. It's normal.*

He hoped those times had, in actuality, been a small part of the big picture. They had been for him. For him, at least, the big picture was the three of them on a blanket with a picnic during the summer outdoor concert series a couple years ago, Kate leaning back against his chest, Cassie leaning back against hers. His girls. And there had been so many days on the mountain together. He used to carry a bag of M&M's in his pocket and dole them out whenever Cassie got discouraged or Kate got irritable. She'd call him her sugar daddy and laugh, and the tension would ease. He remembered sitting next to Kate during Cassie's second-grade talent show performance. Cassie had hopped on her pogo stick for the duration of a whole Disney song—not to the rhythm of the music. She'd just hopped and hopped with a big smile on her face. "I've never been so proud," he had whispered to Kate. She'd laughed, but she had felt it, too. She had been the only other person in the whole world who could have possibly understood what he was feeling in that moment. Those moments were the big picture. Those moments where they were so strongly partners—family.

He carried the basket of laundry up the stairs to his bed, where he dumped it out. He folded the towels first and then the clothes, making a pile for each person. When he was done, he put his clothes in his drawers and put Cassie's pile on her bed. He held Kate's pile for a moment and actually considered putting the clothes away this time instead of back in the hamper as he had done every week since she'd died. He wondered whether he could fold laundry just once without thinking about how he had wasted Kate's life if he just put her laundry away this time. In the end, he made a baby step by putting her pants away, but he dumped the rest of the pile back into the laundry hamper. He couldn't stand thinking of her regret, but neither could he stand the sight of family laundry without some of her things in it. He just couldn't.

After school, Cassie told Mike that she was going to a friend's house to work on homework. He was dozing on the couch since his twenty-four-hour shift the day before had been relatively sleepless.

She went out the front door with her book bag but doubled back around to the shed, where she ditched her bag and found a shovel. She took it and walked down the alley, where she could remain hidden until she finally reached the edge of town. There, she cut through a pasture to the riverbank below.

The river still flowed in the middle, but the sides were covered in ice and snow. She stayed near the cut bank, where she knew she was on solid ground, and there she began to dig through the snow to the stones below. She tried to get a shovelful of cobbles, but they were frozen together. She chopped at the ground in hopes of breaking some of them loose. She desperately needed to hear from her mother. It had been so long since she had heard from her, and as Christmas drew near, her grief had heightened. She would not have believed it possible, but it was indeed worse.

A few cobbles broke loose and she dropped to her knees to examine them. *Please let there be a heart,* she thought. *Please, please, please.* But she didn't see any or hear her mother's voice. She dug for two hours and found nothing. Finally, she sat down and gave up.

She went home the way she came, traded the shovel for her book bag, and walked in the house.

Mike was awake. "How did the homework go?" he asked.

"Pretty good," Cassie answered. "Afterwards we made a snowman," she said, to explain why she was soaking wet.

"Oh, that sounds fun," he replied.

She climbed the stairs and changed into dry clothes. Then she crawled into her bed, under the down comforter, spread her homework out in front of her, and tried to care about it.

"So, Lisa," Eric began, "how was your date last night?"

Lisa stood in front of the stove, simmering freshly grated ginger in butter, the first step of her gingerbread recipe. "What makes you think I was on a date?"

"Tom saw you leave in your date jacket and waited by the window until you came home," Eric said.

"What a stalker," Lisa muttered.

Hans shouted from the other room, where he was finishing his birthday movie for the fourth time, "Who was Lisa on a date with?"

Lisa looked at them and shrugged. "No one. I'm not dating anymore. I went to the movies by myself."

Hans walked into the kitchen and put his empty bottle in the recycle bin.

Eric popped the top of another beer. "Lisa just announced she's not dating anymore," he told Hans.

"You're not dating anymore?" Hans asked.

"Nah. I haven't figured it all out yet, but I was talking to Howard about it," Lisa said.

"Uh-oh," Jill said, and snickered.

Lisa continued, "And he said that like it or not, marriage is how a man shows a woman respect in this culture, and that by avoiding men who want marriage, I've also been avoiding men who will respect me. I'm afraid I might have to get married at some point."

Hans and Eric thought about that silently, which made Lisa suspect it might be true.

Jill raised her eyebrows and looked at all of them. "I have firsthand knowledge that marriage doesn't guarantee respect."

"No, I know that," Lisa said. "I just think that it's possible that while marriage doesn't guarantee respect, no marriage does in fact guarantee disrespect."

"Define disrespect," Eric said.

"Being regarded as just another vagina. Never being introduced to someone's family. The last guy I dated told me he didn't even want a girlfriend. He didn't want romance. It was too intimate and he had just gotten out of a relationship. He didn't want another relationship. He just wanted a friend he could have sex with. And I went along with it for a few weeks because I wanted sex, too. But unlike him, I wanted to sleep next to someone. And I wanted to wake up the next day and make breakfast together. I'd run into his mom at the grocery store . . ."

"Ah, so it was a local boy," Eric said, looking at Hans, trying to figure out who it was.

". . . and I'd say hello just like normal and pretend that nothing was going on, and I'd hope that she didn't know that we were spending time together, because if I wasn't his girlfriend, what was I? Just his whore friend? I don't want to be a whore. I want to be respected," Lisa finished.

"So, it's a boundary issue," Jill said.

"Yes," Lisa agreed.

Eric said, "Yeah, I was having problems dating many years ago and then I figured some things out and have been able to avoid unpleasant situations."

"True, that." Hans nodded. "Last October, I was dating this smokin' hot chick, and I was happy because I was getting laid, but then Eric saved me by telling me about the two critical questions."

"The two critical questions?" Lisa asked.

"Yeah," Eric answered. "Does she have hobbies? And does she get along with her dad?"

Hans went on, "Turns out the smokin' hot chick had never known her dad and she didn't have any hobbies either."

"Good thing he figured it out then," Eric said, "or working out her father issues with Hans would have been her new hobby."

"No one wants to be another person's hobby," Hans said. "Now *that* is a boundary problem." He paused and then said, "Tom would say that men's strengths are physical, and women's strengths are manipulating relationships, particularly to try to entrap men."

"Yeah? Well, Tom is an ass," Lisa said, staring them down.

Still, Jill considered what truth there might be in Eric's philosophy. She and her father didn't have a good relationship. After all, he believed she was going to the Terrestrial Kingdom instead of the Celestial Kingdom—a lower level of heaven than he would be in. It was impossible to have a healthy relationship with a dad who didn't think you were good enough in God's eyes. And Jill didn't have hobbies, exactly, but she did have a career. She didn't think David had ever been her hobby, but had she tried to work out her father issues with him? Maybe so. Unlike her father, though, David thought she was good enough. Or at least he used to.

"If ever there was a case for abstinence," Lisa said, "Sparkle men are it."

But at least the men in Sparkle didn't pretend to be something they weren't, Jill thought. At least they were direct about the nature of the beast, and women were given every opportunity to enter into entanglement with full disclosure or avoid it altogether. At least they didn't pretend to be anyone's husband.

Just then Tom walked in through Lisa's back door. "Hey, Lisa, how was your date?"

"I was just saying that if ever there was a case for abstinence, Sparkle men are it," she replied.

"Is that your plan now?" Tom asked.

"It's been my plan for a couple weeks now," Lisa said.

"Hm," Tom said. "Yeah, me too."

Lisa busted up laughing. "Sure it is. And how's that going for you?"

"You don't believe me? I'm hurt. I really am." Tom helped himself to a beer from her fridge.

"Hey, who do you think could go the longest without sex?" Eric asked. "Besides Jill, of course. No offense, Jill."

"None taken," Jill said, and poured herself a glass of water.

"I have more self-control than all of you put together," Lisa said.

"Did you hear that, Hans?" Eric asked.

"Those sounded like fighting words," Hans said.

"I smell a wager," Tom said. "How 'bout this: Starting today, we all count all the days in one stretch we go without sex. If you go longer than all of our days combined, we give you free labor on your attic remodel for Jill. I think we could finish the attic faster than your carpenter goons are going to finish the rest of your house. If, however, you do not exceed all of our sexless days combined—"

"Wait," Eric said. "I'm trying to think of a prize that would be better than having sex. I think this wager is a bad idea."

"It's okay," Tom said. "I can do this by myself."

"Ooo," Lisa said. "This just got more interesting, and P.S., I think you'll be doing it by yourself a lot."

"Now those sound like fighting words," Hans said, and then

looked at Eric and mumbled quietly, "We're totally getting out of this."

"But if I win," Tom said, "I get to take sexy naked pictures of you and turn my favorite into a poster, which I will proudly hang on the inside of my closet door, which I will open and look at when I feel lonely." He gave her a daring smile.

"Ooo!" Eric and Hans said as their eyes grew wide.

"Don't do it, Lisa!" Jill shouted, horrified.

"So tell me about the remodel," Lisa said, unshaken. "Actually, let's go up to the attic now, and really specify what you're going to be doing."

While Lisa and Tom went upstairs, Hans and Eric, from the threshold of the bathroom door, began flicking bottlecaps into the dirty mugs in the sink.

"I'm out," Jill said. "It's been a long day." She put on her boots and opened the back door.

Eric looked at the clock. "And it's about time for the late shift," he said, so he and Hans made their way out the door as well.

"Game on," Lisa said as she came down the stairs, excited about the prospect of her remodel.

"Game on," Tom echoed, excited that Lisa wouldn't be sleeping with anyone else for a while. He'd agonized through the night before, believing she was out with some creep. He wanted her for himself. Now maybe he'd just bought himself enough time to make that happen.

At the bottom of the stairs, they realized they were alone. Tom smiled, helped himself to another beer, and made himself at home on her couch, where they watched the rest of Hans's birthday movie together.

chapter seven

• • •

SNOW REPORT FOR NOVEMBER 30

Current temperature: 22F, high of 28F at 2 P.M., low of 19F at 2 A.M.
Light snow. Winds out of the south at 30 mph with gusts up to 35 mph.
36" mid-mountain, 44" at the summit. 1" new in the last 24 hours.
3" of new in the last 48.

"You don't have to knock," Cassie said to Jill, who was standing on the doorstep. "You can just come in." She left the door open and walked away.

"Well, I don't have a key and the door should be locked," Jill replied as she walked in the house.

Cassie didn't answer. Instead, she went into the living room and turned the television up loud.

Jill unpacked the groceries and wondered whether this was a battle she wanted to fight, and if so, whether she really stood a chance at winning. She poured Cassie a large glass of lemonade and brought it to her.

"Is this volume really comfortable to you?" Jill asked, playing dumb.

"Yes," Cassie snapped. "And I'm not going to turn it down. It's my house."

"Oh, I wasn't going to ask you to turn it down," Jill replied. "I was just going to make sure your father took you to an audiologist as soon as possible to get you a hearing aid. I know kids often don't like wearing them, but you have long hair and it will cover it up." She smiled sweetly and returned to the kitchen to start dinner.

And when the lemonade hit Cassie, as Jill knew it would, and she went to the bathroom, Jill took the cord that connected the cable box and the television set and hid it in the dryer, confident that Cassie was not going to be doing any chores and therefore wouldn't find it in there.

"What did you do to the TV?" Cassie asked when she returned, angry.

"It just stopped working," Jill replied.

"Really," Cassie said, unconvinced and impatient. "I go to the bathroom for two seconds and the television stops working in that improbable window of time?"

"Good use of the word *improbable*!" Jill said. "I'm impressed! Have you been studying probability in math or science?"

"Why are you here, anyway?" Cassie asked. "Dad says you're a nurse. If you're a nurse, why do you need to be a babysitter?"

Jill paused to think about her reply and then said, "Sometimes something happens in life that changes everything."

"You probably just like my dad."

Jill closed her eyes, shook her head, and said, "Good talk, Cassie," as she walked back to the kitchen.

Cassie followed her. "He's not available."

"Wow, you're really making some bold assumptions. You know what they say about assuming."

Cassie looked at her blankly.

"When you assume, you make an ass out of you and me."

"Did you just call me an ass?" Cassie asked. For a split second, Cassie looked at her just as Kate used to—as though she didn't understand or was pretending not to understand.

"So what will be your favorite thing about living in Arizona, Cassie? The sunshine?"

"I hate you."

"Well, there's something you can enjoy doing in Arizona. It's almost as fun as skiing," Jill shot back.

Cassie stormed up the stairs, slammed her door, and kicked it.

Jill made burritos, left a plate in the refrigerator for Cassie, and then read a book in the living room.

And later that night, when Cassie screamed from her night terror, Jill went to her room and paused outside the door for a moment before she reached for the doorknob. When she tried to turn it, she found the door was locked. She stood there for the longest time, unsure of what course of action would make things better and what course of action would make things worse. In the end, she went downstairs and heated a mug of milk in the microwave, then stirred in a package of Swiss Miss hot chocolate with marshmallows and brought it back up the stairs.

She knocked softly. "Cassie? I made you some hot cocoa."

The room was silent.

"I'm setting it outside your door, so don't trip on it."

With that, Jill retreated to her own quarters.

The next day, Jill sat quietly over a cup of tea while Cassie went about her morning business. She wondered what, exactly, she had gotten herself into but figured ultimately that she had dealt with patients who were much more difficult than this.

Cassie rushed in, grabbed a breakfast bar and a banana, and made for the door just as fast as she could. No words were exchanged.

Jill was retrieving the cord she'd hid in the dryer when Mike came in.

"Hi!" he called out.

"Hey," Jill replied.

"So, how'd it go?" He seemed so optimistic.

She hated to crush him and winced just thinking about it.

"Oh," he said.

"Yeah, I thought it might be better, too, but when I arrived, she was ready for war."

"How's that?"

Jill recounted the evening's events and concluded with, "I'm not sure where we go from here."

Mike pursed his lips and nodded slowly as he thought. "Would you be kind enough to give me twenty-four hours to try to turn this around? I really want this to work. I think Cassie and I need to have a little heart-to-heart tonight."

"Sure," Jill said.

When Jill returned to the Kennel, she found a box. It was from David. After checking out the selection of underwear available at the grocery store, she was grateful to see a huge stash of her own. On days when the one pair she showed up with had been dirty, she had somehow tolerated wearing two horrible pairs that she'd bought at the drugstore, which creeped. Also in the box were some cotton long-sleeved T-shirts, cotton sweaters, cotton socks, yoga pants, a fleece jacket, a little nightgown, and running shoes. Jill surveyed all of it and realized how useless most of it was. Well, cotton would be nice in the summer. Fortunately, David also included a check for a thousand dollars. Still, that wouldn't buy her gear and the clothes she needed for a winter on the mountain. It wasn't going to solve many problems at all.

When Cassie arrived home from school, she noticed things were different. The table was set and on her plate was a Southwest Airlines ticket. Her dad was in the kitchen, cooking. It smelled like chicken and gravy—her favorite.

She walked into the kitchen. "What's going on?"

"I wanted our last dinner together for a while to be special," he said plainly.

"What are you talking about?" Cassie said, panicked.

"Well, I thought I was going to have to ship you off to Arizona on Thanksgiving, and then Jill came along and saved the day. I figured it was clear to you that she was your big second chance . . . and your last chance. I guess that's why it just broke my heart to hear how you treated her. I thought you loved me more than that. I thought you would do your part to make sure that you and I could stay together. But, I guess I was wrong to assume that. Anyway, I wanted our last dinner together to be special, so I'm making your favorite."

Cassie was speechless.

"What did she do that was so awful, anyway?" Mike asked.

Cassie's mouth gaped, but no words came out. Finally, she said, "Nothing. She was nice."

"Hm." Mike continued to peel potatoes. Neither of them spoke for a moment, and then he said, "I put two suitcases in your room. Why don't you go get started figuring out what you're going to take with you?"

Cassie didn't move and didn't speak.

Mike looked up. "Do you have regrets?"

Cassie nodded.

"Well, you could call Jill and invite her to dinner, and try to make things right."

Cassie took a big breath and nodded.

Later, when the three of them sat down together, he let Cassie stumble through her apology. And when Jill accepted it, he wanted to throw his arms around both of them.

chapter eight

• • •

SNOW REPORT FOR DECEMBER 16

Current temperature: 18F, high of 26 at 1 P.M., low of 15 at 5 A.M.
Clear skies, winds out of the southwest at 10 mph.
45" mid-mountain, 53" at the summit. 1" new in the last 24 hours.
6" of new in the last 48.

Ever since Mike returned from the last call, he had been cleaning. He cleaned the bay. He washed the truck. He took apart the chain saws, cleaned them, and put them back together.

Pete had been around long enough to know that's what some of the guys did when they had something to work out. He stayed in the office writing up his reports.

Ben was preparing chicken, potatoes, and green beans for dinner and shaking from time to time. It was the first time he had been to a scene like that. He had been warned, but he never could have imagined how horrifying it could be. When the roast and potatoes were in the oven, he walked out to the bay. "Need help?" he asked Mike.

"Nah, I got it," Mike said.

Ben paused a moment too long before going back inside.

Concerned, Mike turned around. "Are you all right?"

Ben shrugged. "Are you okay after that call?" he asked.

Mike shook his head. The call had bothered him, too, but for a different reason. Mike had been to other calls where someone had eaten a gun. He knew to expect teeth embedded in the ceiling and brains dripping off it. He had seen a man's face with the rest of his head blown off the back more than once. He could even tell you what caliber of gun was used based on the damage. But this time, it bothered him for a new reason.

"That was messed up," Ben said.

"It was," Mike agreed. He turned back to the chain saw he was working on, wanting to be finished with the gruesome memory. But he could feel Ben still looking at him. Finally he said, "I just keep thinking how hard Kate fought for her life, while this guy just threw his away. It makes me really mad."

Ben nodded sympathetically. "Yeah."

"You know, in my mind I have this room with a big steel door and a lock, and I just put all those ugly calls in there. I don't even look at the door. I know what's in there. I don't need to look. But ever since Kate died, it's like I'm not able to keep that door shut," Mike said.

Ben paused to consider that. "When I go home, there's no one there, and you know, sometimes if I'm just coming off a call with a dead person, I feel like they're following me. I mean, I turn around and don't see anyone, so I know they're not . . . but I don't know. I used to have a motion detector light in my backyard that I kept on all the time, and now I turn it off. I know it's stupid, but I'm afraid that if it goes on and I look out there, I might see a ghost. When I think about it during the day, I know it's like a kid who thinks there's a monster under the bed and that it's ridiculous. But at night, I don't know. I kind of lose it."

"It's nice having someone at home—another grown-up, I

mean. I miss it. It was like Kate's just being there pulled me into a different world—one without a whole bunch of dead kids and people who shot themselves and each other," Mike said. "She sort of normalized my world."

"It would be nice to have someone at home," Ben said.

"You'll have that," Mike reassured Ben. "You're going to see some ugly shit, brother. And just when you think you've seen the worst, you'll see something even uglier. But you're going to get to save the day sometimes, too, and that feels good. Plus, you know, one day you won't be the new guy anymore, and you'll be helping us trick some other poor bastard into buying us all ice cream all the time instead of you."

Ben smiled. "I got Dreyer's mint chocolate chip—your favorite. You know this isn't going to go on forever, though. I've already bought ice cream for my first call at the station, for the completion of each weekly probationary training, for my first fire, and now for the first baby delivery in the field. This well is running dry. After this, I only have to buy you guys ice cream when my picture is in the paper, which will be never, because I ride in the backseat."

"You're a pretty boy, Beano. Marcia from the newspaper is going to put your photo in there a lot," Mike teased. The guys started calling Ben Beano after chili night his first week at the station, and it stuck.

"You're the one driving in all the parades, Magoo," Ben countered, calling Mike by the nickname he earned on a call once when the icy fog was so thick that he couldn't see anything and was driving blind through all kinds of danger. As Ben turned to leave, he said, "I like peanut butter cup, just so you know. I mean, the Christmas parade isn't far away."

Mike laughed, put the last chain saw back together, and went inside to set the table while Ben finished dinner. He felt a little better. But the holiday season was just beginning. It was an extra tough time to watch people lose a loved one, and on many of their calls, that's exactly what he saw. And this year, for Mike, it would be even tougher.

In his mind, he tried pulling the door to the ugly room shut. He imagined he was holding on to the doorknob, a foot on the wall on each side of the door, pulling with all his might. He pulled and he pulled, but the door just wouldn't close.

When Jill arrived at Cassie's house on their sixth night together, Cassie was looking at a poor progress report and a long list of homework she had failed to do.

Jill sat beside her and looked at the list. "Looks like we've got our work cut out for us."

"I'll never be able to do it all. I can't concentrate." Cassie pushed the list away in defeat.

"We'll get through it together, kid. I'll help keep you focused," said Jill.

So, Cassie opened her math book, and Jill walked her through three long division assignments. By the third, Cassie had it down enough that Jill could go make a big salad. "Do you like your salad plain, or do you feel adventurous?" she called out to Cassie.

"Adventurous, always," Cassie replied.

"Kids aren't supposed to like adventurous meals," Jill said, and added Craisins, walnuts, garbanzo beans, and feta cheese to the salad, then brought it in for a working dinner.

"This is good," Cassie said. "I never would have thought to put Craisins on a salad."

"I never would have expected a ten-year-old to like Craisins on a salad," Jill said.

"It's fun to blend new flavors together." Cassie turned the page and started on equivalent fractions. "I like fresh things. Mom always made fresh things."

Jill helped Cassie list factors of different numbers and find least common denominators, until at last she was caught up in math. Next on the list was writing. Her progress report said that she had earned a zero so far, having turned in absolutely nothing.

"She didn't list any assignments. What were your assignments?" Jill asked.

"Usually we just write in journals every day. Before Thanksgiving, we were supposed to write about what we were thankful for," Cassie explained.

"Of course," Jill said. "The obligatory Thanksgiving assignment. Did you do it?"

"No," Cassie said. "I didn't feel thankful for anything. What am I supposed to write? I'm thankful that my mom's dead?"

Jill didn't react. "Right. I get it," she said, and thought.

"Everyone says they get it, but no one gets it," Cassie said.

Jill raised her eyebrows. "You're not the only one to have a great big loss, kid."

"Yeah, I know. My dad had one, too," Cassie said, getting sassy.

"You know what, Cassie? Don't give me attitude. I'm not your enemy here. Look, here's what we're going to do for that assignment, okay? You're just going to lie and say all the junk you think your teacher wants you to say. It's okay to fake it sometimes and just jump through the hoops. Sometimes when everything's going wrong, that's just what a person has to do. You know? It's not going to make anything better to have to do fifth grade over."

"I wasn't giving you *attitude,*" Cassie said with even more attitude. "I just don't like it when people tell me they know how I feel. They don't know how I feel."

"Yeah? Well, Cassie, I don't like it when you assume to know how I feel, either. Just so you know, today was my due date. This was the day I was supposed to have a baby. But back in October, my baby died. So, no, I don't know what it's like to be a kid and lose my mom and have to face the holidays without her. But I know what it's like to go into the holidays thinking that everything's wrong, and feeling such emptiness that you wonder how you'll ever be okay again."

Jill got up and went to the bathroom so Cassie wouldn't see her cry, and wondered if she went too far, wondered if that was an appropriate thing to say to a ten-year-old. She splashed cold water on her face and looked at her reflection in the mirror. "Pull it together, Jill," she told herself, took a few deep breaths, and walked back out to Cassie and her homework. She didn't make eye contact. She simply sat back down.

Cassie had written a half page about what she was thankful for—a home, her dad, her cat, enough food, clean water, skiing, and that she got to stay here with her dad instead of moving to Arizona with her grandparents, and for Jill, who helped make that happen by babysitting her when no one else would.

Jill read it over her shoulder. "Don't forget that I don't feed you frozen dinners," she said.

Cassie smiled and wrote, "Plus, unlike my other babysitter, Jill doesn't feed me crappy frozen dinners. She makes good food. And she doesn't breathe weird like Nancy, either."

"You might want to make a different word choice than 'crappy,'" Jill said, so Cassie erased it and changed it to "disgusting." "And don't start your sentence with 'and.'" Cassie erased that, too, and capitalized "she." "How long is it supposed to be?" Jill asked.

"A page," Cassie answered.

"What about friends? Can you write about friends you're thankful for? That would fill space."

"I don't have any friends."

"How is that possible?" Jill asked.

"I just stopped talking to all of them, and now none of them talk to me either," Cassie explained.

"Why'd you stop talking to them?"

Cassie shrugged. "What's there to talk about?"

Jill looked at Cassie a second too long and then decided to just leave it. "Uncle Howard would say nature. Yes, nature. You can fill a lot of space writing about the wonders of nature."

"*Uncle* Howard?" Cassie asked. "Howard on the mountain with the books?"

"That's the one," Jill said. "What has he made you read?"

"A year ago he made me read *Hope for the Flowers* so I wouldn't feel disillusioned when I won the Olympics one day. He said I should question what real success is."

Something about hearing a ten-year-old use the word *disillusioned* made Jill smile. She shook her head. "That's my uncle," she said, and cleared dinner plates while Cassie filled up the rest of her paper about nature.

"Good job," Jill said, glancing at it. It was already an hour past Cassie's regular bedtime. "It's late. Let's get this packed up. Hopefully checking all that stuff off your list will help your dad go easy on you."

"Thanks," Cassie said as she packed her bag. Then, without looking at her, she said, "I'm sorry."

"What are you sorry for?" Jill asked, confused.

"I'm sorry about your baby. And I'm sorry I was a brat."

Jill nodded. "Thanks," she said, and left it at that.

Lisa rolled out more cookie dough and stamped it with her gingerbread man cookie cutter. She was hopeful that the ginger would kick Jill's stomach into gear, just like the gingerbread had seemed to help. Jill needed to eat more, and Lisa considered it her duty to make sure it happened.

Tom knocked and let himself in the back door. "I smelled something good!" He looked at the sheet of cookies cooling on the stovetop and gasped. "Cookies!"

"Yes, cookies," Lisa said, softened by his boyish excitement.

As he reached for one, he noticed how the heads of one row were wedged in between the legs of the row on top of them. "Dear God, Lisa, what are your gingerbread men doing to each other? It's like a gingerbread orgy down there! You made porn cookies!"

Lisa whacked him on the butt with a spatula. "Only you, Tom Cat. Only you."

Tom opened the closet door and moved Lisa's picture to the first square on his Chutes and Ladders board. "Delicious," he said. Then he moved her to the second square. "And sexy turns today, Lisa. Nice ass."

"You like?" Lisa asked playfully. She rubbed her hand on one cheek, flouring the pocket of her jeans.

He gave her his best sexy look.

"Take me off your board, Tom Cat, deluxe mimbo. Getting into your bed would be like getting my driver's license renewed. First I'd have to take a number. Then I'd have to wait for you to say"—she held an invisible microphone to her mouth—"'Number eighty-six! Number eighty-six, please step up to the bed and take your clothes off!'" She followed her announcement with a fuzzy microphone noise.

As Lisa razzed him in her usual way, she could have sworn she saw a brief flash of hurt, as if he had never considered that any lover of his wouldn't feel special, given his legacy—even if, in truth, she was.

But he forced a smile and said, "Oh, a take-a-number machine! That's brilliant! Finally, some form of crowd control! I'm going to go look for one now!" He took a cookie and started for the door. "All right, I've got stuff to do. Thanks for the cookie," he said, and left.

Lisa watched him trek to the Kennel through her kitchen window and wondered what just happened.

She walked over to the closet door and took down her Candy Land board. She wasn't that woman anymore. She studied Tom's Chutes and Ladders board for a moment, and all evidence pointed to this abstinence thing being very temporary, so she left his up.

Then she looked back out the window, saw Tom's bedroom light come on for a few minutes and then go off, and again, she wondered why he had left so quickly. Had she offended him? Was that really possible? She had always thought there were ways in which Tom had depth, and then there were ways in which he did not.

She thought about the dads who dropped their kids off at ski lessons. They were a completely different breed of man. And although she saw them daily, they were exotic and unfamiliar. They were something she couldn't even learn about because they were identified and claimed before Lisa even knew they existed. The sorting had already happened, and she'd missed it. Now she was stuck with the Peter Pans. Nope. She wasn't going to do it. There had to be something better—even for her. If God could part a sea for Moses, certainly He could find her a better man. She made a decision.

She finished her cookies, put on her boots and her sassy date jacket, and walked down to the Catholic church. Like the other two churches in town, it was small—not much bigger than her own house—but it had charm. She walked up the steps, opened the heavy door, and walked up to the first altar. She made the sign of the cross, kissed her fingers, and touched Jesus's face on the picture before her. It seemed she had the whole church to herself, so she went ahead and walked slowly up the long aisle to the altar in the front of the church, feeling the wood give a little under her feet, hearing a board creak now and then. This was what she came to light a candle for—this aisle; so she really let herself feel it. It was like the way the ski instructors practiced on each other before ever teaching for real, or like doing CPR on Ressessa Annie before ever using it for real. It was her dry run-through.

She couldn't quite picture it, couldn't quite picture looking at the church through a veil, couldn't quite picture flowers and ribbons, even though she had been to enough weddings in this church to be able to picture at least that, and she couldn't quite picture who might be waiting for her in the front. When she looked up and imagined someone in a tux, he always had Tom's face. Ug. As if.

When she reached the front, she put three dimes in a collection box and took three little candles. She touched their wicks to the flame of a candle left burning, said a couple of Our Fathers, and then whispered a prayer—a prayer for faith, and for strength, and for an end to this particular kind of bottomless loneliness.

chapter nine

. . .

SNOW REPORT FOR DECEMBER 21

Current temperature: 20F, high of 23F at 3 P.M., low of 17F at 4 A.M.
Mostly cloudy, winds out of the southwest at 5 mph.
49" mid-mountain, 57" at the summit. 4" new in the last 24 hours.
5" of new in the last 48.

Jill watched a young man squat down next to his wife in the FAR. She had hit a tree with her face, and judging by the damage, at high speeds. Her nose looked broken and her eyes were swelling and turning black. Abrasions covered her right cheek, along with a deep slice that went from the corner of her mouth all the way up to her ear. Her husband had left her in the FAR while he went to get his car and had just returned to pick her up.

"Ready?" he asked her.

"What if my face is ruined?" she mumbled out of mostly closed lips as she held a bag of snow on her nose.

"Oh, baby, your face isn't ruined. You're going to be just fine."

Jill's eyes welled up as she watched the tenderness exchanged between them.

"You don't need to worry about that. You're going to be fine," Jill assured her. "The doctors are going to put you back together really well."

As her husband walked her to their car, Jill thought about marriage vows, about how he was keeping his. And she thought about the marriage vows she had taken. She didn't promise to love David only if he loved her and kept his vows. She promised to love him through good times and bad. She made a *promise.*

As the day wound down, she finished up her paperwork, restocked the bandages, folded the wool blankets on the beds, and finally signed out and locked up. She walked home thinking about vows, about good times and bad, and attempted to find some memory to hold on to.

Last year, as they'd decorated their tree with angels, David had said, "Wouldn't this be more fun with children?"

Jill looked at him and said yes. She looked deep into his eyes to see just how much he meant it, whether he meant it lightly or whether he meant it deeply, and near as she could figure, he was doing the same. They both meant it deeply.

That night, they made love with a different intention and a different intensity. It was beautiful, in fact. It was souls merging and miracles and everything a person wanted conception to be. Jill was deeply disappointed a few weeks later when it was evident they hadn't conceived. They had two more months of disappointment. Each time, Jill felt as if she had failed. And each time, David held her and whispered in her ear that she didn't need to be sad, that everything was okay, that maybe their child didn't want to be a Virgo or a Libra or a Scorpio, and that would always make Jill laugh because David was the last person to believe in astrology.

When she finally saw the plus on her pregnancy test, she went to the library and checked out *Linda Goodman's Sun Signs,* and that night at dinner she opened it up and began to read aloud about people born under the sign of Sagittarius—athletic and fun, prone to sticking their foot in their mouth, and phobic of being fenced in.

"I'm a Capricorn," David said.

"I'm not reading about you," Jill replied. "I'm telling you what our child is going to be like." And the look in his eyes said, *What? Really? Is my dream of being a dad really going to come true?* David was fairy-tale happy. Jill had been surprised just how happy he was. "You're going to be a dad," she said.

He stood up, leaned across the table, and gave her a powerful kiss.

That was a good moment. If she could take one moment out of her life to put in a frame and hang on the wall, it would be that moment. It was so hard for her to believe that a year after that moment, she was one hundred and eighty degrees away from it. And as much as she wanted to look to that moment for something to hang on to, here was the thing about that moment: It was never coming around again. At least not with her. David might have that moment again with someone else. He could. And he had been so happy, why wouldn't he? Why wouldn't he want that moment again? Why wouldn't he want a woman who could give him that?

When she got home from work, Eric was outside the Kennel in the sun, wearing his cowboy hat and holding a Corona in one hand and a hose that snaked from the laundry room window in the other. He was rinsing off a five-foot-tall cut fir tree. Seemingly endless suds foamed and grew as the water hit the branches. Jill could hear someone vacuuming inside the Kennel. She walked up, stood next to Eric, and just watched. He handed her his bottle of beer. She took a swig and handed it back. Out of the corner of her eye, she could see him looking at her, but she was still avoiding eye contact as much as she could these days. One sympathetic look from anyone could send her into sobs.

"Looks like there's an interesting story here," she finally said.

Eric nodded. "Yeah, well . . . we thought maybe you needed a Christmas tree."

"And a very clean one at that," Jill said, genuinely touched.

"Nothing but the best, Jilly." He took another swig of beer. "Hans and I poached this one from the United States Forest Service just this morning, brought it down on the cat, and hid it behind the house. We were very proud of ourselves."

"Most poachers are," Jill said. She cracked a little smile.

"This morning, while you were at work, the three of us brought it in, put it in the stand, and began to hang lights. It was at this point that we noticed millions of tiny bugs dropping off the branches. At first, none of us said anything because, you know, acid flashbacks can happen. But finally Hans went, 'Is it me, or are there fuckin' bugs everywhere?'" Eric imitated Hans's voice perfectly, making Jill laugh for a moment. "That's when Tom began to scream like a little girl. Come to find out, he hates bugs. I think he's had crabs two or three times. Maybe that's why. Anyway, it's been two hours and he's still vacuuming."

"That's generally not an indicator of good mental health," Jill said.

"No, sadly, it's not. So Hans and I threw the tree in the yard and Tom came out with that can of Raid and gave the tree a thorough dousing. We gave it a good shake and then brought it back in, but it stunk too bad and gave us all a headache, plus we worried that it might be significantly more flammable, so I said, 'Hey, I know, let's wash it!' And since Tom wouldn't let me take it in the shower, I brought it out here with the dish soap, and, well, I don't know. It seemed like a good idea at the time. It's been about an hour now and it still stinks. Tom's pissed because he needs to take a shower to wash the psychosomatic bugs off him and I used all the hot water on the tree. I thought it would cut the oily bug spray better."

Jill wasn't sure whether to laugh or cry or do both. "You know, this is the nicest thing anyone has done for me in a long time—maybe ever. I love this tree." She blinked back tears.

Eric looked at her like a deer in headlights for a second, and then he held out his beer arm, gesturing for her to come in for a hug, so she did. And it felt good. When she began to break away, Eric said, "Yeah, you're not going to want to go in there. Go to Lisa's for a while. Hans has gone to work, but Tom's a wreck and the house stinks. It's my night off, so I'll come over and let you know when Tom finally gets a shower and the place airs out."

Jill smiled. "Thanks," she said.

"Pine beetle?" someone called out. It was Uncle Howard. He had his backpack on and was headed back toward the resort.

"Little baby ones, sir!" Eric called back.

"The hardware store is having a sale on artificial trees," Howard offered as he approached. "Sure, they smell like plastic, but you could just hang some of those pine tree air fresheners on them—you know, the ones that people have in their cars?"

"Sweet idea, Howard," Eric said.

Howard came over to give Jill a hug. "Happy Solstice," he said. "It's uphill from here starting tomorrow."

"I sure hope so," she replied. "I'm waiting to feel a change."

"Well, be patient. In March and September, around the equinoxes, the length of the day can change three or four minutes, but around winter and summer solstice, it only changes by a few seconds. It's a slow climb out. Conserve energy, hunker down, and wait. Spring is coming again, and then summer," said Howard.

"Sometimes I wonder how much more I can take," she whispered.

"All of nature does," Howard replied. "Go spend time with the aspen trees. They'll tell you how it works. They'll tell you to look to your roots for energy. They'll tell you there's warmth below the surface."

Jill gave him a sweet smile. She loved him so much, even though she only understood about half of everything he said. He tried.

"Well, your yard is going to be an ice rink tomorrow," Uncle Howard said to Eric. "Do you have skates? You and Tom could put on a show and, you know, wear those little sparkly suits. You could charge admission. I'm sure it would help you get girls."

Eric gave him a courtesy laugh, and with that Uncle Howard waved and walked away.

Jill walked over to Lisa's house just as Lisa walked out onto her front porch with two new boxes of Christmas lights. "They're magenta!" she exclaimed. "How funky is that?"

"Pretty funky," Jill said. "They'll match this." She pointed to Lisa's lacy lingerie hanging next to her ugly wool socks on the clothesline on her porch.

"I heard about the tree incident," Lisa said.

"Can you believe how sweet those guys are?" Jill asked.

Lisa snorted. "Hey, we should grab Tom and Eric and sneak into the hot pool at the hotel."

"You know, I don't think I'm up for it, but you guys should definitely go. I think the chlorine might help kill Tom's psychosomatic bugs."

"Sure?" Lisa asked.

"Yeah," Jill answered. "You know, the Kennel guys get a bad rap. They're really all heart."

"Shh . . . don't let that get out," Lisa said.

Mike and Cassie sat across from each other at the dinner table that now seemed uncomfortably large and empty. Mike watched her chew her enchilada, hoping she would offer the answer to the question he was wondering—why she hadn't mentioned the Christmas program. She offered nothing.

"I read in the paper that the Christmas program is tonight. Aren't you in it?" he asked.

Cassie's chewing slowed as she thought about how to answer. "I didn't tell you because I don't want to go."

Mike took another bite and waited to see if she would offer a reason. She didn't. He swallowed and then asked, "Why?"

Cassie looked at him as if it were obvious. "Really? Would you want to stand in front of a couple hundred people and sing songs that make you think about spending Christmas without Mom? Would you want to stand there and try not to cry and know that people were looking at you and feeling sorry for you?" Her eyes welled up and her cheeks got blotchy.

Mike nodded. "I understand," he said.

They ate in silence for a few minutes.

"I don't know what to do this year either, you know," Mike said. "You're going to have to help me. We're going to have to figure it out together, because I don't know what I'm doing."

Cassie chewed and nodded. They looked at each other, terrified.

"I guess I was worried that if we did holiday stuff, it would just draw attention to the fact that it's Christmas and Mom isn't here. But not doing holiday stuff isn't helping us forget. Should we get a tree?" he asked.

Cassie thought about it and nodded. "We should get one tonight."

Mike smiled. "I'd like that," he said.

They took their dishes to the kitchen. Mike rinsed them and put them in the dishwasher while Cassie started putting on her layers. He joined her in the glassed-in porch, where they kept their coats and boots.

"I miss your snowflakes in here," he said. "Usually before Christmas, you cut out snowflakes and tape them all over the windows."

Cassie looked at the empty windows and nodded sadly. "I'll make you some snowflakes," she said.

"I would like that very much."

They walked around the house to the garage, where Mike took the sled with the red runners off the wall and a coiled rope off a nearby hook.

"Do you want me to pull it or do you want to?" he asked.

"You pull it," Cassie said.

"Want a ride?" he offered.

"Nah," she said, and took his hand instead. He swallowed hard.

They walked down the sidewalk together hand in hand, toward the little park beside city hall where the Shriners sold Christmas trees.

"This is a pretty nice moment," Mike said.

"Yep," Cassie agreed.

"Maybe we'll end up having a lot of nice moments like these, and each one will help us endure all the sadness in between."

Cassie gave his hand an extra squeeze. "Yeah," she said.

"Nice stars tonight."

Cassie looked up and saw some stars that formed a connect-the-dots heart. "Do you think that's where Mom is?"

"Sometimes," he answered. "And sometimes I think she's right beside us."

"Do you think she's right beside us now?" she asked.

"Nah, I think she's riding on the sled."

Cassie laughed. "Yeah, she would do that, wouldn't she?"

"Standing up, like it was a surfboard," Mike said.

"Let's decorate the tree with pictures of her."

"That's a nice idea. I like that idea." *Breathe in,* he told himself. *Now breathe out.*

They walked in silence for a bit. The condensation from their breath froze on their eyelashes and hair.

"This is the longest night of the year," Mike said.

Cassie paused and replied, "Every night is the longest night."

"Yeah, it sure seems that way, doesn't it?"

Christmas lights were strung above the little park outside city hall. Like everyone else in town, the Shriners knew Mike and said their hellos. And like everyone else in town, they were saddened by the sight of Mike and Cassie without Kate.

Mike picked up a tree from where it was leaning against a rack. He spun it so Cassie could see it from all angles.

"That one looks good," she said.

"Don't you want to shop around?" he asked.

"No. That one's good." She could feel people looking at them.

Mike paid the Shriners twenty bucks, tied the tree, and then tied it to the sled. "Which way do you want to go?" he asked her.

She pointed toward downtown. Every window was lined in little white Christmas lights, and boughs of greens were stretched across the street. Big red ribbons hid the speakers that played hammer dulcimer holiday music from the lamp-posts. It looked like a town where nothing bad ever happened.

"It still looks magical, even though it's not," Cassie said.

"What looks magical? The town?"

"Christmastime," she answered.

"Oh, Cassie, Christmastime still is magical. It just hurts a little more this year. That's all."

"It hurts a lot more this year," she said.

"Yeah," Mike agreed. "I know."

Where people had shoveled the sidewalk in front of their shops, the sled scraped. A few businesses were open late, and a few tourists were out shopping, but since the locals were at the school for the Christmas program, the streets were relatively empty. Mike and Cassie walked a couple blocks and then turned up one block to their street.

Cassie took Mike's hand again and he shut his eyes tightly for a second.

"We should probably make cookies, too," Cassie said.

"Yes, let's do that," Mike said, grateful that they seemed to be figuring out the whole holiday thing together.

Lisa and Tom walked past the bellboys and in through the colossal doors of the historic Sparkle Lodge. A massive chandelier hung in the lobby and a bouquet of flowers that almost rivaled it sat on a table below it. Everything about the lodge was elegant—red carpet, dark wood, red-and-gold floral wallpaper.

Straight ahead was Carlucci's Italian Bistro, the fine Italian restaurant where Lisa's father had been the head chef and manager for decades. It still bore his name.

"Every time I pass that place, there's this split second when I forget my dad is no longer there, and I forget how old I am now. For that moment, I have this strong impulse to run back to the kitchen and see him like I did when I was a little girl," Lisa said.

Tom put his arm around her and gave her shoulder a little squeeze.

They walked past the front desk down the hall toward the spa. They paused in the hallway to pretend to gawk at the pictures of famous people who had stayed there, like the guests always did, and then when another couple was making appointments with the spa receptionist, they slipped by, pretending that they were just going out the door to look at the pool.

Outside, they quickly ducked around a corner and shed their clothes all the way down to their swimming suits.

Tom shuddered one last time before he submerged himself completely in the hot pool and imagined all the bugs floating away. He ran his fingers through his hair vigorously underwater before coming up. Then he inspected the surface of the water to make sure they weren't floating there, alive, waiting to hop back on him. Satisfied that he saw nothing, he sat back against the wall just as Lisa stepped in next to him.

Across the pool sat a couple with Long Island accents loudly debating politics, and next to them was an older gentleman by himself who wore a thick gold chain that rested in his bushy chest hair. Closer still sat two couples with Texas accents reminiscing about a trip to Mexico.

Lisa rolled her eyes and said, "I so understand why the rest of the world hates American tourists."

"Do they stress you out, darling?" Tom asked. "Let me help you with that." He reached up to massage her shoulders.

"Oh, your charms aren't going to work on me, Thomas. Eric told me how you two and Jason checked out all the massage videos from the library and practiced on each other to hone your seduction techniques—that is until you all got so good that you had to stop before you seduced each other. I'm on to you."

"Once again, Eric is telling stories."

"He said Jason says the massage videos are the whole reason he is married today," she said.

"Eric is a masterful storyteller," Tom said.

"Is that so?"

"Oh, Lisa, relax. You're my friend. Come here," Tom said.

Lisa gave him a suspicious look before she turned and let him massage her shoulders.

Tom admired her graceful neck, the way her shoulders were both delicate and strong. He felt her loosening up until she could hardly sit up straight anymore. That's when he pulled her back against him so that her head rested on his chest. The rest of her sort of floated above his lap.

"What are you doing, Thomas?" Lisa mumbled.

"Chill, Lisa. You're my dear friend. Sex ruins friendships. I'm never going to try anything with you." The red of her bikini top kept catching his eye. He looked at her luscious breasts floating in front of her and ached to touch them.

"No, it doesn't," she said. "We've both had fuck buddies before."

"They were our fuck buddies because we knew it could never work with them," he said simply. "You and I could never be fuck buddies. I know that. So, no worries. I'm not putting the moves on you. This is just nice."

"Wait. You're saying you would never have sex with me because you think it could actually work with us?"

"Uh-huh," he said.

"Yeah, that makes total sense," she said sarcastically.

He didn't reply. He just kept his arms around her and enjoyed the weight of her resting on his chest. He shut his eyes and moved his face close to her head, his nose an inch above her hair, and he smelled her uniquely Lisa smell. He wanted to hold her tighter but fought his instincts and loosened his hold instead. He leaned back and looked at the stars. As much as he didn't want to, he found himself thinking that this moment felt something like a gift from God.

Lisa floated away just a little, lifted her chin, and filled her lungs. But each time she started to float away, Tom's fingertips pulled her back. Eventually, he just kept his hands under her back, not really holding her up but ready to if she needed him.

He tried not to miss the feeling of her weight on his chest, but he did, so he pulled her back so that her head rested on his heart again. He folded his hands around the bottom of her rib cage.

"Sometimes I feel like Jilly's experience with love has been like food poisoning . . . and mine has been like quietly dying of thirst," Lisa said quietly.

Tom didn't know what to say, so he looked at the stars. But they didn't give him an answer.

"Do you ever feel like that? Like a part of you is dying?" she asked.

"Yeah," he finally said.

Lisa put her hands on his. "This is nice," she said. "I needed this. I didn't even know how much."

A little smile spread across his lips. "I knew," he said.

They stayed that way, dozing off and on, until Orion slipped behind Sparkle Mountain. Tom thought about not saying anything and instead just spending the night there with Lisa, but he knew he should get at least a couple hours of sleep before work the next day. "It's bedtime," he finally said, although he didn't want to.

Lisa took Tom's shriveled hands in her own and opened his arms. She slid out of them but didn't let go of his hands right away. She gave them an extra squeeze before she finally released him. They got out of the hot water and made a mad dash for their towels. Keeping their towels wrapped around them, they slipped their bathing suits off underneath and put their fleece layers back on without exposing themselves. They stepped into boots, put on gloves and stocking caps, and together walked back through the hotel lobby and out the front door.

Outside, the world looked different to Tom. He had never noticed how much the little white lights all over the bare trees looked like galaxies. The stars above seemed brighter than ever. He couldn't help himself. He reached for Lisa's hand and held it as they walked home.

They reached her sidewalk first. Tom let go of her hand. She gave him a little hug. He put his arms around her carefully, awkwardly, and then let go. She walked up the path to her house and let herself in through her unlocked door, and when she shut it behind her, Tom placed his hand on his heart.

On his way over to the Kennel, he passed Stinky Tree. It had been stuck upright in the snow and covered with Playboy automobile air fresheners with pictures of topless women on them. Big black plastic spiders also hung from several branches. He laughed. Word traveled fast in Sparkle.

chapter ten

• • •

SNOW REPORT FOR DECEMBER 24

Current temperature: 15F, high of 19F at 1 P.M., low of 9F at 4 A.M.
Clear skies, winds out of the southwest at 20 mph.
50" mid-mountain, 58" at the summit. 0" new in the last 24 hours.
1" of new in the last 48.

Cassie opened her eyes and turned her head to look at the picture of her mother on her bedside table. "Merry Christmas Eve, Mom," she whispered. She bit her quivering lip. She didn't want to be one more thing that made her father sad, especially this morning. It was enough that she had screamed and cried in her sleep last night. It had been one of those nights, leaving her feeling heavy and stiff, particularly her eyes, which she struggled to keep open.

This should have been a good day. For years Cassie had looked forward to the day she could finally ski in the Christmas Eve torchlight parade. And now here it was, but it was not going to be as she had imagined it. It was not going to be with her mom. She couldn't imagine a torchlight parade without her mother in it. Year after year her father had let her sit on his shoulders while they watched the lights come down the hill until they turned into people they recognized, and at last they saw her mother. She always flashed them a winning smile as she skied through the two rows of spectators to the garbage can where the skiers extinguished their flares.

This year, her father would be standing alone and watching Cassie instead of Kate negotiate the steep bumps on the Exterminator. It broke Cassie's heart to think of her father standing there all alone on Christmas Eve. She wanted to revise her Christmas Eve dream so that she and her dad could stay together, but a plan was a plan, and any deviation from it would only draw attention to all the ways everything was wrong and all the ways she was still not herself.

Look down, baby, she heard her mother say inside her head. It seemed cruel to hear her mother's voice when she was not on a bar of river cobbles. It seemed like a cruel memory or a cruel figment of her imagination.

She lifted her head and looked down at her bed. She examined her pillow, the wrinkles in her sheets, and the shadows. Nothing. She let her head fall back onto her pillow, wincing with disappointment.

Look down, look down, she heard again. She wanted to yell at her own mind to shut up. *Look down,* she heard again.

Cassie inched her way over to the side of her bed and hung over the edge. Half of the little braided rug that lay next to her bed had been flipped up and folded over by her father's foot last night as he'd rushed to her side. Under where it had been, Cassie saw a heart in the grain of the wood. Her tears hit it and splattered. She reached behind her for a pillow and held it to her chest since she couldn't hug her mother.

"I don't know how we're going to get through today without you," she whispered.

Only a select few people were invited to ski in the torchlight parade: ski patrol, ski instructors, and ski team members who were ten or older. So Mike stood near the lodge and watched as Cassie stepped into her bindings. Kate used to volunteer to time the races and loved this fringe benefit. Mike wasn't able to be that involved. His work schedule just didn't allow for it.

Technically, Cassie wasn't on ski team this year, but Coach Ernie had a history with her and hoped it would get her back in the game. He knew she had been looking forward to this day since she could walk.

Cassie seemed so alone to Mike as she shuffled toward the lift all by herself. He gave her every opportunity to change her mind. But here they were. Tonight he wouldn't be watching his wife ski down the steep mogul run with a flare in her hand. Instead, Cassie would finally get to do it, and Kate would miss it. Or maybe she wouldn't. Mike didn't presume to know. He hoped she'd see. And he ached as he watched Cassie, still so small and all alone, shuffle away from him.

Just then, Jill skidded to a stop at the bottom of the lift. "Hey, Cassie!" she called out. Cassie turned to see her and looked relieved. Jill skated up the empty ski patrol lift line, meeting Cassie at the front. "Hey, Scooter, can I ditch my poles with you?" she asked.

"Sure," he said, and took them.

Cassie, knowing what to expect, had left hers behind, so Scooter offered her a hand and pulled her up to the blue line where they met the chair.

"You're the best, Scooter," Jill said.

"That's what all the girls say," he replied.

Jill laughed.

Mike watched the lift whisk them off together, and something in his heart swelled a little. Gratitude. Gratitude for good timing. Gratitude for the right person coming along when you need them the most. Gratitude for some warmth and mercy in this world.

"I patched up your teacher yesterday," Jill said to Cassie on the lift. "She's nice."

"What was wrong with her?" Cassie asked.

"She had a big wipeout, and somehow her ski hit her in the face and sliced her a little. It wasn't bad. She'll be fine. But we were talking about you and talking about your writing."

"Uh-oh," Cassie said.

"I proposed something which maybe you'll like or maybe you won't, but it's an idea, and your teacher supports it if you're into it. She also said you could decide if she got to read it and that if you didn't want her to, she could just flip through your pages and see that you wrote."

Cassie was uneasy. "Okay . . . ," she said apprehensively.

"Consider making yourself a memory book about your mom where you write down your favorite stories and traditions and, you know, just memories. Whatever it is you most want to remember. Maybe little things, maybe big things, I don't know. Obviously, it would be all up to you. But it would be yours, and it would be writing, and it would be meaningful. It would be something you would always treasure, and if you have kids one day, it might even be something you share with them. You could illustrate it if you wanted, or scan photos and include them. I don't know. You could put your collection of writings in a binder and decorate it and make it really special."

Cassie was avoiding eye contact, looking off into the trees instead.

Jill worried that she had gone too far and interfered too much. "So, anyway, I wasn't trying to tell you what to do or anything. I was just trying to help," she said.

Cassie was still silent.

Jill tried changing the subject. "You know, this Christmas Eve is nothing like I thought it was going to be, but I'm excited to ski in the torchlight parade."

"Me too," Cassie said.

"If I crash and my light goes out, will you save me?" Jill asked.

"As long as you save me if I crash and my light goes out," Cassie replied.

"Deal," Jill said.

A few chairs behind Jill and Cassie sat Lisa and Tom. They passed a carton of eggnog back and forth.

"So, I've been wondering," Lisa said. "What happens with our bet if we both break down and have sex on the same night?"

"I'd have to say the bet would be off," Tom said.

"Hm," Lisa said. She had been thinking a lot about their soak, about being in his arms, about holding hands on the walk home. It was stupid, she knew, but she had been thinking about it.

"Are you plotting to seduce me in order to get out of this bet?" Tom joked.

"No way, pal." She sniffed the air. "Do you smell that? It's the smell of my attic being remodeled." Still, she feared she had already given herself away.

Tom laughed, handed her the carton, and then slipped his

hand behind her back to point at Eric, who was grooming a slope far off in the distance behind them. "Bummer Eric couldn't be here this year."

"You totally just did that so you could put your arm around me," Lisa said.

"Oh, Lisa, honestly. Don't be ridiculous." He let his hand drape over her shoulder and made like he was going to go for a breast.

"As if you could even find any girl parts under all these layers. Ha!" Lisa said. "It's like chastity armor."

Tom laughed, put his hand back up on her shoulder, and kept it there.

And even though she didn't want to admit it to herself or anyone else, she liked it.

At the top, Uncle Howard and Coach Ernie sipped hot buttered rum.

"Jill!" Coach Ernie called out. "I heard you were back in town! And you found my favorite kid on the mountain! How great to see you both!"

"Oh, Coach Ernie, great to see you, too!" Jill said with a huge smile, skied over, and gave him a big hug.

Uncle Howard handed her his thermos cup with hot buttered rum. She took a sip and handed it back. "What kind of energies will this infuse me with?" she asked.

"The tranquillity of the Caribbean, and the gentleness of cows," he answered.

Lisa and Tom skied up to them. "Can I top you off with a little eggnog, Coach?" Lisa asked. "Breakfast of champions."

"Ah, Lisa, you always were my favorite," he said. "But this

year, I've chosen a holiday beverage a little bit lower in saturated fat."

"Good choice, Coach," Tom said.

Lisa held out the eggnog for Uncle Howard, too, but he put up his hand and said, "I'm good."

Coach Ernie looked at Lisa and Jill and said, "It's nice, you know, seeing you girls together on the mountain again."

"What about me, Coach?" Tom asked.

"Oh, Tom, it's nice, you know, seeing you chase girls on the mountain always." He laughed. "Yeah, whenever you weren't where you were supposed to be, I'd just look for groups of girls, and eventually I'd find you."

"Ha!" Lisa laughed accusingly.

"I think you girls should ski in the Powder Eights this year. You've won it before. You could do it again," Coach Ernie said.

"Oh, I'm not at the top of my game, Coach," Jill said. "I think those days are over."

"When you get to be my age, you can say that, but not until then, Jilly Bean," said Coach Ernie. He was by far the oldest man on the mountain.

Uncle Howard took a cowbell out of his pocket and struck it with his flask until people were quiet.

"Light," he began. "It is the spirit within each one of us. It is what unites us. As we see these lights on the outside, let us reflect on our lights on the inside. Light is truth." He struck a match and held it to his flare, then held his flare out so Jill could ignite hers. "Let us spread the light."

No one knew for sure exactly what Uncle Howard really meant, but listening to him say a few words about light on Christmas Eve each year was part of the tradition, so they did. And everyone tried to look as if he made perfect sense, so that they wouldn't appear to need a book to help them understand. One confused look could lead to an unsolicited book from Uncle Howard that they would feel obligated to read, no matter how mind-numbing it might be.

Jill held her flare out so Cassie could light hers, and then Cassie ignited Coach Ernie's, and on and on until everyone's flare was lit.

"And now, let us take our light into the darkness," Uncle Howard said, and he, with Coach Ernie right behind, slowly led the way, holding their flares out away from their bodies with one hand, and one by one, everyone followed carefully. They snaked down the steep hill in full view of the guests both in and outside the lodge, where the party was already getting started.

After the parade, people would dance to Christmas songs and Uncle Howard would put on a Santa suit and try to talk children out of video games and into books. And at midnight, Uncle Howard and eight friends would leave the party to don sleigh bells and snowshoes and run through the streets of Sparkle so that little children in bed might hear and believe in, in Howard's words, "intangible and limitless possibilities."

Jill knew Christmas Eve was supposed to be magical, but it was impossible to let go of how she thought it should be magical and just let it be magical in a different way.

She passed another light-up Santa on her way home and thought about how, as a kid, believing in Santa made Christmas magical and how when she learned that there was no man in a red suit who lived at the North Pole making toys for all the girls and boys of the world, Christmas seemed a lot less magical for years after that. And only when she really let it go did she start to see the essence of Santa everywhere—all the acts of charity, all the generosity, and the mindfulness of how precious children are. Only then did Christmas become magical again.

Jill hoped maybe it would be the same way with love—that once she gave up her idea of what love was supposed to look like—marriage and romance—maybe she would begin to see love everywhere in infinite forms. *Maybe believing in one true love was like believing in Santa,* she thought, and in the same way she would wish for every child the experience of believing in Santa, she would also wish for every young person the experience of believing in true love. *Before you discover it's a load of shit, it's magical,* she thought. *It really is.*

Inside the Kennel, Jill greeted the dogs and then went back to her room, where she reached under her bed. There, she had stashed three pairs of wool socks, three tangerines, three chocolate bars, three candy canes, three lottery tickets, and three six-packs of Fat Tire Amber. For each pair, she put one sock in the toe of the other; filled the rest of the sock with the tangerine, chocolate, and lottery ticket, and put the candy cane in so it stuck out. Then she carried the six-packs out to the corner of the living room with the woodstove and put them next to the wall. She set a stocking on top of each six-pack and fastened a name tag to each.

As she backed away, she realized it had been her wish to hang three stockings this year. It seemed tragically funny to her that though it wasn't remotely in the way she had envisioned it, her dream had come true.

As midnight neared, Lisa made her way to the coat corner and began looking for hers.

Tom noticed and approached her just as she slid her arm down one of her sleeves. "Walk you home?"

Lisa found this situation awkward. Her renewed faith seemed private, yet if she simply told him she wasn't going home, he would take that to mean she was meeting someone and proclaim victory in their bet. She did not want Tom to take sexy pictures of her and hang them in his closet, so she told him the truth. "I'm going to midnight mass."

"I can walk you to mass just as easily."

"Wait, what's going on? You want to walk me places?" Lisa asked.

"Yeah. There are a lot of drunks out tonight. I want to make sure nothing happens to you."

"There are a lot of drunks out on Christmas Eve?"

Tom motioned to the room full of people behind him.

"I don't think Coach Ernie and Howard are threats," Lisa said.

"Okay, I want to make sure you don't sneak off and cheat on our bet."

"Ah," Lisa said with a smile and a nod. "That sounds more like you. Sure. You can verify that I am indeed going to mass."

"Why are you suddenly going to mass? Are you meeting someone there? Is there a new Catholic man in your life?"

"No, I'm not meeting anyone at mass," Lisa said.

"Are you going to sneak out of mass and meet someone?" Tom asked. "Or are you going to mass until it's so late that I'm asleep, at which time you'll sneak over to someone's house?"

"You want to sit through mass with me and then walk me home to verify that I am not cheating on our bet?" Lisa asked a little incredulously.

"Yes," he said.

He put her hand in the crook of his elbow as they walked to the church quietly. Inside, it was crowded. They squeezed their way into a pew.

Lisa tried not to let Tom distract her from her prayers. It was her first Christmas mass in at least a decade, and she really wanted to think about her sins just going away. She really wanted to think about the opportunity to be renewed, to begin again, to make better choices and create a better outcome.

When it was over, they waited their turn to step out of the pew and into the aisle, and both were keenly aware that they were walking back down the aisle together, not terribly unlike a newly married couple. Lisa was telling God silently, *See, this is what I have available to me, and therein lies the problem*. He was going to have to send her something better than this.

On the walk home, though, the Christmas spirit overtook her. Tom put his arm around Lisa, and Lisa let him. Neither spoke. They walked past the Kennel and to Lisa's sidewalk, where they hugged. Tom kissed the top of her head. Lisa wasn't sure what to make of that, but she chalked it up to Christmas.

"Merry Christmas," she said.

"Merry Christmas," he answered, and she disappeared inside her house.

chapter eleven

• • •

SNOW REPORT FOR DECEMBER 25

Current temperature: 29F, high of 28F at 3 P.M., low of 4F at 4 A.M.
Snowing, winds out of the southwest at 10mph.
53" mid-mountain, 61" at the summit. 3" new in the last 24 hours.
3" of new in the last 48.

Mike's shift had fallen on Christmas, but Ben offered to cover for him since he had no family outside of the brotherhood at the station. He said it made no difference to him, and that spending Christmas at the station was spending Christmas with family. Even though he acted as though it were no big deal, to Mike it was as much a heroic save as anything he'd ever done.

Mike stared at the Christmas tree, the presents, and then looked over at Cassie's stocking hanging by the fire. Kate's foresight made it feel a little less like doing it completely by himself, but it still had been deeply sad the night before, putting presents out without her, knowing it was the first of many years of doing this on his own.

He stood and looked, once again, at the decorations that

hung on the tree. Cassie had made them using copies of old family pictures. He studied several with Kate on them.

Cassie had slept late, and Mike was glad. It was going to be a hard day, so the shorter it was the better. Eventually, though, she appeared at the top of the stairs.

Cassie guessed her dad had been looking at the pictures on the tree. She could tell he had been crying.

"Merry Christmas," he said.

"Merry Christmas," she said back.

"Grandma and Grandpa called last night. They send hugs and kisses and are going to call you later today."

"That's good," Cassie said. "I wish they were here."

"I know. Grandpa's back is getting better, but he just wasn't well enough to make the trip."

As she looked at the whole scene in front of her, it felt as if she were in some sort of dream. She couldn't begin to absorb it. She stood there feeling numb.

Mike opened his arms for a hug and Cassie walked to him. He put his arms around her and kissed the top of her head. She felt his tears fall on her hair. "Before your mom got really sick, she went Christmas shopping for you." He pointed to the fireplace.

First, she took her Christmas stocking from the fireplace and brought it over to her mom's chair. She sat down and Socks jumped up in her lap. Cassie took out each gift in her Christmas stocking and carefully unwrapped it: hair accessories, flavored lip balms, sunblock, fancy pens and pencils, bubble bath, stickers, and two pair of lightweight wool socks with snowflakes on them. At the bottom was a tangerine and a small bag of bad-tasting chocolates wrapped in gold foil and stamped to look like coins. She got them every year.

When she was done with her stocking, she moved to the tree, where she unwrapped a wooden box with little copper triangles and tin strips nailed onto it to make angular designs. It looked like a treasure box. Cassie opened it and found a note taped to the top: "I thought you might need a pretty place to put our heart-shaped rocks. Love, Mom." Inside the treasure box, there were more presents.

She opened the smallest one first. It was an opal pendant on a silver chain. A little note inside read, "Are you wondering where my jewelry box went? I wrapped up all the pieces that were special to me for your future Christmases and birthdays and graduations. I wanted you to have this one first. It was the first Christmas gift your father ever gave me. I love how it sparkles. Love, Mom."

Cassie looked at her dad. "Is it okay if I wear it?" she asked.

He just nodded as tears streamed down his face.

"I need your help," she said.

Mike stood and took the necklace from her. He held it in his palm for a moment, remembering how he had done the same thing that first Christmas with Kate. He opened the tiny clasp between his thumb and finger and reached out to put it around his daughter's neck. The necklace had now begun chapter two. It was still Kate's and yet it wasn't.

The next gift was another wooden box, this one a recipe box containing a few recipes written on cards inside, along with blank cards and a heart-shaped cookie cutter. A note read, "If you make sugar cookies every Christmastime, I'll be there in spirit. I never could resist them, you know. Love, Mom."

After that, Cassie opened a delicate silver picture frame

with a picture of her mother and her in it. There was no note with this one. Cassie put it down and paused to try to remember the day it was taken. She couldn't. It was just their faces. It could have been taken anywhere.

Finally, she opened the last gift. It was a book with a cover that tied shut. Cassie felt uncomfortable untying it, undoing something her mother had done, but she wanted to see what was inside. She let the pages flutter through her fingers. All the pages were full of her mother's writing. She read the first page: "When someone you love dies, it's normal to lose your faith. I don't want you to lose yours. I want you to believe there is a force bigger than you in this world, a loving and compassionate force. I want you to believe that your life has meaning and your existence has purpose. And when life is hard, I want you to believe that you'll be given the strength to endure it, and that it will get better. I want you to have the peace in your heart you can only have when you believe there is a reason for everything, even if you cannot see it. All of those beliefs are sustaining me and strengthening me now. You and I never really talked about faith. In my family, a person's relationship with God was considered a personal thing. I figured if I kept taking you to the Church of the Rising Chairlift, you would find some kind of divinity and order in nature and build your own relationship with God. But I fear that you may not have had enough time to develop your own faith before you had to deal with my loss. Each day, I'll be writing a prayer so that I can share my faith with you. I love you, Cassie. And I believe that when you read this, I will be in a good place, still loving you and your father with all of my heart."

Cassie held the book to her heart. "Did you know about this?" she asked her father.

Mike nodded.

"Have you read it?" she asked.

He shook his head.

Even though Cassie knew the presents were just things, they seemed like a time capsule back to her mother—the book especially.

She tied the ribbons on the book and put it, along with the other things, back in the treasure chest. She shut the lid but loved knowing she could open it whenever she wanted or needed to, and that inside a new conversation with her mom awaited her.

Jill woke and lay in bed for a few moments, thinking of all the Christmas mornings she would not be watching her joyful child run to see what Santa left for him.

Thankfully, her thoughts were interrupted, if only momentarily, when Lisa opened Jill's door, ran toward her, and dove on her bed. "Merry Christmas! Merry Christmas!" she sang. She held a gift bag.

"Merry Christmas," Jill mumbled, and made herself smile.

"Come to my house! I made cinnamon rolls and I'm about to scramble eggs."

Jill looked at the clock. Six-thirty. She sat up and gave Lisa a hug. "Santa came for you," Jill said, and looked at another gift bag—this one on the floor.

"Goody!" Lisa exclaimed as quietly as she could so as not to wake the cat crew. She picked it up and began to unwrap its contents: Aubrey Natural Sports Bath, a cranberry-orange-scented candle, a pair of amethyst-and-silver earrings, a journal, SmartWool socks, a gift certificate for a ski wax, and a stainless-steel water bottle. "Yay! I love everything! Now you! Okay, some of these things are to help you cope with the Kennel and were meant to be funny."

Jill dug into the bag Lisa brought for her and found latex gloves, shower sandals, antifungal powder, and floral-scented Lysol. Next were things to help Jill cover up the bad smells: incense and a spicy-scented candle. Lisa also gave her a chunk of obsidian "for psychic protection" and had put a small print of "Saint Liberata, invoked against unwanted suitors and burdensome husbands," in a silver-and-turquoise frame.

"You definitely need that if you're going to live at the Kennel. It needs to be hung above your bed," Lisa said.

Lisa had one last gift for Jill—a rose quartz pendant on a silver chain to help heal Jill's heart. Jill put it on, touched it, gave Lisa a heartbroken smile, and said, "I think it's working."

"Let's make Tom's Christmas wish come true and wake him up by jumping on him," Lisa said.

Jill shook her head. "I don't really have that kind of relationship with him."

"Okay, I'll fly solo on this one," Lisa said.

Jill lingered a few minutes before getting out of bed, dressing, and tiptoeing to the front door, where she stepped into her boots.

Lisa and Tom made their way to the living room. Tom looked at the beer and gasped. "Santa came!" he exclaimed in a whisper voice. He emptied his stocking, put all the goodies in his coat pocket, looked at Jill, and said, "Thanks, Santa."

On their way out, Jill looked at the thermometer. It said four degrees. Her nose hairs froze immediately and her eye water thickened.

When Lisa opened her back door for them, Christmas music and the smell of cinnamon rolls wafted out. Lisa began to sing along with "Feliz Navidad." Tom gave her a kiss on the cheek and sang part of the song with her. Lisa proudly served up her whole-wheat cinnamon rolls with dried apricot chunks, Craisins, and almonds and then turned her attention to scrambling eggs.

"Is there anything more heavenly than cinnamon rolls?" Tom asked.

"Mm . . . ," Jill said as she unrolled her soft, warm roll and bit off the end of it. "So yummy. Oh, Lisa, this is so nice."

Lisa replied, "I wanted to have mimosas, but since we all have to work today, it didn't seem prudent. Juice or coffee?" she offered.

"Anything going on tonight?" Tom asked. "Cat party?"

"I don't know," Lisa said. "Remember last year? We were all so beat, we just wanted to go to bed."

Tom gave her a suggestive look. "Okay, Lisa. Tonight we'll celebrate in bed."

Jill rolled her eyes.

"Pardon me, Tom?" Lisa said. "Did you say celibate in bed? Yes, that's exactly what I had in mind."

"Ha! Well played, Lisa," Jill said.

Tom just smiled and took a sip of coffee.

"Mind if I check my e-mail real quick?" Jill asked.

"Help yourself," Lisa said.

Dear Family and Friends,

Merry Christmas! Blessed be this holy day, this day when God sent his only begotten son, Christ, our salvation. During this season, my thoughts often turn to King Herod, who ordered all babies under the age of one to be killed because he felt threatened by the new King. How divine King Herod didn't kill the Baby Jesus, for without Jesus, we'd all be damned. We delivered this message along with volleyballs and soccer balls to orphanages this morning, and hope our proselytizing takes root. Pray for all of us here.

Love,

Elder and Sister Anthony

Super, Jill thought, feeling sorry for all the Kenyan children who had been bribed with balls to sit through her parents' scary story. She remembered having to sit through that interminable story every Christmas morning before opening presents. The story itself made less sense than ever to her.

She looked at the clock and logged off. Then she and Tom said thank you again and rushed off to work.

The morning was relatively quiet. They had only one injury in the FAR—a local guy in his early twenties with no family. He sat with a bag of ice on his knee, looking depressed.

On her break, Jill went to see Uncle Howard. He had Christmas lights strung around the window and a plastic wreath on the door of his little apartment below the lodge. Jill knocked, and when she heard him shout, "Welcome!" through the door, she opened it.

"Merry Christmas!" he said, and gave her a big hug. Jill held it together and followed him to his table. He handed her two presents shaped like books. "Here," he said.

Jill bent one to see if it flexed like a book, which of course it did. "I wonder what it could be!" she teased. Before she opened it, though, she reached into her backpack to take out the bottle of mulled spiced wine she had gotten for him and half a dozen cranberry-orange scones from the Sparkle Café. She remembered Uncle Howard heating mulled spiced wine in an electric teapot around Christmas when she was a teenager.

He admired it, read the label, and smiled. "Don't mind if I do," he said, and went off to find a corkscrew. He returned and put a couple of scones on napkins for them.

Jill opened her gift. "*A Country Year,* by Sue Hubbell," she said, and read the back to herself. "This looks really good."

"When I described the type of book I wanted to find for you, not even knowing if it existed, Roger at the bookstore handed me this. He said it's one of his sister's all-time favorites. It does look good," Uncle Howard said.

Jill opened the next one. "*Tales of a Female Nomad,* by Rita Golden Gelman." She flipped it over to read the back of that one, too.

"Both authors write about their incredible lives after their divorces," he said.

Jill winced. She couldn't imagine staying married, but she couldn't imagine being divorced, either. Still, Uncle Howard's good intentions were obvious. "Well, thank you very much," she said.

They sat and ate their scones. "Mm! These are good!" Uncle Howard said. "Hey, have you heard from your parents? How's my sister?"

"Yeah, they're telling all the African children about King Herod and how we'd all be damned if he succeeded in killing baby Jesus." Jill shrugged and rolled her eyes. "Lately, I've been remembering these monthly fast and testimony meetings at the Church of Latter-day Saints. As if fasting wasn't torture enough, we had to go listen to everyone talk about what a worthless piece of trash they would be without their family and the Church. And we were expected to do it, too, so I'd get up and bear my testimony. But, you know, while no one told me I was doing it wrong, I was never given genuine praise for doing it right. I mean, I knew what genuine praise was from winning the spelling bee, acing a math test, or winning a track event, and I knew what patronizing praise was because I watched the rest of the kids get that, and I was keenly aware that at church, at best, I was given patronizing praise. Truly, I couldn't figure out how I could have loved God more. I read my scriptures, I quoted prophets, I felt guilty even though I hadn't done anything bad, I put a bunch of flowery words before the word *Lord*—I did everything. And it was never good enough. Maybe it's because I simply could never be meek enough."

Uncle Howard listened, shook his head slowly, and said, "No, you are not meek."

"I hate it that all these years later, it still makes me crazy."

"Anytime our truth is denied, it can make us feel crazy," he said.

"I wonder who I would be today if you hadn't rescued me from all that," Jill said.

"Maybe in Africa with your parents, handing out volleyballs and talking about damnation." Uncle Howard smiled, then paused for a moment and asked very tenderly, "How are you doing today?"

She knew he was talking about her loss. "I've got to say I'm having a tough time today," she answered quietly, her voice cracking once. "I keep thinking that this isn't how it was supposed to be."

Uncle Howard nodded. "If you can, judge less and observe more. Try it, Jill. Instead of thinking about how it was supposed to be, just look at it and watch it and think, Hm, isn't this interesting? You might see some opportunities you would have missed if you were still blinded by your attachments."

That sounded nice and all, but not particularly realistic for her today. Still, Jill said, "I'll try that."

"It's powerful," Uncle Howard said. "It's the secret to contentment and happiness."

Jill looked at her watch. "Oh, sorry, Uncle Howard, but my break's just about over. I have to get back down to the FAR." She put the books he gave her into her backpack. "Thanks so much for the books!"

He patted her on the back as he walked her to the door. "Merry Christmas, Jilly."

"Merry Christmas to you, too, Uncle Howard. I sure do love you."

"I love you, too," he said as she walked out into the cold.

Jill put her skis back on and glided along a little ridge while deciding which route she would take down. The tourists were starting to come out now that they were done with their Christmas morning rituals, so she skied the easiest way down, looking for anyone who might be in trouble, but all she saw were happy families skiing together.

The FAR had a few more guests in it than when she left, but all in all, it was quiet compared with what she knew it would be like tomorrow. Still, by the time the last person left the FAR at the end of the day, and the other patrollers were done sweeping the mountain, Jill was tired. She picked up, signed out, and went home. Lisa was right. She did just want to go to bed.

On her way home, something about the Christmas lights on the houses made Jill's heart ache. She remembered coming home in the middle of the night after working night shifts back when she'd just started her nursing career. David always left the Christmas lights on to welcome her home. It was such a little thing, really, but something about those lights always made her feel loved and so lucky to be coming home to a man who loved her. Now she looked around at the Christmas lights and thought about how just last night she'd wondered if she would come to see love everywhere as she had come to see Santa everywhere, and it occurred to her she did. Christmas lights still looked like love to her, even though they didn't look like love for her.

When she reached the Kennel, it was dark. Eric and Hans had forgotten to turn on the Christmas lights. It was a stark contrast to her early days with David. In addition, the only ones to greet her at the Kennel tonight were the dogs. They seemed happy to see her, though. *Maybe that's enough,* she thought. *Maybe it's enough to have dogs that are happy to see me.*

Eric had left Jill a bottle of red wine and a Christmas cactus in her room with a card. Inside, he had simply signed his name. Hans had left her a Whitman's Sampler. Jill was surprised and wondered if they had done that ahead of time or if they'd rushed off to the grocery store after seeing she had done something for them. Jill guessed the latter. Still, she smiled at their gifts.

When she went to the bathroom to brush her teeth, she discovered Tom had left her a gift on the bathroom counter. She unwrapped it and found three bars of soap from a local soap maker: lavender, wild rose, and cinnamon. They were all wrapped in pretty fabrics and smelled heavenly. She wondered how Tom came to pick out such a nice gift, and it crossed her mind that maybe he had slept with the soap maker. Whatever the case, it was a lovely gift.

Before she crawled into bed, she found herself missing David badly, so she called him, but she only got his voice mail. "It's a tough day, isn't it?" she said. "You're the only person in the whole world who would understand. I've been thinking about how hard grief is, how it makes us temporarily insane, but also about the good times and about the vows we made, and I want to keep my vows to you. I just would like to spend the winter here and heal, so that when I come back, it really does feel like a fresh start. Is that okay? Call me."

She lay in bed waiting for him to call, but he never did, and her stomach sank as she realized that he might be spending Christmas with the woman he had slept with. Even if he couldn't be her husband on this night, she had hoped he could at least have been her friend—the only person in the world who might be feeling her loss. She had hoped for at least a call, just to let her know she wasn't all alone in her grief. As time ticked by, she realized that the phone was not going to ring and that she was all alone in her grief.

Tom had gone out for drinks at the Gold Pan and had a nice holiday buzz as he walked the streets back home. But outside the door, he heard Jill's sobs, and it sobered him immediately.

Tom considered his options. He was going to require some backup, so before going into the Kennel, he went over to Lisa's. He opened the door without knocking. "Lisa?"

She sat watching *It's a Wonderful Life* on TV, looked up, and said, "Thomas, I said 'celibate,' not 'celebrate.' "

"No, it's Jill," he said. "This one's too big for me."

Lisa opened Jill's door, came in, and put her arms around her.

"It was supposed to be my baby's first Christmas," Jill sobbed.

"I know," Lisa said.

"I'll never get another chance to have that. I hemorrhaged and they had to perform a hysterectomy."

"Oh," Lisa said, and gave Jill an extra squeeze.

"I told David to sing to him because I couldn't sing to him. I couldn't sing to my own baby. I never got to sing to my own baby! I wanted to, but I couldn't stop crying. God, I hope he sang to our baby!" Jill covered her face with both hands and gasped for air as more sobs racked her body.

Lisa just held on until Jill finally fell asleep. She knew there were no words.

Then she snuck out of Jill's room and into Tom's. He was lying on his back under the covers with his knees bent. Stout slept on the bed next to him, near the window.

Tom looked over at Lisa in his door and waited.

She came in, lifted the covers, and crawled in next to him, fitting her back in close to him. He rolled over on his side and put his arm around her. She put her hand over his.

"Thank you," she said.

He held her tighter.

"Thank you," he replied.

chapter twelve

• • •

SNOW REPORT FOR DECEMBER 31

Current temperature: 18F, high of 21F at 2 P.M., low of 14F at 4 A.M.
Clear skies, winds out of the southwest at 45 mph with gusts of up to 70 mph.
56" mid-mountain, 64" at the summit. 0" new in the last 24 hours.
2" of new in the last 48.

So, are you doing okay these days?" Eric asked Jill as she sat in the groomer next to him, eating pizza. Jill thought his voice was like one of those motel beds that vibrate when you stick quarters in it. It was low and sexy and made her cheeks tickle. Yes, the Kennel men were charmers.

"Uh-huh," Jill answered as though everything were fine, and took another bite.

Eric looked at her a little too long.

"You know, don't you?" she asked without looking at him.

He paused. "Yeah," he said. "Tom told me. That's so rough, Jill. I'm sorry."

She just nodded and looked at her pizza. "Quick, change the subject," she said.

"So, I'm sure you remember the Dirtbag Ball—Sparkle's raunchy prom where that year's ultimate ski bum is crowned the dirtbag king or queen . . . usually someone who crawled out of their VW bus in the resort parking lot each morning all winter smelling like body odor and their three dogs, ate a slice of leftover pizza, and caught first chair up the mountain."

Jill laughed. No one had ever summed it up so perfectly.

"Well, I've been putting together my Dirtbag Ball costume," he continued. "A couple years ago I wore duct tape pants, but they were too hot, so last year I changed things up to make them more workable. I made duct tape shorts to go with my duct tape vest and tie. I didn't get to wear them last year, though, because I lost a bet and had to wear a dress instead."

"Bummer," Jill said.

As midnight approached, Eric drove to the top of the mountain near the others, pointed the cat toward where the fireworks would be, and turned it off. To their right was Hans with Lisa in his cat, and on the other side of them was Tom, who had ridden up with someone Jill hadn't met yet.

"Hang on," Eric said, and stepped outside. High winds nearly blew him over as he walked to the base of a little tree and came back in with a bottle of champagne. "Whew!" he said.

Just then, his phone rang. "Yeah," he said into it. "It's way too windy . . . Okay. Later." He hung up and put the phone back in his pocket. "Everyone is staying in the cats. It's wicked out there."

Jill didn't mind. She liked being warm.

He opened the door, popped the cork, and held the bottle outside while it spilled over. Then he handed it to Jill and she took a swig while he shut his door. When she handed it back, the first fireworks began exploding and Eric leaned over for a New Year's kiss. "Happy New Year, Jill," he said, and planted a soft one on her. It was a little too long to be what Jill would call a friendly New Year's kiss between buddies. But then it was over and he took a swig of champagne.

"Happy New Year," Jill replied, a little flustered.

"You're going to have a much better year," he said. "I made all kinds of good wishes for you while I was kissing you, so they're going to come true."

"Really? Is that how it works? I didn't make any wishes for you," Jill said.

"What? You've got to make some good wishes for me. Come on, let's do it again," he said.

"Hold on," Jill said, and took a really long swig of champagne. As her inhibitions subsided, she unbuckled her seat belt so she could crawl partway over the console in the middle. She gulped a little more champagne and handed it back. He leaned over for the kiss. "Wait," she said, and held up a finger. "I have to think. This wishing thing is a big responsibility."

"Come here, you goof," he said, and put a hand behind her head to pull her in for a kiss—still no tongue, but definitely more passionate. Jill tried to think of at least one good wish for him, but her mind went blank. All she could think of was that she wished he'd stop smoking pot every day and take better care of his health. "Sorry if that was a bit much," he said, "but I really wanted your good wishes to come true."

That made Jill laugh. If only he knew what they were, he wouldn't. Outside, big explosions of red, purple, white, and green filled the sky.

"What?" he asked, alarmed that she was laughing. "What did you wish?"

"Well, what did you want me to wish for you?" she asked.

"Health, happiness, good snow, good crops, good hunting season—you know, the standards," he said.

"Uh-oh," she said. "Then I screwed up." She laughed some more and rubbed her forehead. "I'm really sorry. God, I hope you don't have a bad year all because of me."

"Quick, Jill! Do-over! There's still time! My future is at stake!"

This time, Jill put her hand on his cheek and kissed him very gently and very sweetly, and she wished for him all the things he desired. He had one hand on her arm and the other on her thigh. The kiss ended slowly and just as tenderly as it had begun. "Okay, I nailed it that time," Jill said with a big, proud smile.

"I made another wish for you, too."

"Thanks," Jill said, and crawled backward back into her seat to watch the rest of the fireworks. Eric handed her the bottle and she took another drink.

"You're a good kisser," he said.

"Thanks. You too," Jill replied, as if it were the most normal thing in the world. "Wait, is it weird that we just kissed three times?" she asked.

"No," he said. "They were New Year's kisses."

"Oh, good," Jill said. *Of course,* she realized. Eric likely kissed several women a season, or even a month. For him, it was definitely not a big deal. They could have slept together and for him it still would not have been a big deal. And of course it was strange to her. She hadn't kissed anyone other than David since she was twenty.

She did feel some satisfaction at having kissed another man besides David. Like maybe she had evened the score just a little. She didn't want to feel that way, but she did. Then she began to wonder if David had also just kissed someone tonight. She wanted to believe he hadn't, but in her gut she had a feeling that he had. Still, Jill felt kissing Eric put her on more even ground with David. She was no longer guiltless. And she also understood something about how a person could feel something good and exciting with a new person, and how it was possible to get caught up in it and not to think about your spouse.

The ball in Times Square was on TV along with thousands of people excited for the promise of the new year. Cassie watched them with disdain. "How did they pick this day to be the beginning of the year, anyway?" she asked.

"I don't know," Mike answered. "The sun doesn't do anything special on this day. The moon doesn't do anything special on this day. I have no idea who pulled this day out of a hat."

"It seems like a big bunch of crap to me," Cassie said.

"Let's use the word *baloney* instead."

"Like in an hour everything is going to be all perfect and new, like everything that sucked about last year will be gone. . . . It's just crap," Cassie said.

"Baloney," Mike corrected again.

"Tomorrow we're going to wake up and everything that sucks is still going to suck."

Mike didn't really like that word choice either, but he decided now might not be the time to pick that battle. Now might be the time to simply hear his daughter. He wasn't sure what to do, but he figured getting away from the TV might be a good first step. "Want to snowshoe up the little ridge and watch the fireworks?"

"Sure," Cassie said.

So they got dressed and trudged up a ridge to a little knoll not particularly far up on Big Daddy, and although they were tired, it felt good. It felt good to simply move forward in the little ways that they could. It felt good to move forward instead of lie down and give up. Mike carried a backpack with two nylon chairs that folded up into skinny tubes, a bottle of sparkling apple cider, and a little coconut cake someone had left at the station as a thank-you, and when they reached the knoll, he took it all out, popped the cork, and handed Cassie a fork.

They sat there for a few minutes in silence, just looking at the night sky together. The Milky Way was so thick with stars, it was practically blinding. Cassie took a few bites of cake and handed it back to her dad.

Mike was thinking about how on years when he'd worked on New Year's Eve, Kate had walked to the station for her midnight kiss. One year he was on a call and missed it. He thought about how it must have been hard to be his wife, to be alone at some pretty important moments, to be robbed of holidays, or at least holidays at home, birthdays, all that. Before she told him about the lump in her breast, when he knew something was wrong but wasn't sure what, he wondered if the distance he felt was the cumulative effect of all the times he had let her down—all those little disappointments.

"I'm cold," Cassie said.

"Then let's go," Mike replied, and he folded up the chairs and put them back in his backpack along with the uneaten cake. He carried the bottle of sparkling cider as they walked away since he couldn't put the cork back in it.

The fireworks started as they walked down through a sparse glade of young trees. They paused for a moment to watch a few, then kept walking.

When they reached home, Cassie ran herself a bath while Mike made cocoa. She took a mug into the bath with her, stirred the little marshmallows until they melted into the chocolate, and then sipped away at it until her core began to warm again. Halfway through the cup, she watched the designs the remaining melted marshmallows made. Some spots looked like hearts. And she looked at the surface of her bathwater, where the bubble bath had all popped down to a simple soapy layer, and saw hearts in that, too.

It made her wonder if they were messages from her mother like the stones, messages that the new year would be better, or if the hearts in her cocoa and in her bath just meant that hearts were everywhere if you looked for them.

chapter thirteen

• • •

SNOW REPORT FOR JANUARY 1

Current temperature: 17F, high of 22F at 2 P.M., low of 12F at 4 A.M.
Clear skies, winds out of the southwest at 20 mph with gusts of up to 30 mph.
58" mid-mountain, 65" at the summit. 0" new in the last 24 hours.
0" of new in the last 48.

The next morning, Jill slipped into the shower sandals that Lisa gave her for Christmas, grabbed her toilet paper, and made her way to the bathroom like every other morning. This morning, though, she noticed Eric's door was open. She poked her head in and confirmed that his dog, Ale, was the only one sleeping in there. Eric hadn't come home last night. Just then Tom walked out of the bathroom and gave her a questioning look.

Jill just raised her eyebrows, shrugged, and passed Tom. She went into the bathroom and shut the door, and while she brushed her teeth, she looked at her reflection and wondered if she was actually feeling a little possessive of Eric. At no point had she projected herself and Eric into the future, living on a farm part-time or in the Kennel part-time as a married couple. She couldn't picture it. What she realized was that when he gave her the New Year's kisses, he affirmed that she was desirable. She wanted him to keep affirming that, but instead he replaced her with an undoubtedly sexier woman and affirmed Jill's worst fear: She wasn't *that* desirable. It was just ego stuff, she knew, but it still compounded the damage done by David.

At the end of the day, Eric stopped in on his way to work just to say hi to Tom and Jill. "Happy New Year!" he exclaimed, a little too happy for Jill's comfort. Happy in that way a man was after he had a *very* good night.

"Hey, Eric. Looks like your new year is off to a great start," she said curtly, and then went to the back, where she restocked first-aid kits.

From the back room, Jill heard the mumbling of a brief conversation, and then Eric shouted, "See you later!" to her. She shouted it back and wondered if he had picked up on her tension. She hoped she hadn't been that obvious. After Eric left, Tom and Jill went to their lockers to get their gear, then rode chair five to begin their end-of-the-day sweep to make sure all the guests were safely off the hill.

On the chair, Tom said, "Look, Jilly, I saw the way you looked at Eric when he stopped by."

"Really, Tom? And how was that?" which came out a little too bitterly, giving her away.

Tom gave Jill one of those "assess the situation" looks before he spoke. "Hear me out. I'm about to tell you the ultimate man secret."

Jill laughed, easing the tension. "This should be good."

"Males are born to do one thing," he began. "They have one purpose in life, and that's to have sex with females."

"That's a secret?" Jill laughed.

"Listen, you may think you know it, but I'm about to help you know it on a deeper level. In many species, males have to fight other males to be the one that has sex with the female. The ones who win these fights and get the girls are the alpha males. Now females are born to do one thing and that's have babies." He suddenly realized how that might sound to Jill, but he kept going. "A female, in most cases, anyway, can only get pregnant by one male, and since there's no shortage of them, she doesn't need to fight. Meanwhile, the male can get several females pregnant, which is his goal, even if he's not conscious of it. He needs to spread that sperm far and wide because chances are that even when he's done fighting other males, his sperm is fighting the sperm of other males. There are no guarantees that he did his job, so his job is never done. This is the nature of men. Are you following me so far?"

Jill rolled her eyes and nodded.

"Good, okay. Now here comes the tricky part. In some species, the males who stand no chance of competing with other males in the conventional ass-kicking way have figured out that if they show a female some gestures of helpfulness, she'll give him access to the hooch. He may not spread his sperm far and wide, but at least he impregnates somebody. He may even go so far as to provide the female and her offspring with food in hopes of having access to her again. But make no mistake, this is not the preferred strategy of the male. This is the beta male strategy. That's why Scooter is the only one of us who has a girlfriend—he's the ugliest. And Paul and I totally screwed up Jason's back last year in the Ski Patrol Olympics when we went off a little cliff with him in the sled, so on some level Jason knows he's weak and can't go to battle over women. That's why he got married. If only we had put Paul in the sled instead. Anyway, this stuff is hardwired. It's imperative you know the difference between alpha and beta males."

"Are you serious?"

Tom nodded.

"What are you?" Jill asked.

"You need to ask? I'm an alpha. I fuck a lot of women. However, I noticed I've begun to lose some of my hair, so in the foreseeable future, it's possible it won't be as easy for me to get into the pants of so many women every ski season. See, soon I'm going to have to change my strategy and lock in one woman before I go completely bald, so at least I'm getting some from somebody."

Jill said, "Ah. So, you're trying to tell me Eric is also an alpha male."

"Yes. And maybe there are moments when you wish he loved you, but here's the thing—he already does. It's just that alpha male love looks different from beta male love. Eric's idea of love means he would help you if you ever needed help, especially if that involved having sex with you. Let's say you wanted revenge on your ex-husband so you devised a plan to trick him into thinking you wanted to spice up the marriage by tying him up for some hot dirty sex. Then once he's tied up, you let Eric out of the closet and let him go to town on you so your husband can have that image etched in his mind the way you have that woman riding him etched in yours. Eric would do that for you. It may seem like a big favor to ask, but in providing it, he gets to have sex with you *and* outcompete another male. It's every man's fantasy. Well, it would be if it involved fucking more women."

"And what about David?"

"David used to be a beta male. He was probably some geeky little bookworm in school, right? While the football players hosted big frat parties filled with drunk, loose sorority girls, he was in the library. He knew ultimately he'd outcompete the football players over time, but he couldn't do it right then, so he put a little energy into winning you over, sealed the deal by marrying you, and then stopped putting energy into you. He simply capitalized on his investment by nailing you on a regular basis. Then one day, all his library time finally paid off. He became a businessman with enough money to buy food for a whole harem. The single women looked at this and thought half of that pie was still bigger than the smaller whole pies being offered elsewhere, and so desired your husband. He realized he was no longer a beta male, but had finally graduated to alphadom and capitalized on the mass breeding rights he worked so hard for.

"I'm telling you this because women take it all so personally, and it's not personal at all. It's *Wild Kingdom*. No matter what you do, no matter how sweet and hot you are, you are never going to make an alpha male adopt the mating strategy of a beta male—period. The only time that will appear to happen is if the alpha knows the next time he locks horns with another male, he will likely lose. Then the alpha male will make the shift. It's not personal, though—just good timing for the woman."

Jill looked stunned, so Tom explained, "Howard loaned me some books on sociobiology."

"Clearly you've thought about this a lot," Jill said.

"I haven't just thought about it, Jill. I've lived it."

"So where does the miracle of love fit into your *Wild Kingdom* philosophy?" she asked. She could see the end of the lift approaching.

"Jill, Jill, Jill. Come on. You went to nursing school. Most people think love comes from the heart or soul. The heart simply pumps blood, so love can't be created there. Where is the center for what appears to be a person's soul? The brain. And what is created there, Jilly? That's right—dopamine. What does dopamine do? Creates feelings of love and euphoria. How do we get our brains to create more? Drugs, massage, and/or sex. Boil it down and it's all just dopamine. The good news is that you can also get more dopamine pumping through your brain by skiing fast, hence the multiple snowgasms of which Lisa speaks."

Their feet hit the ramp and they stood up. Tom, on the inside of the turn at the bottom of the ramp, took the lead. Jill followed a few feet behind him and to his right as they swept Lollygag.

Jill thought about what Tom said and wondered if he was right or whether she had just chosen to hope Eric would boost her ego because she knew there was no real possibility of anything serious happening between them.

Lollygag was an easy run marked with a green circle. To Jill, the joy of the easy run was just pointing her skis down and giving it all over to gravity. Little dips and turns combined with high speeds made it feel like a roller-coaster ride. She went on autopilot, letting her body function without her brain while she admired snow on the trees and the mistletoe that grew in the treetops. Sometimes on runs like these, she'd see the flash of a red fox running through the woods next to her or little chipmunks treasure hunting under the lift. That's when it always happened. Today it was a snowshoe hare that caught her eye. She caught an edge and was airborne long enough to contemplate how the false sense of security that led to her wipeout was likely a factor in her marital problems as well.

Fortunately, Tom was ahead of her and didn't look back before she got up. He had explained to her recently that there was an ugly necklace with a wooden corkscrewlike thing on it called the Auger that was passed from patroller to patroller. No one wanted it because whoever had it on payday had to buy all the other patrollers flaming shots at the Gold Pan. A patroller with the Auger could relieve himself of it if he saw another patroller fall while skiing in uniform. Jill didn't know if Tom had the Auger, but she was glad he didn't see, just in case.

She pulled into the lift line a minute or two behind Tom, long enough for him to realize he'd lost his chance. What started as an amused look grew into a big smile. "Really? On Lollygag?" he said, and brushed some snow out from the crack between her goggles and her helmet. "Gaper."

"I have no idea how that snow got there," Jill declared with a smile.

"I have a pretty good idea," Tom said, and skied up to the chair-loading line.

Jill followed him. "You can't prove anything," she said.

"Hey, Scooter," Tom said. "I want you to notice the snow in Jill's helmet."

Scooter looked and asked, "Good run?"

Tom answered, "Oh, it was great. It was *Lollygag*."

Jill gave Tom a little punch while Scooter snickered.

"Wet T-shirt night at the Gold Pan," Tom told Scooter.

"I'm a no-go," Scooter said. "Hot date with my girlfriend."

"The man-to-woman ratio up here is six to one. I still can't figure out how you got a woman," Tom said.

"I just asked your mother and she said yes," Scooter replied.

"Oh!" Jill said just as the chair came up behind them and lifted them up and away.

"Who knew the secret to unloading the Auger was not to take your partner down the burliest runs, but to take them on Lollygag, where they'll . . . what, were you looking at nature? Oh, that's beautiful. I can't believe I missed it." He paused for a moment, thoughtful, and then said, "I might still get a beer out of this anyway."

"How's that?" Jill asked.

"Two. Two beers. Good beers. Fat Tire Ambers. That is the

cost of me not including 'Jill ate it on Lollygag yesterday' during morning announcements tomorrow, and/or including it in the Peter Book."

The Peter Book was a journal that was brought out every payday at the bar during drinks, where the patroller who did the stupidest thing during the pay period had to write his or her story and then read it aloud. Jill hadn't attended any of these payday events but was hearing more and more about them. She was more than self-conscious enough to find the whole prospect mortifying.

"Done," she said. "Would you like your beers at the lodge or at home?"

"Oh, I think the lodge has a nice ambience. Plus, that's where the babes are."

"Of course," she said. "Hey, Tom? Back to what you were saying before, how does birth control play into all of this? I mean, if all males want to get as many females pregnant as possible, why the condoms?"

He nodded. "Excellent question, Jilly. Beta male strategies were written into law because beta males, smarty pants that they are, were writing laws while the alphas were busy having sex. If an alpha male is paying child support to five women, he's no longer desirable. He can't afford to ski or look good or buy girls drinks, so he doesn't get laid. Now the beta males can weasel in for some action. Child support makes mating more complicated for alphas for sure, but make no mistake, the biological imperative to have sex with as many women as possible is most definitely hardwired."

They passed the signs on the chairlift poles instructing them to be prepared to unload. Then their feet hit the ramp and they were off to sweep Meander, another easy run.

"You go in front this time!" Tom called, hanging back. "I've only got a week to get rid of the Auger!"

When they were done sweeping, Jill went to the bar and ordered Tom his two bottles of Fat Tire Amber and one for herself. As she walked toward Tom with the beer and reflected on all his big brother advice, she realized he was the brother she never had. When she returned, they clinked beers, said cheers, and took a drink.

Lisa walked in, spotted them, and, as she made her way toward them, began to peel off her hat, goggles, neck gator.

"See, Jill, women take just one look at me and begin to peel their clothes off," Tom said.

"Clearly it's your alpha man smell," Jill replied.

"Clearly," Tom agreed.

"Tom's been giving me his *Wild Kingdom* take on relationships," Jill explained to Lisa.

"Is that right?" Lisa asked.

"Tell me about Lisa's mating strategy," Jill prompted. "Listen to this, Lisa."

"I've given this a lot of thought," Tom began, "because it could be one of two things. Okay, the females of many species show signs when they're fertile, thereby letting the males know it's their big chance, but human females hide their fertility. We never know when they're in heat, so if a male wants to increase his odds of impregnating her, he needs to stick around for a few weeks. And how does he get her to tolerate him this long? He's nice to her. Why? Because he really likes her and cares about her? No. Because he wants to have sex with her. That's all. Simple as that. So if Lisa can make several men think there is even the slightest chance they might get lucky, she can get them to do all kinds of nice things for her. Sven will fix her roof. I will shovel her sidewalk. Cody will make her dinner, and so on."

Lisa nodded. "That's a fact. Men will do anything for women if they think they have even the slimmest shot."

"That's one possibility. The problem arises when we consider what would happen to Lisa if she actually got pregnant. She'd have no help because she hadn't wanted to seal the deal before she let the father into her pants. In this culture, we men have done a truly remarkable job making our mating strategy—promiscuity—fashionable. A lot of women like Lisa aren't even questioning what's in their best interest anymore, and that bodes well for us alpha males.

"In many species, some females prefer to mate with an alpha male even though that male will be long gone by the time their baby is born. See, the female wants her offspring to have alpha male qualities—maybe good looks, athletic ability, maybe a good singing voice, a large stature—so that the next generation will be able to compete well for a good mate or lots of mates and pass on the genes. But you generally see that in scenarios where there is little hope and so little food that the female will send her offspring out on its own sooner than usual. The alpha female strategy is, of course, to lock in a partner to help her long term, so by adopting the alpha *male* mating strategy, the female forfeits her ability to be an alpha female. See, no male is going to invest long-term energy into a female if he thinks the likelihood of her child being his is not great. These things were hardwired long before paternity tests." Tom looked quite pleased with himself and his display of brilliance.

Lisa got quiet. She scanned the room. "Excuse me," she said, and walked over to talk to a group of ski school instructors.

"Uh-oh," Tom said.

"Yeah," Jill said. "That was some killer mating strategy you displayed just now. Good thing you gave it a lot of thought."

"You're going to help me fix it, right?"

"Repeat after me, Tom. Ready?" Jill said, "I, Tom . . ."

"I, Tom . . ."

"Do hereby renounce my brilliant alpha male theories as complete and utter crap," Jill said.

"But they're not crap," he said.

"As long as you believe that, Lisa's off-limits," Jill said. "Really, Tom, what kind of friend would I be if I helped Lisa hook up with a man who sees her as a plan B? She's no plan B. You know what? None of us are. We're women, Tom—women. And we're blessings, even if all of you are too stupid and blind to see it."

Jill took her beer and left him there to think about it.

Cassie had taken her mother's cookbooks off the shelf and was leafing through the pages, mostly looking at pictures, when Jill arrived.

"You look like you're on a mission," Jill said.

"I just got to thinking that there's not a lot I can do, you know? There's not a lot I can do to make things better now. But I could learn to make really good food, and that would make my life a little better. And it would make Dad's life a little better, too."

"Brilliant," Jill said. "Hey, I had an idea for making things better today, too. I was thinking about how if I helped you win a season pass, it would almost be like my service paid for itself."

"Talk to me," Cassie said, which cracked Jill up.

"Does the mountain still have the Dummy Downhill, you know, where you make a dummy on skis and they launch it off the ski jump and whoever's goes farthest wins a season pass for next year?"

"Why, yes, it does," Cassie replied, again making Jill laugh. Then they looked at each other with their best cunning and sly expressions and nodded their unspoken pact: They would dominate the Dummy Downhill.

Later that night, after dinner was cleaned up and homework was done, Cassie excitedly sketched ideas for their dummy. It was the first time in a long time she actually felt excited about something, and that it was a project with Jill made it complicated. Cassie wondered whether Jill was replacing her mother so slowly that she didn't even realize what was happening. And Cassie wondered whether she was letting her. Was it a betrayal to her mom to have fun with Jill? Would she slowly start to forget things about her mother as Jill became a bigger part of her life? She wondered whether she should take a couple steps back from Jill while she figured it out. Probably. But she couldn't quite bring herself to do it.

chapter fourteen

. . .

SNOW REPORT FOR JANUARY 6

Current temperature: 23F, high of 24F at 2 P.M., low of 19F at 1 A.M. Increasing clouds, winds out of the southwest at 30 mph with gusts of up to 45 mph.

61" mid-mountain, 69" at the summit. 0" in the last 24 hours.

0" of new in the last 48.

After Cassie went out the door for school, Jill continued to try to get the burned waffle out of the waffle iron without scratching the nonstick surface. She was deep in her own thoughts when Mike came in.

He took off his coat and boots, paused to look at Kate's picture as he walked through the front room, and made his way to the kitchen. Something about him seemed different, something in his demeanor had changed.

As he walked into the kitchen, Jill handed him a glass of orange juice.

"What's going on?" she asked.

He paused and leaned against the doorjamb. "Tough night," he said.

"Yeah?" Jill asked.

He nodded. "Sometimes we see things—bad things. I had to go on a really bad call last night."

She waited. After a long pause, she said, "I didn't last one whole day on my shift after returning to work. They brought in this meth addict pregnant lady who gave birth way too early. She didn't even want to see her baby, so I stayed with him while he died. It brought me to my knees, you know, seeing someone take something I wanted so much for granted and throw it away."

He nodded. She understood. She understood perfectly. She understood how ugly this medical field could be and how it was even uglier after a loss. It was such a relief to be with someone who understood. He looked away for a moment and then said, "Cassie said you lost a baby. I'm so sorry."

She nodded back. "Yeah, that may not have been an appropriate thing to share with her, but she was giving me attitude on my due date and I needed her to let up."

"I don't think it was a bad thing for her to realize that everyone has their heartbreaks, and that just because someone looks fine doesn't mean that they are."

They had never really had a conversation where it seemed appropriate to look into each other's eyes for any length of time, and now that they were, Jill saw so many things: pain, of course, but also compassion, and nonjudgment, deep concern, and something like endurance or tolerance—something that would continue to withstand it. Continue to withstand all of humanity's heartbreaks. Continue to withstand Cassie's. And continue to withstand his own. And she saw something warm and she saw something that was searching, although she didn't know exactly for what. Maybe answers. Maybe something to fill the empty places everyone had. Maybe someone to fill the empty places everyone had. She shrugged as though she didn't know, and after a short pause she asked, "What happened last night?"

He took a deep breath and let it out. "Car wreck with two sixteen-year-old boys. Mangled. Just mangled. It took us a long time to get the driver's body out. Meanwhile, some witness must have made some calls. I pulled this dead kid out and was holding him in my arms, and I turned around, and there were his folks, looking at us, devastated. Just devastated."

Jill shook her head. Tears brimmed in her eyes. She wanted to take him in her arms and tell him everything would be all right, but she didn't because it wouldn't. Everything would not be all right. So instead, she just continued to listen.

He said, "Yeah, you know, death is a part of life. I get it, but it's one thing when Grandma dies of heart disease. It's another when it's a kid, and the causes aren't natural."

Jill understood this. "I used to see birth defects from time to time that were so severe that the baby didn't even look human. I think that was the thing that got to me the most. I'd watch these parents try to grasp that the child they had been dreaming of was not going to have any kind of quality of life, but thanks to us, they weren't going to leave this world, either. They were just going to spend a lifetime in purgatory." Memories of babies and parents flashed through her mind, and she wondered how they were doing now.

Mike rested his head in his hands. "Sometimes I come home, and I'm just so happy that Cassie survived another day. There are days that seems nothing short of incredible. I mean, in any given neighborhood in any part of the country, every twenty houses or so, someone is dealing with some big shit. I don't mean natural stuff, but really bad stuff."

Jill just nodded.

"I'm sorry. I didn't mean to wreck your day," he said, suddenly self-conscious.

"You didn't wreck my day. I've been there. Usually it's not the dead ones that get you, but their survivors." She went back to cleaning the waffle iron.

"What do you remember about Kate?" Mike asked.

Jill didn't know how much to divulge. He wanted to hear good things, she knew. "She gave me an apple once when I forgot my lunch, and it surprised me because I never had the feeling she liked me. Mostly, my memories of her are of her racing. She was fearless. She was a force."

He smiled sadly. "Yeah. She was." He poured himself a little more orange juice and then asked, "So you weren't friends?"

"We weren't enemies," Jill replied. "I see her in Cassie sometimes. She's a force in her own way."

Mike raised his eyebrows as he nodded in agreement. "You should have seen her before Kate . . ."

Jill nodded.

"When we crossed paths on the sidewalk this morning, she handed me a grocery list for all the ingredients in the dinner she wants to make with you, and then asked if we could hit the hardware store for PVC pipe for the dummy project. I can't tell you how nice it is to see her excited about things again. Thanks for that. You've been really good for her. She really likes you." Jill noticed the dimples at the corners of his mouth when he smiled just a little.

"Well, it's mutual," she replied.

Then the dimples disappeared as he paused and then said, "I worry about her."

"Time," Jill said. "Or so they tell me."

"Well, thanks for listening," he said.

Jill could tell he was finished. "I'll see you the day after tomorrow," she said.

He followed her to the door. "See you."

"Take care," she replied, and let herself out.

After Jill left, Mike walked up the stairs to his bedroom. He lay down on his side of the bed and looked over at Kate's side. What he remembered was the sense that she was always miles and miles away.

"How come you never tell me about your day?" she'd asked him once. There was nothing particularly soft about the way she'd asked, nothing that would lead him to think she could be any kind of comfort, even if she could understand, which she couldn't. It was almost a challenge. "I can tell when you've had a bad day, you know. You're distant."

He had pulled a three-year-old out of a pond that day, and it just hit too close to home.

"I don't want to talk about it. Talking about it with you doesn't help. It doesn't help to get it off my chest. You haven't seen a whole bunch of dead kids," he'd said.

Kate had rolled over, turning away from him. He had rolled over on his side and put an arm around her, but it did no good. Neither one could bridge the distance between them.

When Jill stepped out of the bathroom, the sheriff was waiting for her near the door of the FAR. "Jill Fritz?" he asked.

"Yes?" she answered, alarmed.

"I have something for you from the great state of Texas," he said, and served her with papers. "Sorry to be the bearer of bad news." He turned and left.

She was speechless. She examined the petition for divorce. David had filed for a no-fault divorce, stating the reason simply as "unsupportability." The other document was a notice of a hearing for temporary orders in less than two weeks. She would need to find and hire a lawyer somehow, take time off from both of her jobs, and get back to Austin.

She hated the word *divorce,* and now here it was about to be stuck to her like a stain that couldn't be removed. For the rest of her life, she'd check the divorced box on forms. It was going to be part of her identity. Divorced.

When Jill walked into the Kennel after work that night, Lisa was sitting with the guys on the couch, mesmerized by the TV.

"Lisa, you're in the Kennel," Jill said, shocked.

"We're watching *The Bachelor,*" Tom said, poured Jill some wine, and handed it to her. "We take a generous sip every time someone says 'amazing,' 'incredible,' 'like,' 'connection,' 'oh, my God,' and whenever anyone toasts or someone cries."

"I like to watch other women get dumped," Lisa said plainly. "It's been really healing for me."

Horrified, Jill shot Lisa a look. "Huh?"

Lisa explained, "It makes me feel normal, you know, to see that everyone feels like they were robbed of their rightful destiny when they get dumped. But it doesn't mean they were. Like this guy is totally wrong for that girl, and yet, when he dumps her, she's going to go on and on like he was her soul mate. They all do. He's not their soul mate. He can't be all of their soul mates! That's obvious to any objective observer. So I like to imagine that God is up there when I'm getting dumped and watching me like I'm watching them and thinking, Oh no, honey, he is definitely not for you. Believe me, this is for the best."

Someone on the show managed to get four drinking words into one sentence, so they all took four drinks and then watched the bachelor dump some girls. The jilted ones went outside to cry. Everyone drank some more. Jill was drunk in about five minutes.

"This is more painful than calling a woman after sleeping with her," Hans said.

"See?" Lisa asked. "Don't you just want to go, 'Hey, chica, that bozo made out with five other women last night! He's no prize!' "

"So a man who has played the field is no prize?" Tom asked, looking right at Lisa.

There was an awkward standoff moment, and then Jill announced, "David served me with divorce papers today."

"That fucker," Lisa said. "Jilly, you've got to believe me, it's for the best. You're going to be much happier from here on out."

Jill held up one finger. "And you know what else? . . . I forgot. Wait. Oh. You know what else? Even if no one ever loves me again, I am going to be much happier from here on out. Because I get to ski and that's all I need to produce dopamine."

"That's right," Lisa said. "We've got snow. We don't need sex."

The men rolled their eyes at one another.

"I have to go to Austin in two weeks for a hearing," Jill said. She turned to Tom and said, "Boss, I'm going to need a few days off."

"No problem," Tom replied.

"I'm going with you," Lisa said.

"Oh, Lisa, that's sweet. You don't have to," said Jill.

"I'm going," Lisa said definitively. "All right. It's time for me to get my beauty sleep." The show was over.

Jill walked her to the door and hugged her before she left. Three dogs immediately replaced Lisa and Jill and sat on the couch with Tom, who had flipped to a movie with fast cars and shooting guns. Eric and Hans had moved into the kitchen and were making marijuana cookies.

"Hey, Tom," Jill said. "I'm drunk."

"That's okay," he replied. "I'm drunk *and* stoned."

Jill went to her room, found her cell phone, and held it for a moment while she contemplated all the girls on *The Bachelor* who felt their destinies had been stolen. Seeing just how hopelessly indignant they were should have helped Jill make a better choice, but she drunk-dialed her old phone number anyway. While it rang, she looked at her clock: It was eleven forty. Austin was an hour later, which meant it was past midnight there. After the fourth ring, it went to voice mail. David's voice said, "Leave a message and I'll get back to you as soon as I can."

"Will you, David? Will you really get back to me as soon as you can? Because I called on Christmas, and you still haven't called me back. You just sent a sheriff to give me papers instead," Jill slurred, and started to cry. "David, is it because I can't have kids anymore? Is that when I became so worthless to you? Is that why you had to replace me? Is it just that you want to be a dad so bad? Is that why? I'm just trying to figure out how someone who knew me so well could think I was so worthless. But it's okay, because I get to ski and you don't and I don't need you. All right. Well, I hope I didn't interrupt your hot sex with that home-wrecking whore. David, I really hope you get a very bad disease and your dick burns and blisters and then just falls off."

She hung up and walked back out to the front room. "I just drunk-dialed my husband."

The guys looked up and waited for some clue about what the appropriate reaction might be.

Finally Tom broke the silence. "Well, I don't know why you would want just one husband when you can have this platonic harem here at the Kennel." He began to rub his own chest. "All this manliness plus you get to ski every day. Why would you want to trade that for one lousy husband in *Texas*? Look, those guys make cookies. Did your husband make cookies?"

Hans held up a cookie, fresh from the oven.

"Why, no, he didn't," Jill said, and doubled over with laughter until she cried.

Tom continued. "I mean, do you really ever want to have sex again? Because you could if you wanted to. Any one of us would be happy to nail you, right, guys?"

Hans shrugged.

"Absolutely," Eric said.

Jill laughed even harder.

"But," Tom continued, "we don't expect to have sex with you. We don't feel entitled to have sex with you. You could live with us and we'll put oil in your car, and not demand sexual favors in return. I really think you ought to reexamine what you want out of life because I think you'll find that you have it right here."

"I really don't want to ever have sex again," Jill said as if it were a big epiphany. "I've been through enough."

"See?" Tom said. "Stay with us and you don't ever have to have sex again."

"That's right," Hans said. "We'll love you and screw other women."

"Oh," Jill said. "You guys are so sweet. You really are the best husbands a girl like me could ever have."

"But if you ever change your mind about the sex, I'll make you even *more* glad it didn't work out with your husband," Eric said with a wink.

Jill blushed. "Thanks, sweetie. It's nice to have choices. And P.S., you have the sexiest voice in the history of the world."

"Oh, that's just the start," he said.

Then Tom interrupted, "Now go get some sleep, dear, because I think we're going to have a big day with the storm on the mountain tomorrow."

"Big storm coming," Hans told Jill. "I can feel it in my knees."

Eric said, "My knees are like having two big painful barometers with me everywhere I go." He broke out the giant bottle of ibuprofen and passed it around. "I'm a big fan of the vitamin I chaser." He threw back a shot of tequila with his pills.

Jill said, "You all can't go eating pills like M&M's."

"Not pills—vitamin I," Hans corrected.

"Very important supplement," Tom added. "And isn't it you that eats antacids like Neccos?"

"It's just calcium," Jill said. Then she paused and pretended to hear something. "Sh . . . wait. Do you hear that? It's your kidneys screaming for mercy."

They all pretended to listen.

"I can't hear them over my screaming knees," said Eric. "Can you, Tom?"

"That's a negative," Tom answered.

Jill shook her head, petted the dogs good night, and then stumbled down the hall, relatively happy, all things considered. She loved her platonic harem.

"Just you wait, Jilly Bean! You'll become one of us yet!" Tom called after her.

"Never!" she shouted back lightheartedly.

It all got Lisa thinking about how women change after men have screwed them over. She remembered how irritable and irrational her own mother had been after her father's indiscretion.

Once, Lisa had come home from school and walked straight into the kitchen, where pots and pans steamed away on the stove as usual. It had felt so good to be home from school, back in the smells of herbs and spices, in the savory steam that felt like fur, back in the warmth that was her mother's essence. While her mother looked for something in the fridge, Lisa walked over to the stove, picked up a wooden spoon, stuck it in the sauce, and brought it up for a taste.

"No!" her mother shouted as she slapped Lisa's hand, knocking the spoon out of it. "That is only for your father! For your father only!" Lisa still didn't know how her mother got across the kitchen so fast.

She stood there for a moment, stunned. No experience in her whole life would have ever led her to believe she'd be struck for tasting sauce. Tears bubbled up from deep inside her, and she started to cry. She looked at her mother to see if she would comfort her, to see if she had any idea how much all of that stung.

"No more tasting sauces, Ragazzina. Very important. Now stop crying and go outside and play." And that was all she said.

Thinking about it now, so many years later, Lisa still felt mad. And drunk enough to pick up the phone. She didn't care that it was almost two o'clock in Florida. She wanted answers. After seven rings, her mother finally picked up.

"Ragazzina?" It was her mother's name for her—an Italian term of endearment. "Is everything okay? It's so late!" Her mother sounded panicked.

Lisa said, "Mama, do you remember when I was little and you slapped my hand for tasting the sauce? Why did you do that?"

"Lisa, have you been drinking?" her mother asked.

"Yes, but that's not the point. I want to know why you slapped me for tasting sauce."

Lisa's mother laughed softly and then took a breath. "Oh, Ragazzina, I am sorry, but after your father was unfaithful, I was so angry that I put dog shit in all his food for about two years. You were about to taste his sauce, and I didn't want you to eat the dog shit."

Lisa sat on her end of the phone, stunned. Then slowly she started giggling, until at last she erupted into full-blown hysterical shrieking. Her mother joined her. They laughed and laughed until they cried.

Finally Lisa said, "Okay, Mama. I think I can sleep now."

"Okay, then, Ragazzina, I love you!"

"I love you, Mama," Lisa said through her laughter.

In the middle of the night, Cassie put one of her pillows on top of the other and draped the white fuzzy bathrobe over them on the bed. Then she brought over the treasure chest full of rocks and set it down. Carefully, she got on the bed and curled up against the pillows. When no one was looking, she often did this—pretended to sit on her mom's lap. Sometimes, figuring that she was ten and too old for such things, she would pretend that she was simply sitting next to her mom; but other times the smaller girl inside her, the one who wanted to be on her mom's lap, would cry louder, and she would give in. Tonight was one of those times. She opened the treasure chest and took out the rocks one by one, admiring each and realizing their individual stories were beginning to fade a little.

She took out some notebook paper and began to write the stories before she forgot them completely. She sketched each rock next to the corresponding story. Eleven pages. All together she wrote eleven pages. She couldn't believe it.

And suddenly, she was remembering all kinds of other things she didn't want to forget either, but there was too much to write in one night. So she made a two-page list of all the things she wanted to remember to write about, and just having that list of things she didn't want to forget made her feel better.

chapter fifteen

• • •

SNOW REPORT FOR JANUARY 16

Current temperature: 10F, high of 13F at 2 P.M., Low of 2F at 5 A.M.
Clear skies, no wind.
63" mid-mountain, 72" at the summit. 0" new in the last 24 hours.
1" of new in the last 48.

Of course Jill had thought about it. Mike was handsome. And unlike David, he was honorable. Of course she had looked at their family pictures and wondered why she hadn't been lucky enough to marry a man like Mike.

And yes, it was as obvious to her as it was to everyone else that they were both single and about the same age. It was equally obvious that they both had been through too much. Not only that, but recently. The traumas were still very, very acute. Far too unbearably acute. But still, she thought about it.

Ever since his bad day, she had been thinking about their conversation and about how much she liked who he was.

It was easy to imagine a different set of circumstances as she cleaned up the kitchen at his house, especially in the morning when he came home from work. Easy to imagine for just a moment or two that she had married him instead of David. And even though the fantasy was never particularly detailed or involved—it was just a feeling for a moment—she always felt stupid when the moment passed. Guilty, too. Somehow, it just felt wrong. Even though Kate had passed, Mike still felt married to her.

Nonetheless, Jill found herself excited to see him on her mornings at their house. She wished she didn't, but she did.

She pulled blueberry muffins out of the oven just before Cassie had to run out the door. Yes, she had made Mike muffins. It looked as though she'd made them for Cassie, and sure, she had made them for Cassie, too, but really she wanted an excuse to sit for a minute with Mike before she left.

"What are these crunchy things?" Cassie asked as she bit into one.

"Millet," Jill answered.

"I like it," she shouted as she opened the door and headed out.

Mike walked up the sidewalk just in time to intercept her. They hugged a few seconds longer than a normal hug, and as Jill watched through the window, she wondered if it was because Mike had another difficult shift and a call involving a kid, or if it was about Kate.

"Mm! Smells good!" he said as he walked in.

"Hi!" she said, and smiled. *Is it obvious?* she wondered. She hoped it wasn't obvious. *Stupid, stupid, stupid. Get it in check*, she said to herself.

But he put a muffin on a plate, poured himself some juice, and sat down at the table. And something about that, about him sitting in his chair, and the other chair slightly askew, was like an open door or an invitation. And as she sat in her place with a muffin on her plate and a cup of hot tea, it struck her that it wasn't really male company she looked forward to on these mornings; it was understanding.

Uncle Howard and Jill rode the chairlift in silence. He poured trail mix into his mouth. "You're quiet," he said.

"Lisa and I are driving back to Austin tomorrow. I'm dreading it. All of it. Seeing David again. Court. All of it," Jill said.

"Did you find a lawyer?"

"Yeah," Jill replied. "Wes Heusser. This hearing won't really have much to do with the divorce. The judge is just going to make a ruling about how our finances should be handled until the divorce is final."

He nodded. "Well, here's what you're going to do, Jill. You're going to go and watch yourself participate in it. You're going to think, Hmm, isn't this interesting? But you're not going to judge it. You're just going to observe, and by doing so, you'll be able to see the truth as you've never seen it before. It will give you peace. You're going to imagine pink fluffy clouds around you in the courtroom. Negative words and intentions may come flying at you, but they'll hit the pink fluffy clouds and lose their momentum. They'll never touch you. No matter what comes flying at you, don't catch it. Step aside and let it fly by. Think of all those words as if they were balls bouncing around the room, like dodgeball. If you don't catch them and throw them back, they'll all lose their energy and end up on the floor behind you. Go through the motions in the physical world, but don't participate on an energetic level."

Jill listened and nodded. "I'll try," she said.

He put his arm around her and gave her shoulder a little squeeze. Then he added, "And take some Sparkle water with you, too, so that if you start to wilt while you're there, you can drink some Sparkle essence."

"Okay," Jill said as the chair reached the ramp. They put their skis on it. "See you later, Uncle Howard. I love you." She stood and slid down the ramp.

He nodded and waved a pole at her as he glided off in the other direction. He loved her, too.

chapter sixteen

. . .

SNOW REPORT FOR JANUARY 19

Current temperature: 1F, high of 5F at 2 P.M., low of –7F at 5 A.M. Snowing, no wind.

64" mid-mountain, 73" at the summit. 4" new in the last 24 hours. 5" of new in the last 48.

Lisa had sat in the courtroom the day before, watching lawyers trying to spin Jill's life and state of mental health in different ways. She looked at David and seethed. Here was Jill, who always followed the rules; Jill, who had nothing but good intentions in her heart. And here was the man who screwed her. Lisa imagined all the vengeful things she wanted to do to him.

You'd have to be an idiot to get married, Lisa thought. *It just sets you up to get screwed.* But then she reached up and touched the crucifix she wore around her neck, and wondered how she was going to rectify this.

In the end, the judge seemed to think Jill was a woman who had been through enough and ordered David to pay for everything until the divorce was final, as well as provide her with a thousand dollars a month to live on. It would help Jill, for sure. The judge also gave an order for Jill to be let in the house the following morning to get her things. Lisa had anticipated this. It was the reason she had come.

Now, as they approached the house, Lisa was stunned. She was in no way prepared for the opulence of Jill's home. Still, she kept her focus and surveyed the yard until at last, she found what she was looking for.

David had already packed Jill's things in boxes, which were stacked neatly by the door. Lisa didn't trust him and walked through the house with Jill, trying to get her to take things that looked valuable, things she could pawn if she ever needed to. But Jill didn't want any of them.

Upstairs, they walked down the hall. Lisa put her hand on a doorknob of the first room, but before she opened it, Jill stopped her. "That's the baby's room. I don't need anything in there."

"Sorry," Lisa said, unsure of the right response.

They descended the stairs and surveyed the living room. Jill went to a shelf and opened a photo album. "I know that later on, I'll wish I had some pictures of these last fifteen years. It's just so hard to think about going back and looking at my marriage, at the good times . . ."

"Do you want me to go through them and pick out the ones where you look prettiest?" Lisa offered.

"No. But thanks," Jill answered.

With that, Lisa went to work in the kitchen. She searched the cupboards for ingredients to some complete and simple dish. She opted for chili. Mexican spices could hide anything. She filled the Crock-Pot with beans, onion, hamburger, stewed tomatoes, and spices.

"What are you doing in there?" Jill called out from the other room.

"Oh, you know. It was so nice of David to pack all that stuff and save us all that time, so I just thought I'd make him a special dish of my mom's to express our gratitude," Lisa answered.

"That's not like you," Jill shouted back.

"I'm a Carlucci. We cook. That's what we do when we don't know what else to do."

That explanation seemed to satisfy Jill, so Lisa put a plastic bag in her pocket and carried a box to the car so that she could discreetly get what she needed. When she returned, she finished the chili, dipped two bowls into it, emptied them, and stuck them in the sink so David would think they had eaten it. *Genius,* she thought to herself.

Then she loaded all of Jill's belongings into the car, and when Jill came outside with a plastic sandwich bag full of photos, they drove away together and left everything else behind.

Pete, Mike, John, and Ben all served themselves big bowls of Ben's chili and took them to the table.

Pete spoke first. "Magoo," he said to Mike, "we're concerned."

Mike looked up, worried. Was he not doing his job well enough? Was he dropping the ball? Did the guys feel like they couldn't count on him?

"It's not healthy for a man to go this long without sex. How long has it been?" Pete continued.

Mike felt awkward but relieved. He shook his head. "I don't know. A long time."

"We're not proposing you go out and find a new wife. We know you're still healing. We just think you need to get laid," John said.

"Fact," Pete said. "Men who don't have enough sex get prostate cancer."

"You're making that up," Mike said.

"*Prevention* magazine, September twenty-eight, 2006. I showed Barb the headline and read her the first two sentences. I didn't read her the part where it said no partner was necessary. And I've been getting it five times a week ever since. You know how Barb loves a good cause. God, I love that magazine," Pete said.

"Do you at least have some good spankavision?" Ben asked.

Mike blushed. "I've got a kid in the house, so no, I don't have any spankavision."

"This is not good," John said. "This is not good at all."

"Look, do you really think Kate would want you to be celibate for the rest of your life?" Pete asked.

Mike shrugged.

"Look, Barb wants to fix you up with someone," Pete said.

Mike shook his head. "No fixups," he said. "If it's meant to be, it will happen naturally."

"How about the babysitter, Magoo?" Pete asked. "Why haven't you nailed the babysitter?"

"Because I don't want to have to find a new babysitter," Mike said. "And she's going through a divorce. She's actually in Texas now. There was some hearing or something. Howard is covering for her."

"Texas?" Pete asked.

"Texas," Mike said.

"Well, that's grounds for divorce right there," Pete said.

Ben helped himself to another bowl of his chili and said, "Word on the street is that she found her husband in bed with another woman."

"I didn't know that—about her husband," Mike said. "She lost a baby when she was seven months along last fall. I don't think she's in the mood for love."

"Okay, so no babysitter," Pete said, and wiped some chili out of his bushy mustache. "No babysitter and no fixups. That leaves hookups. Ben here is prepared to take you to the bar and help you find easy women."

Mike laughed.

"If you want, Barb and I can come along, too. I'm sure she'd be happy to help pick you out an easy piece of ass for the sake of your prostate. Hey, I'd like to propose a toast. To *Prevention* magazine," Pete said, and raised his glass of milk.

The other men raised their glasses, too, and clinked them together.

"I think this intervention went well," Pete said. "Do you need to sleep at home tonight? We could hold down the fort without you."

"Thanks. That would be good," Mike replied.

"Did you like Jill's husband?" Cassie asked Howard, who was preparing some coconut-curry lentils.

He shrugged.

"How come they're getting divorced?" she asked.

Howard shrugged once more. "It's really not my business."

"Do you think she'll get married again?"

Again, he shrugged. "Do you think your dad will get married again?"

This time, she shrugged.

"Kind of hard to think about right now, isn't it? I think Jill feels the same as that. Too soon to tell," he said.

"Did you ever get married?"

"Nope," he said. "Here, stir this while I chop more onion."

She took the wooden spoon from him. "Why not?"

"Marriage isn't for everybody. I know all the Disney movies

end with people getting married, and that's what kids think a happy ending looks like, but it's not that simple."

"Did you ever meet anyone you wanted to marry?"

"Nope. Did you?" He somehow managed to keep a straight face.

"No! I'm just a kid!"

Howard shrugged again and chopped another onion.

"Is Jill sad about her divorce?"

"Yes," he answered. "Take a spoon and taste that. What do you think?"

She took a spoon from the silverware drawer, dipped it in the pot, and tasted it. "Good." She paused for a moment and then asked, "Do you think my mom watches when Jill is here?"

Howard shrugged. "Do you?"

"Sometimes," she answered.

"Do you get the feeling it's okay with her?"

Cassie shrugged just like him. "I think so. I mean, people probably don't get jealous in heaven, and she'd probably be pretty glad someone is taking care of me so I can stay here with Dad, right?"

Howard nodded. "Do you ever see her?"

Cassie shook her head. "Sometimes I think I hear her, though."

"Yeah? What does she say?" he asked.

"She helps me find special rocks."

"Hm. Does she ever visit you in dreams?"

"I don't know. I only remember the bad ones," she said.

"After my mom died, she would visit me in dreams. We'd talk about stuff—not always important stuff or anything, but boy, it was so nice to see her and so hard to wake up and miss her," he said.

"I never thought about you having a mother. I mean, of course you did, but I just never thought about it before."

He laughed a little. "My father died when I was in high school and my mother never married again. She somehow raised us by herself. She was a waitress at the soda fountain down at the drugstore. On Fridays, my sister and I would go there after school and she'd treat us to a milkshake."

"Do you wish she had? You know, remarried?" Cassie asked.

"I guess it would have depended on the person. There were times when I knew she was lonely and sad, and I knew it was that special kind of lonely that a kid couldn't fix."

"You never wish you had a wife?"

"No, I never wish I had a wife. Sometimes I wish I had a love, though."

"I hope you fall in love," she said.

"I hope you fall in love, too," he replied.

She laughed and rolled her eyes.

chapter seventeen

• • •

SNOW REPORT FOR JANUARY 22

Current temperature: 18F, high of 18F at 7 A.M., low of 12 at 12 A.M.
Light snow, no wind.
75" mid-mountain, 84" at the summit. 1" new in the last 24 hours.
1" of new in the last 48.

Snow used to just be snow. This was what Mike thought about as he walked home in the morning. He missed looking at snow like a child or a tourist. When he was little, snow was opportunity, or even the freedom of a snow day. It was fun. And now, as he watched it fall, he could see its graceful beauty, the dance each flake did as it tumbled to earth. But it took effort. His first thought when he looked at snow was always, *Accidents*. What used to be magical, elegant, and pure, was now simply the predecessor to carnage.

And it struck him that it wasn't so different with women. Since Kate died, his first thought when he looked at a woman was simply that he never wanted to feel this way again.

Walking up the sidewalk, though, he could see Jill in the kitchen window, and as with snow, he felt the conflict of recognizing her beauty and the dread of the inevitable disaster that beauty surely hid. She looked up, caught him gazing, and smiled. His first thought was, *Nothing lasts.* With some effort, he could remember how it was when he was a teenager, that moment when the girl he liked finally smiled at him. . . . What victory! What a miracle! But now, he simply knew too much. He knew the realities of marriage. He was not so foolish as to believe that any couple escaped the bad times. It was part of the deal. And he knew now about the parting—about the untold misery and suffering of the parting.

The blue jays jumped from branch to branch in the bare cottonwood trees that lined the street. There was so much beauty all around him, yet every day he walked right by it thinking about all the ugliness and tragedy in his world.

He looked back up at Jill. She was looking down at the sink. It was so nice to come home to her. It was. She was warm and kind. He could appreciate her beauty without being sucked into a dangerous situation. He could. From his safe place, he could simply sit and admire all the ways she was beautiful.

As they sat at the little table in the kitchen, she told him about the hearing, about how her husband's lawyer tried to make her look crazy, about the judge's ruling, about watching her husband get into a car with the brunette afterward, about going back to her house for her stuff, and about having to go back in a few months for the actual divorce court. She looked weary. Still, when he looked at her, what he saw was this: goodness. And it was beautiful to him. He didn't need to get involved in it. And although he wondered who this husband was and what kind of dirtbag would put her through more suffering, he didn't need to take it on. He could simply sit in his chair and appreciate her beautiful goodness.

chapter eighteen

• • •

SNOW REPORT FOR FEBRUARY 13

Current temperature: 28F, high of 31F at 2 P.M., low of 27F at 5 A.M.
Snowing heavily, winds out of the south at 15 mph.
81" mid-mountain, 90" at the summit. 22" new in the last 24 hours.
38" of new in the last 48.

Somehow Jill's body made it through another brutal day of hiking across ridges in waist-deep new snow to do avalanche control and then digging out lift towers for the rest of the day. Another patroller had a rotator cuff injury that was acting up, so he needed Jill's spot in the FAR, and Jill therefore was recruited to step up her duties. Fortunately, almost three months on the mountain sweeping runs at the end of every day, and skiing on all her days off, trying to keep up with Lisa, Eric, or whoever wanted to join her for a few runs, had transformed her. She hardly recognized herself.

She was uneasy doing control work, but Tom had made her his partner, and while she learned the ropes, they bombed and ski-cut the easiest places that needed it.

When four o'clock rolled around, she hobbled to Cassie's house. It was one of those cold days where the snow squeaked under her boots and her breath stuck to her eyelashes and froze. It was the day before Valentine's Day, and everywhere she looked there were reminders of a holiday that she would have rather forgotten.

Cassie had about forty-five minutes of being alone from the time she got home from school to the time Jill arrived, and in that time, she usually got her homework done. When Jill arrived, she was bursting with anticipation. "Oh, Jill!" she sang.

"Cassie, I can tell you're up to something," Jill sang back.

"Uh-huh!" Cassie replied excitedly.

"Could it be what's for dinner?" Jill asked, sniffing the air.

"That's part one!" Cassie replied. "I hope you know how to use chopsticks!"

"We're making something from the Orient?" Jill asked.

Cassie just nodded with her very best wait-and-see smile.

"Part two?" Jill asked.

Cassie nodded again. "Oh yes, part two: I found an old sleeping bag in the thrift store Dumpster that we can use for the hang glider on our downhill dummy, and we can use the stuffing to stuff the rag doll."

"Excellent score, Cassie. Well done. Your father will be so proud that I turned you into a Dumpster diver," she joked. A week earlier, they had pulled some worthless old skis out of the thrift store Dumpster.

"Yeah, not so much," Cassie replied. "But we don't have to tell him."

Jill just laughed. "What first?"

"First we sew," Cassie said, and led Jill out to the garage.

They had been constructing a dummy that looked like Cassie on a hang glider. PVC pipes were used to make the frame of the hang glider. Two poles rested in concrete that they had poured into outdated ski boots. The boots were mounted to the skis, and the skis were secured a couple feet apart by two pieces of plywood that they screwed to the tops. Now Cassie stuffed the rag doll that was going to hang from the bar, while Jill sewed the nylon onto the frame of the hang glider.

Socks found his way into the garage and rubbed up against Cassie.

"Someone sure loves you," Jill said.

Cassie leaned over and Socks rubbed her cheek against Cassie's. "You should get a pet," Cassie said, and went back to stuffing the doll.

"Hm," Jill said. Just three months ago, she would have said pets were germy parasite carriers, leaving behind a trail of dander and dust mites. Lately, though, they didn't seem as bad as she thought. The Kennel dogs had grown on her.

When they finished working on the dummy for the night, they went to the kitchen. Cassie instructed Jill on how to cut the vegetables and then went on to measure rice and water. After that, she set about measuring ingredients for a spicy Thai peanut sauce.

Jill turned on the radio in the kitchen so they could listen to reggae while they cooked. Cassie stopped what she was doing and turned it up louder.

When they finished cooking, they sat at the table together. Jill sat in Mike's chair, took one bite, and said, "You know, I think you have a gift. Maybe after you win the Olympics, you'll open your own restaurant."

"That would be awesome!" Cassie said.

"Hey, we should bake something for Valentine's Day. You could surprise your dad," Jill suggested. Thinking of her husband spending a romantic Valentine's Day with his new love was a really difficult pill to swallow. Her spirits were low. And she thought if she had been feeling low, Mike had likely been feeling even lower.

"Yeah," Cassie said, but her demeanor changed.

"When we finish dinner, we'll go to the store and get a vision," Jill said.

"Sure," Cassie said.

Cassie and Jill walked down the baking aisle, trying to decide between making a cake or heart-shaped sugar cookies, but it was getting late, so they decided on a cherry cake. They picked out a can of pink frosting and a tube of red so Cassie could write a Valentine's Day message.

As they looked at Red Hearts candies in a little bottle and contemplated whether artificial cinnamon flavor would go well with the cherry cake, Cassie heard her mother say, *Look down.* At first she saw nothing, but she squatted anyway, as if she had to tie the lace on her boot. From that angle, she could see a single Sweethearts candy hidden just under the bottom shelf. As she blew the dust off the white candy, she could see that it said "Forever" in pink letters. Cassie closed her hand around it, took a big breath, and blew it out slowly. As she stood, she put the candy in her pocket. Her eyes teared up, but she collected herself before anyone saw.

While Cassie and Jill walked home from the grocery store, they talked about their vision for the cake they would make. But half of Cassie's mind was on her father's sadness. It was like a lead apron at the dentist. His sadness was so heavy that she couldn't begin to lift it, no matter what she did.

She remembered all the people at her mother's service, most

of them her grandparents' age, who said, "Oh, don't cry," or, "Be strong for your father." She had tried. She had really tried. She had tried not to burden him with her tears. She had tried to be strong for him. She made him paper snowflakes and learned to cook healthy dinners. Now she would make him a cake, and even though she would put her whole heart into it, she knew he would still feel sad. It would be his first Valentine's Day without her mother, and there was no way around the reality of it. She could make him the greatest cake in the world and it wouldn't begin to lift his great sadness. Something about it all made her tired now. She wondered how much longer she could keep trying, how much longer she could hide the depths of her own sadness, how much longer she could just put on a happy face and make a happy cake.

It was at that moment she saw Socks lying on his side in the road, mouth open, body bent at an impossible angle. She screamed, "No!" and ran down the slippery sidewalk, too blinded by horror to care if she fell. She picked up his broken body and fell to her knees, shaking. Everyone was dying.

Then Jill's arms were around her, holding her against her chest, rocking her gently. Cassie's mouth gaped for air. She was slightly aware of the animal noises that escaped her and of the snot that poured from her nose and froze to her upper lip. And soon the weight of her dead cat was noticeable. She let her hands rest on the road underneath it, looked to the sky, and howled. She wanted her mom. She let her mom see how devastated she was. As much as she hadn't wanted to burden her mother, she could no longer shoulder it alone.

Then Jill was lifting her as headlights approached and slowed. Socks's head and tail hung down, still limp in Cassie's hands. The car pulled off to the side of the road and parked. Tom got out. "Jill? What happened?"

"We just found Cassie's cat. He'd been hit by a car," Jill answered.

Tom put his hand on Cassie's shoulders and said, "Cassie. Cassie, can you look at me?" She felt her eyes roll over to him and look at his face. "I'm going to bury your cat for you." He slipped his hands under Socks and took him from her. Her wailing escalated for a moment as she realized this was the last time she would ever see her friend. "Take her inside and get her warm," he said to Jill.

"Thanks, Tom." Jill set Cassie's feet on the ground but continued to hold on to her. "Come on, sweetie," she said gently, and led her into the house. She let go of Cassie, then took off her bloody gloves, coat, and snow pants and set them in a pile near the door. Finally she guided Cassie, still wailing, to the couch near the woodstove.

Tom crept in, relatively unnoticed, for matches and newspaper.

Cassie, no longer worried about burdening anyone with her sadness, unleashed seven months' worth of tears in Jill's arms until at last, exhausted, she slept.

After Cassie fell asleep, Jill looked out the window and watched Tom with a shovel in the back of the yard near the alley. He shoveled aside the flaming logs and dug deep where the fire had softened the frozen soil. Then he buried the cat and shoveled snow on top of the fresh grave.

Jill waited for him to come in, but he didn't. He just walked back toward his car and drove away. She wasn't sure how to thank him but thought warm leftovers and hot cocoa might have been a good start.

It struck her hard how it was often the ordinary acts that

were angelic. Maybe there were angels in the sky and maybe there weren't. Maybe angels helped arrange for Tom to be the one to drive along right at that moment. She didn't know. But what she did know was that there were angels on the ground. She did know that Tom stopped the car, got out, and buried a kid's dead cat. He didn't have to, but he did. It was a small act, but it was huge. And that made Tom an angel to her, one no less divine than any angels that might be in the sky.

Tom drove the two blocks from Mike's house to the Kennel. Next door, Lisa was shoveling the huge pile of snow the snowplow had left all around her car. He parked, and for a moment his headlights shone on Lisa. She started disco dancing.

As Tom got out, she shouted, "*American Bandstand* spotlight dance! Woo-hoo! So, Thomas, been out prowling?"

He wasn't in the mood for it. "Nah. Hey, hang on a sec," he said, subdued, and then went up to his own door to get another snow shovel. He walked back over to her and helped her dig out her car.

"So, what . . . no boob report?" Lisa heckled.

He stopped shoveling for a moment and just looked at her.

She noticed, stopped, and looked back. "What?" she asked.

"I just spent the last few hours thawing out a part of Mike's yard so I could bury his daughter's cat for her. I'm a nice guy, Lisa. I'm a good guy. But you treat me like I'm this big asshole, like I'm *no prize*. Weren't those your words?"

"We've heckled each other like this for years, Tom. What the hell? I don't understand," she said.

"No, you don't." He started shoveling again.

She walked closer to him. He kept shoveling. She reached out and touched his arm. He froze.

"Hey," she said. He still didn't look at her. "Hey," she said again.

He stood up straight and met her eyes. "Lisa, I . . ." He couldn't bring himself to finish. He looked down at her looking up at him, concerned and confused. He put a gloved hand behind her head and kissed her softly. He pulled back only a little and looked up from her lips to her eyes. She looked up from his lips to his eyes, and she didn't seem angry, so he kissed her again, this time longer. And instead of just letting him kiss her, Lisa kissed him back.

He was afraid to break away, even just for a moment, afraid that if he gave her an opening, she'd bolt. He was afraid to say anything that might wreck the moment. But he didn't want to overwhelm her with his passion, either. He wanted her to know what was in his heart. He wanted her to know that he would treat her with tenderness. He wanted her to see a side of him she didn't know existed.

Lisa's kiss grew more urgent, and Tom wasn't sure if it was him or if she was letting herself go on autopilot. He pulled his lips away, rested his forehead against hers, summoned all his courage, and looked into her eyes.

He saw uncertainty.

He let his hand slide from behind her head down her arm to her hand. He took a step back and placed her hand on his heart, covering it with his own hand. He closed his eyes and hoped she could feel it, because he couldn't find the words.

When he opened his eyes, Lisa looked worried. He looked down, let go of her hand, picked up his shovel, and walked back to the Kennel, feeling somewhat defeated but not completely hopeless.

chapter nineteen

. . .

SNOW REPORT FOR FEBRUARY 14

Current temperature: 22F, high of 28F at 2 P.M., low of 18F at 5 A.M.
Snowing, winds out of the south at 10 mph
93" mid-mountain, 115" at the summit. 12" new in the last 24 hours.
36" of new in the last 48.

From the doorstep, Mike could look into his house and see that Cassie and Jill were still asleep on the couch. His first thought was that Cassie must have had another rough night, because she should have been in school by now. His second thought was how thankful he was to have someone watching Cassie who clearly cared a lot about her. His third thought was simply how soft they both looked—soft and kind. He waited an extra moment before turning the doorknob. Cassie was sleeping on her back, but her head had rolled to the side just a little, into the crook in Jill's arm. Jill's feet were on the footstool and her head was bent uncomfortably forward, turned slightly toward Cassie. *Her neck is going to hurt today,* Mike thought. He looked at Jill's face, and while he had always thought she was pretty, suddenly she looked so much more than pretty to him. He had an impulse to touch her cheek. Then he noticed Kate's bathrobe balled up in Cassie's arms and felt guilty for even thinking it.

He slowly turned the doorknob, trying to be silent, but Jill stirred and opened her eyes. She crawled out from underneath Cassie. She was wearing long underwear, and Mike didn't mean to, but he noticed her curves.

He walked in and whispered, "Sick?"

Jill shook her head. "Socks was hit by a car last night. She took it *really* hard. I just couldn't throw her into school without letting her debrief a little more."

The lines between Mike's eyes deepened, and Jill could tell that he had been attached to the cat, too.

"I'm sorry," Jill said.

"It's okay. You did the right thing. I'll take her to school later."

Jill nodded, stepped into her clothes, picked up her things, and headed for the door, but as she passed Mike, she squeezed his arm. "No, I'm not sorry she's late for school—I'm sorry about Socks," she said.

"Death happens. Socks was a cat," he replied.

And even though Jill knew he was saying that for his own benefit, she said, "But Socks was part of your family, and one of the few comforts Cassie has had. Somehow, he made the house warmer."

Mike looked down and nodded.

She gave his hand one more little squeeze before she let it go, put on her parka, and left.

Mike went out the back door, picked up his splitting maul, and started splitting rounds. The wood was nice and dry, but he hit it with great force anyway, sending the fractions flying.

"Goddamn cat," he muttered as he chopped. "Goddamn cat."

What timing. What timing, he thought as he brought the heavy maul down again and again. *Goddamn cat.*

Jill walked over to Lisa's. They both had the day off and planned to ski.

"Hey, girl," Lisa said as she answered the door. "Tom told me you had an intense night last night."

Jill took a big breath. "It was a hard one. Tom totally saved the day."

"He does that sometimes," Lisa said, and went off to gather her things. Jill noticed that Lisa didn't take the opportunity to insult him.

"Mind if I check my e-mail?" Jill asked. "It's been a while."

"Go right ahead," Lisa answered.

Jill logged on and shouted, "Oh, goody! My parents sent Valentine's wishes!"

"Super!" Lisa shouted back.

"Listen to this! 'For those of you who are not now enjoying the tremendous blessings of a Temple rather than temporal marriage with promises of eternal companionship, we encourage you to turn your hearts to the Gospel. We pray that you will find your way back, for a marriage without strong moral fiber is destined to fail and only the Gospel can offer you that moral fiber.' "

While Jill read Lisa puttered in her kitchen, putting cups in the sink and unloading the dishwasher. "There you go, Jill," she said. "All this time it was so simple." She dried her hands on a dish towel.

Jill shook her head. "Seriously, wasn't it nice of them to direct that e-mail right at me, but send it to all their friends and family?"

"Well, you could block them."

"Block them?" Jill asked.

"Yeah, block their e-mails. You don't need that shit. You're not genetically obligated to read that shit. Go to 'More Actions' and 'Filter Messages Like These.' It's easy."

"Good to have options," she said as she simply logged out. "Ready."

"Off we go," Lisa said as she picked up an armload of her gear. Together, they walked out.

Jill noticed new purple lingerie on Lisa's clothesline. "Hot date tonight?" Jill asked her.

"Nah," Lisa said. "I'm still trying to get my attic remodeled for you. Plus, it's just easier."

"I'm all about the monk/nun happiness program," Jill replied as they walked to the mountain. "Sometimes, though, I wonder if there is something wrong with me. Not only have I not wanted to have sex with anyone since I lost my baby, I haven't even wanted to have sex with myself."

Lisa seemed to consider that. "I think that's to be expected, given the circumstances."

"I've always been such a healthy woman in that respect, you know? And now . . . I don't know. I think my cha-cha's in a coma." Jill shrugged.

"Aw, sweetheart, I bet your cha-cha is just sleeping. Don't worry. She'll wake up," Lisa said. "Maybe your cha-cha is like a bear that needs to hibernate to save energy during your proverbial winter. There's nothing wrong with energy conservation, especially these days."

"Maybe I'm using all my Kundalini energy to create *my* new life instead of *a* new life," she said.

"Makes sense," Lisa said. "You're giving birth to your new

life. No one wants to have sex while they're giving birth. Not for a while afterward, either, I'm told. P.S., you're totally turning into your uncle Howard."

Jill laughed. "There are worse things than turning into Uncle Howard."

"When he retires or passes on, you'll take over the library and be the one to make the ski team read *Siddhartha*. I can totally see it now." Lisa laughed.

Jill pictured it and smiled. "Never," she said.

Their feet hit the platform and they slid to a spot where they took their skis off and hiked up the snow stairs created by other people who had kick-stepped up the hill. Then they followed the path across a narrow metal grate bridge. When the ridge widened again, they put their skis back on and skated the rest of the way across the ridge to the Horseshoe Bowl. At the top of the bowl, they just stood there for a moment and took in the view all around them.

"I'm so glad I'm not in Texas making meat loaf for David right now," Jill said.

"Amen, sister," Lisa agreed.

They watched two other skiers on the other side of the bowl pick their lines and go. They were the only other people up there.

Jill pointed to a place without tracks. "That's my line," she said. *If only life were as easy as that,* she thought. *If only I could see an untracked place in the world, say to myself, "That's my life," and go.* She skied over to the line she wanted and dropped off the edge.

As she made nice tight turns, she thought about how she

couldn't stop if she wanted to. She realized being in control in skiing or in life wasn't a matter of being able to stop; it was only a matter of being able to change direction.

When she reached the bottom of the bowl, she turned uphill to watch Lisa ski beautiful eights over her line. Then Lisa passed Jill, so she followed her through a lovely glade and over some gentle knolls. She felt the life force strong inside her and wondered when it had returned. She felt glad, so deeply glad. She may not have had any sex drive, but she had life force. Maybe they were degrees of the same thing.

At the chair, Lisa said, "I think I have time for one more lap."

"Ah-ha! So you *do* have Valentine's plans! Busted!"

"Nah," Lisa said. "I just have my heart set on making Tom obscene heart-shaped cookies—you know, like those Sweethearts candies, only with much nastier words and suggestions."

Jill looked at her with raised eyebrows.

"What?" Lisa said. "I just think it would be funny to make those cookies, and he's the only person I can think of who wouldn't freak out if I gave them to him. I mean, I think they would scare Hans and Scooter. They would think I was some nasty cougar with a secret agenda or something. I think these might even scare Eric. They are going to be *dir-ty*."

Jill laughed. "You should make one that says 'Kidney Love.'"

"Shut up," Lisa said with a smile.

Jill held her hands up. "I'm just saying . . ."

"Get on the chair," Lisa said.

They skied another great run, and then Lisa took off to make her cookies.

Jill skied alone and remembered a Valentine's Day long ago that changed her life. She and David were sophomores in college and had no money. He had made her fettuccine Alfredo and a big green salad. They had no taste in wine then, so he poured cheap white zinfandel into two glasses. He smelled especially good that night. He had worn a crisp button-up shirt to give the evening a sense of formality. Candles were lit, and he played a cassette tape mix of romantic but not cheesy love songs, and when Bruce Springsteen began to sing "Lonely Valentine," David said, "You know what I like best about you?"

"No," she said. "I don't," and smiled as she waited for his answer.

He smiled back for the longest minute. "Everything," he finally said.

"That's my favorite thing about you, too," she said.

She knew when he took an uncomfortable breath. "Jill?" he said.

She waited.

He dropped to one knee, reached in his pocket, and presented her with a ring. "Will you marry me?"

And she dropped to her knees in front of him, said yes, unbuttoned his crisp shirt, and attacked him. And when they were done, they lay on the floor and he fed her the fettuccine they hadn't finished at dinner.

Looking back, she wondered whether she would do it all over again, whether she would go through all the pain just to keep moments like those.

Mike worked on Valentine's Day last year. He missed it. It was his last Valentine's Day with his wife and he missed it. It fell during that window of time where he had known something was wrong but hadn't known what she knew—that she was sick.

The night before Valentine's Day, he took her out to dinner. She said she didn't feel well. He thought she was just letting him know not to expect any sex.

The candles were lit. The wine was poured. It should have been romantic, but she was so distant. There was tension. He didn't know why there was tension. He thought she was being passive-aggressive, and it irked him. He hadn't even cared that he worked the next day, on the actual Valentine's Day. He was glad, in fact. This was what he was thinking as he sat at the dinner table with her at Carlucci's Italian Bistro on his wife's last Valentine's Day.

If he had only known. If he had only known, he could have softened her and comforted her the way he was able to after she finally told him. She went to her first two doctor's appointments without him knowing. She didn't tell him until the test results came back. She said she hadn't wanted to scare him unnecessarily. Kate. She always thought she had to be so much stronger than she really did.

And if he had known, he could have appreciated the last Valentine's Day they would spend together. He would have loved her as though there were no tomorrow instead of feeling irritated.

Now he hung his head in shame and his eyes began to fill. He stirred the spaghetti and tossed a salad. As someone who witnessed the fragility of life on an almost daily basis, he of all people should have known something about how delicate life was and how nothing should ever be taken for granted. He guessed that no one ever thought it was going to happen to them.

In the other room, Cassie sat at the dining room table decorating a Valentine's Day cake she had made for him. He paused to watch her for a moment. She was pursing her lips like she always did when she was deeply focused on something. Kate used to do that, too. Sometimes Cassie resembled her so much. It was beautiful and painful all at once.

He stirred the sauce once more and then called out, "Okay, dinner's on."

She brought the cake back in, set it on the counter, and sang, "Ta-da!" as if it were magic.

"Oooo! It's beautiful!" Mike said, appreciating not only her effort, but her stoic attempts not to keep crying about Socks. "That looks like the most delicious valentine ever!" He couldn't change the past. The best he could do was simply not lose another opportunity to appreciate Valentine's Day. "I am the luckiest dad," he said.

Cassie beamed.

He looked at his beautiful little girl, all earnest, all heart, and he most certainly did feel like the luckiest dad.

Tom stopped by the grocery store on the way home. He needed beer, chicken, oatmeal, and a new razor. He put these things in a basket and then found himself in front of the Valentine's Day cards, not really knowing why. He and Lisa hadn't spoken since the kiss, and he doubted they would today. In fact, he was beginning to suspect that his friendship with her, as he had known it, anyway, was over. But if he was wrong, he didn't want to be caught with nothing.

As he stood there, looking at lame card after lame card, he glanced up and saw Scooter walking toward him.

"Who are you getting a valentine for?" Scooter asked.

"Your mother," Tom answered.

Scooter rolled his eyes. "Listen, bro, I have a request. May I please park my uncle's travel trailer next to the Kennel, run an umbilical cord up to it for some power, and use your facilities so I don't have to pump the tank?"

"Good job on the 'may' and 'please,'" Tom said.

"My mom was an English teacher," Scooter explained, and laughed. "Look, Alan, the lift op supervisor, as you know, is a dick. He was making it his special project to find my stash—inspecting employee housing every day in hopes of busting me—"

"And that, my friend, is why we all moved to the Kennel over a decade ago," Tom said. "But go on."

"So then I rented Cody's grandpa's cabin on the mining claim. Cody from the bike shop. Do you know the place I'm talking about?"

"The infamous cabin with the frozen water bed that you have to ski a mile and a half to?"

"That's the one. No electricity. No fireplace. Laura dumped me, so I can't even crash at her house for an occasional night of luxury. I've been totally trying to body thaw that water bed, but it's not happening. I want out."

"Understandable. Make me an offer," Tom said.

"Eighty bucks a month, plus I'll help you guys build a luge track and dig dog holes for you on three of my days off this season."

Tom nodded. "For that, my friend, yes, you may park your uncle's travel trailer in our yard, run an extension cord to the Kennel, and use our facilities."

"Excellent," Scooter said. "Seriously, who are you getting a valentine for? There's not that many women in Sparkle."

"I'm just going to keep a blank one in my pocket for whomever I meet at the bar tonight," Tom lied.

Scooter set down his basket and began to applaud. "Brilliant. Never would have thought of that. Brilliant." He picked up a random card, put it in his basket, and went on his way down the aisle.

Tom continued to look at cards so stupid that they almost

physically hurt him. Eventually, he picked one that was pretty plain. It had a heart on the front and on the inside said "Happy Valentine's Day."

He carried his groceries home. Low clouds accelerated nightfall. They looked as heavy as his mood.

At home, he unpacked his groceries and then picked up a pen and stared at the card. He scribbled on a bill to make sure the ink was flowing. Finally, he wrote, "I know in my heart you're the one. Love, Tom." He put the card in the envelope, wrote Lisa's name on it, and sealed it. He carried it into his room and sat it on his stereo. He figured it would most likely become three-dollar fire starter.

He dug through his music collection for a CD to match his mood and eventually selected R.E.M.'s *Reckoning*. He turned his bedside lamp on and the overhead light off and then just stared at his ceiling, wondering if the damage he had done with his careless attitude toward women was permanent . . . whether Lisa would ever take him seriously.

For weeks, Lisa had planned to make Tom heart-shaped cookies with very nasty messages on them, but after his tender kisses, she couldn't do it. She stared at her two dozen sugar cookies, frosted in pink, and held the tube of white frosting, waiting to write something. But no words came to her.

She paused and looked out her window. The Kennel was dark except for the dim light in Tom's room. Then she turned her attention back toward the cookies, squeezed the tube of frosting, and on each one wrote, "Love." Carefully, she layered them in a box with waxed paper, took a big breath, and walked out her door.

When she opened the front door of the Kennel, Bud Light

made a small bark, almost like a cough. She touched the top of his head and then walked slowly down the hall. She didn't know what she was going to say. She stood outside Tom's door for a moment and then tapped on it twice before opening it.

Tom had rolled his head to the side to see who was there. When he saw it was Lisa, he just waited to see what she would do. He was neither warm nor cold.

She wanted to run. The tension between them was as palpable and unpleasant to her as the metallic taste of pennies.

"I know you are a good man, Tom," she finally said. "I'm sorry for everything I ever said or did that led you to believe I didn't."

He gave her a small nod to let her know he accepted her apology and continued to wait.

Lisa felt an ache in her chest and wondered if it was his pain or hers.

"I would, you know, give you my kidney if you needed it," she said quietly. And then she set down the cookies in the doorway, turned, and began to walk back down the hall. It was all she could do not to run.

"Lisa," Tom said.

She froze.

"Lisa," he said again.

She took a big breath and walked back to his doorway.

"Don't go," he said.

She paused.

He motioned for her to come to him.

She picked up the cookies and shut the door behind her. Then she walked over to his bed, put a knee down on his mattress, and crawled on top of him, resting her head on his chest.

He closed his arms around her, nuzzled her hair with his cheek, and began to rub her back.

Lisa lifted her head and kissed him. The music that seemed melancholy just minutes ago now seemed as sweet and tender as their kiss.

"Wait," she whispered, and pulled back. She pulled Tom's curtain open and lit his candle. Then she kissed him again.

Jill and Eric stumbled into the Kennel after having a couple of beers at the Gold Pan. Well, Jill had a couple. She wasn't sure how many Eric had.

"Sh! The candle in Tom's window means he's entertaining!" Eric said, and turned on the TV. *"Sixteen Candles!"* He rushed to the kitchen, threw a bag of popcorn in the microwave, rushed back, and began to recite the occasional line along with the movie. "It's possible we've watched this a few times," he said.

He retrieved the popcorn, shooed the dogs off the couch, and sat down. "Come on, Jilly. Watch the movie with me. You can snuggle up right here." He pointed to his side.

Jill laughed and sat next to him.

"I love this part!" he said, and offered her some popcorn.

When the popcorn was gone, Jill yawned. The night before had been a hard one, and she had run out of steam a long time ago.

"Lay down and rest your head in my lap," Eric said.

She started to protest and then thought, *Why not?* So she did. And to her surprise, he stroked the hair away from her face. It was soothing, something her mom used to do when she was sick and needed comforting. When had she last been comforted like this? Right after she lost the baby. David had comforted her like this. But now that all seemed like a lie.

Eric laughed at the movie again.

Tears welled up in Jill's eyes, so she shut them. A few tears rolled down to Eric's fleece pants, she assumed unnoticed. She felt so many things all at once. When she looked at it from inside her body, she was grateful for physical comfort, for the way it filled a primal need in a time of so much loss. It was enough to make her love Eric in spite of his limitations. But when she looked at it from outside her body, as if she were floating above it all, she saw herself on a gross couch covered in dog hair in a trailer that smelled like marijuana smoke, being comforted by a man who likely had done the same thing with ten different women since Christmas. It was sad. So she went back to looking at it from inside her body, where the only thing that mattered was physical comfort, where she could appreciate the warmth of a friend and simply fall asleep.

chapter twenty

. . .

SNOW REPORT FOR FEBRUARY 17

Current temperature: 27F, high of 28F at 2 P.M., low of 24F at 4 A.M.
Snowing heavily, with winds out of the southeast at 5 mph.
94" mid-mountain, 104" at the summit. 18" new in the last 24 hours.
25" of new in the last 48.

Snow muffled everything, so the morning was silent. Jill had slept late on her day off. It was nearly ten. She peeked out her window to see almost a foot of new powder and more falling. Flakes filled the sky, at times swirling and at other times merely gliding down gracefully. A part of her wanted to stay in her warm bed all day and wait out the storm. But a bigger part of her knew she would have fun if she could shift gears and see the storm for what it was: an opportunity.

She put on all her layers and opened the door. She paused for just a second and took a breath before she walked out into the seemingly inhospitable storm. It was funny that after all this time on the mountain, she still had that moment of surrendering to a storm. Other people didn't hesitate. She always did. Somehow it seemed unnatural to go out in a storm, much like jumping off a cliff.

She stopped at her locker in the back of the FAR and got her skis. Then she made her way to Scooter's chair. He wore his goggles over his hat and smiled from ear to ear. "How about this storm?" he called out to her.

"Yeah!" Jill said with a big smile. "Hey, welcome to the neighborhood!"

"You like my new digs in your yard?" he asked.

"Oh, super deluxe. And Lisa said the Kennel couldn't get any uglier. She underestimated us."

"That she did, that she did," he said. "We're taking the trash factor to a whole new level. Just wait until I put a couch and a fridge outside of it this summer."

"Sweet. That way we won't have to get up for another beer," she joked.

"You knows it. And I'm thinking about getting a big Rottweiler and naming it Growler or maybe Guinness. When are you going to get a dog and name it after beer?"

"Tough call," she said as the chair came up behind her.

She felt an even deeper degree of solitude in the storm. The resort was quiet. A part of her still wanted to go to the lodge and drink cocoa along with everyone else. Something about goggles almost made it seem as though she were watching the storm from inside a car instead of actually being in it. Lisa had loaned Jill her iPod for the day, and the music now seemed almost like a sound track for the storm. It gave her energy and made her want to move.

She didn't need to hike for good turns in this kind of snow. It was ridiculously thick right on the runs. She traversed over to the Super Bowl and dropped into it. She and Lisa always called that kind of snow heroic, because a person could do no wrong in it. Everyone skied like a hero in that kind of snow. It came up above her knees, which slowed her down some. Instead of making tight turns, she let herself simply free-fall down the mountain in wide, sweeping arcs. She didn't fight gravity. She didn't fight the storm anymore, either. She became a part of it. She held her arms out to the side, pointed her skis downhill, and simply surrendered. Near the bottom of the bowl, the snow deepened. She brought her arms in and cut through part of it and then burrowed through the rest. She couldn't breathe or see but just kept going. She just skied the white room and hoped she wouldn't run into anything. She had joked about needing a snorkel before, but today she really did. Then she surfaced and kept skiing.

She didn't pass another soul. The storm had shrunk her world and offered her complete solitude. She skied in rhythm with the music, dancing her way down the mountain.

She approached a little lip and dropped down a steep hill. Instead of slowing down, she tucked it and flew over. Tree after tree passed in her peripheral vision as she sailed through the air. She remained airborne just above the ground for what felt like seven solid seconds, and then her skis touched down with a gentle *whoof.* She continued speeding down the mountain.

Now that Jill had surrendered to the storm, she was having the time of her life. She tried to figure out how she could apply the same principles to the storms that had raged in her life, in her body, in her marriage, but she couldn't draw the parallels. The only vision she had was the day after the storm, when new snow covered icy patches and bare spots, granting a fresh start.

That's when Cassie flew by her. Jill recognized Cassie's red jacket with the orange stripe down the side. Jill thought she had been skiing fast, but Cassie dusted her effortlessly. Cassie skied off a knoll, grabbed her ski, and spun a beautiful three-sixty. *Yes!*

Jill thought, and watched her land gracefully. Jill pushed herself to go even faster. She never completely caught up with Cassie but stayed on her tail.

At the lift, Cassie turned around to see who was behind her. "Oh, Jill!" she said, and gave her a little hug. "I thought you were my dad."

Jill smiled. "That was a nice three-sixty," she said. "Beautiful!"

"The nice thing about snow like this is that it doesn't hurt so bad to fall on your head," Cassie said.

Isn't that the truth? Jill thought. *What a tricky balance of safety and risk it is that brings out the best in us.*

Mike skidded to a stop behind them. "Hey, Jill, great storm, huh?"

She nodded. "Fabulous."

"Cassie, you're going to give your dad a heart attack skiing like that," Mike said to her, only half-joking.

"Do you mean just trying to keep up with her or are you talking about that incredible jump?" Jill asked.

"You're not encouraging her, are you?" Mike asked with a smile.

Jill faked a frown and shook her head. When he glanced back toward Cassie, Jill slipped her a wink. Kate would have loved seeing her ski like that.

As the three of them rode the chair back up together, Jill wondered what forces might guide three people together in a storm. Maybe chance. Maybe something else. She didn't know, but she felt thankful nonetheless.

Here is what Mike remembered from the rest of that day. He remembered watching snowflakes melt on Jill's nose and cheeks and lips. He remembered how Cassie looked up at her the way she might look at someone who threw her a life preserver when she was too tired to swim any longer. He remembered the way Jill looked at Cassie with an expression that could only be described as love. He remembered watching Jill and Cassie race each other ahead of him, watching them laugh, admiring Jill's figure when she tucked.

At the end of their third run together, Cassie beat Jill to the base lodge.

"Kid, you're so dang fast!" Jill shouted, released her bindings, and walked over for a high five.

Cassie popped out of her bindings and met Jill halfway.

Mike pulled up, stepped out of his skis, and picked up his daughter like a sack of potatoes. "Who wants cocoa?" he asked.

Cassie screamed, "Ah! Jill! Help me!"

Jill was laughing, Cassie was laughing, he was laughing, and for the first time he could remember, the moment lacked for nothing. It felt complete.

He remembered that.

And he remembered standing in line at the cafeteria with three cups of cocoa and looking over at them, taking off Gore-Tex shells and fleece coats, wet hat hair dripping, smiles on their faces, Jill patting Cassie on the back, their delicate faces and smooth skin, their beauty and perfection. He remembered sitting next to Cassie and putting his arm around his daughter. He remembered watching Jill's lips as they met the cup of cocoa, watching the lines under her eyes deepen when she laughed. He remembered that when she talked, he had the luxury of just looking deep into her eyes.

They skied a little more, Cassie showing off her best moves in the air for Jill. Each time, Mike gasped and went rigid until she landed safely.

Then, after the chairlifts had closed, they all walked down from the base through the parking lot to town together, smiling until their faces hurt, joking and teasing. And what Mike remembered most was feeling like a family, like a happy family.

Kate used to give Cassie tips and pointers the whole walk through the parking lot, and Cassie would listen and ask questions. They understood each other. They really did. And Cassie saw it for the act of love it was. But with Jill, Cassie got to just be a kid. And Mike thought that with everything she had been through, she could use more of being a kid.

Most of all, what Mike remembered was feeling happy, truly happy, for the first time in a long while. For the past few months, at best, he could imagine his life being okay. He had not been able to imagine it ever being happy again. But when Jill smiled at him, he started thinking that maybe, eventually, a chance at happiness with her would be worth having to find a new babysitter if it didn't work out.

Hans and Eric were both grooming on the mountain and Jill was at her other job, so no one saw when Tom came over to Lisa's and never left. No one knew the difference. That was the way Lisa wanted it.

Tom was propped up on one elbow next to where she lay on her back. With his other hand, he played with the damp clumps of hair around her face and looked at her adoringly.

She smiled and hid her fear. This thing, this situation, this relationship (oh, she hated that word), could go in so many directions.

"I don't see why we need to keep this a secret. If we keep it a secret, I get to sneak over once every three days when Jill is at work. If we out ourselves, I can be here as much as you'll tolerate me," he said.

"Do you have a secret place?" she asked.

"Oh, baby, I think you know my secret place," he joked.

"No, I'm not talking about that. I mean a place that you go when you need to think or pray or recalibrate . . . a place that's sacred to you."

"Yeah," he said.

"And you know how you wouldn't want a whole bunch of people throwing a kegger at your secret place?"

"Well, I don't know about that. . . ."

"Okay, you know how you wouldn't want a bunch of people defecating in the woods in your secret place and not burying it and leaving their toilet paper everywhere?"

"True. I would not want human excrement all over my secret place," Tom said.

"That's how I feel about this. Gossip is like excrement. I don't want it in my secret place." She put her hand behind his head and pulled him in for a kiss. "This thing feels sacred to me. And I know other people wouldn't see that or understand that. I don't want to explain it. I just want to keep it private and sacred." And later, when he would undoubtedly slip up and sleep with another woman with big boobs whom he met at the bar, as he was sure to, she didn't want anyone to know she was ever with him. She wouldn't want anyone to know she had been that stupid—stupid enough to believe he could ever be different from what he was. She wouldn't want anyone to know he broke her heart. But she told him only one of her two reasons for wanting to keep it private.

"I just feel like I've finally come home. I want to shout it from the rooftops," Tom said. "It feels like the biggest thing that ever happened to me. It's hard to keep it a secret."

"But will you? For me?" she asked.

"I would do anything for you," he said, and leaned over for another kiss.

"Thanks, baby. And as for the one out of three days, you know what they say, abstinence makes the heart grow fonder."

"That's not what they say." He laughed.

"No?" She laughed back. "I think we'll have a lot of fun sneaking around. Ah, here's one: That which is forbidden is sweeter."

"You just made that up."

"I swear to you I did not," she said, and raised her hand as if she were taking an oath. "You know, I feel like when I'm with you and we're quiet, I know the truth, but when we start talking about things, I start to doubt the truth, like words are just clutter that hides the truth that's between you and me."

And to Lisa's surprise, Tom didn't say a word. He just kissed her.

chapter twenty-one

. . .

SNOW REPORT FOR FEBRUARY 18

Current temperature: 24F, high of 27F at 2 P.M., low of 22F at 4 A.M.
Overcast with occasional snow flurries, winds out of the south at 10 mph.
103" mid-mountain, 111" at the summit. Trace new in the last 24 hours.
18" of new in the last 48.

Something was different. Cassie couldn't name it, but something was definitely different. Nothing appeared to look different. She still sat at her desk and looked at the other kids, looked at them and thought about all they didn't know, all the things she'd learned in the last year that they hadn't. Sean Harlson threw chunks of eraser at Renee Van Hoof. Obviously, he liked her. Renee finally looked at him and flipped him the finger behind her back when the teacher could not see. Cassie watched and thought about how completely uncivilized people her own age were. She felt older, more mature, for sure, but that wasn't what was different. She had been feeling that way the whole year.

It was something else that felt different, a lightness. Her body wanted to ski again.

She sat in class and dreamed of skiing again. She hadn't daydreamed of skiing since her mother was diagnosed. When she realized that, she instantly felt a pang of guilt for enjoying life when her mother was not able to anymore. But then she realized that her mother wouldn't want her not to ski, to spend her life sad. Her mother would want her out there on the mountain.

On the board, the teacher demonstrated using multiplication and division to create equivalent fractions. Cassie wasn't sure what the point was. She missed that part. Apparently, mentally checking out during school was something that hadn't changed.

The bell rang for lunch recess, and the teacher instructed them to line up. As she passed the ball box on her way out, Cassie took a jump rope. It wasn't that she liked jumping rope. It just made her look busy. It was something she could do alone. When she jumped rope, no one asked her to join their game. And she figured it was good ski conditioning. Outside, she found a spot under the crowded covered area and began jumping. She watched the other kids. They all seemed so shiny and bright and happy. That hadn't changed. But Cassie no longer felt angry at them for being all those things. That was different.

And she was able to jump rope for the whole recess without getting tired or losing her will. That was different, too.

After ten minutes, another bell rang for the kids to line up to go to the cafeteria. Cassie waited until everyone else was in line before taking her spot near the back. She didn't like going through the line first and sitting at a table alone, watching kids pass and avoid her. When she was in the back, she could just get her lunch and let the lunchroom supervisor guide her to one of the few remaining seats. There was no decision to be made. There was no permission to be granted from other kids. Laurel told her where to sit and she sat, and whoever was next to her tolerated her. There was no need to speak, though sometimes they did. Today, the lunchroom supervisor sat her next to Renee and Alyssa. Hailey was at another table. Clearly, Renee and Alyssa were leaving her out today. Cassie felt so grateful not to be part of that.

"Hi," Renee said.

"Hi," Cassie answered.

"How's it going?" Renee asked. She was trying. Ever since Cassie's mom died, Renee tried to be nice. Cassie had to give her that. She was trying.

"I saw you flip off Sean before lunch. That was funny," she said.

"Yeah," Renee said with a little laugh. "Sean's a jerk."

"Yeah," Cassie said, and then started to eat her lunch. That was it. Their conversation was over. It was enough to ease the tension, but not enough to make them friends. It was just right. Renee turned the other way and visited with the mean girls. Cassie finished her lunch and put her tray away. Usually, she hid in a bathroom stall for the remainder of lunch, just waiting for it to be over, but today she didn't feel like hiding. Instead she stood by a window, looked out, and longed to be elsewhere. She thought about sneaking out of school and hiding in her garage or maybe walking to the river's edge.

Mrs. Peterson, the librarian, walked by on her way to buy a little carton of milk and then passed her again. "Hey, Cassie," she said. "Come with me. I've got a book to show you."

Cassie followed her out of the cafeteria and down the hall to the library. Once in the library, Mrs. Peterson said, "Okay, really, you just looked like you needed out of there, but it wasn't a complete lie because I have a whole library of books to show you." She scribbled a note and handed it to Cassie: *"Please let Cassie come to the library when she's done with her lunch. She's helping me. Mrs. Peterson,"* it read.

"There's your Get Out of Jail Free card," she said. "If you lose it, I'll write you another."

Cassie gave her a little smile. "Thanks," she said.

Mrs. Peterson gave her a wink and sat down to eat her lunch at her desk. "Go find a good book," she said. "Enjoy."

Cassie wandered off to browse the books. She had sanctuary. She had someone at school who understood a little about what she needed. And Mrs. Peterson would notice if she cut out of school early from now on, so she probably wouldn't. Cassie didn't want Mrs. Peterson to think she didn't appreciate her sanctuary. Cassie would show up. That was different. She wandered back to the sports section and selected a biography on Picabo Street.

As she sat among the books, she thought about how none of these things in her day alone were remarkable, but all of them added up to some kind of shift. It almost felt uneasy or itchy. It was a restlessness. It felt like coming back to life. It was expanding. It was discontent. It was wanting more. It was movement.

And three hours later when the day was over, Cassie returned home, went to her room, and opened her mother's book to the next prayer Kate had written.

God, wherever you are and whatever you are, please fill me. Please fill me so full that there is no room for fear. Please fill me so full that I keep on living even when I want to give up. Don't let me give up. I know I'm here for a reason. Whatever that reason is, please guide me toward fulfilling it. Please fill me up so full that any negativity in me bleaches out like mold in sunlight. Root it all out, so there's as much room as possible for you inside me. Fill me, good God, fill me until I overflow with you and spill you all over everyone around me.

In the years to come, Cassie would read that prayer many times and each time it would mean something new to her. But on that day, the words that jumped out at her were "keep on living," and something about them gave her the affirmation that it was okay to do just that.

Tom went to the Pneumonia Shack and called out Jason.

The person who had the Auger could call out anyone and pick the run they would ski together. It was how a person got rid of it. But Tom's motivation for calling out Jason was more than just unloading the Auger. He missed his best friend.

Jason was, in his own words, level five irritated. There were only five levels. As a practical joke, someone had created a very large snack bar sign complete with pictures and prices of tasty treats, put a nice coat of polyurethane on it, and affixed it to the Pneumonia Shack.

Tom looked at it and couldn't stop laughing.

"Are you responsible for this?" Jason charged.

"Oh, I wish I was. This is brilliant," Tom said.

"They used star screws so I can't even take it down. All day I've had tourists pissed at me because I didn't have any Snickers bars to sell them."

"And now I'm about to show you why I'm worthy of my illustrious job title," Tom said as he made a sign that read CLOSED. As he wrote, he heard scratching from inside the wall. "How's Roger?" Tom asked.

"Roger's excrement composting in the walls has helped keep the shack a little warmer this year," Jason replied.

Tom duct-taped the CLOSED sign to the snack bar sign. "Wala. Problem solved."

Jason applauded. "Well done, Tom. Well done."

"And now I'm calling you out to ski Waterfall with me so I can unload this." Tom reached inside his jacket and pulled out the ugly corkscrewlike necklace.

"I can't be buying everyone drinks. I've got to put that money in a college fund for Junior now," Jason said.

"Well then, let's hope you don't fall."

Jason shut the door to the shack and followed Tom across the ridge to the impossibly steep run. In keeping with the rules, Jason dropped first. He made tight, expert jump turns. Snow had piled up on a few large rocks that stuck out of the frozen waterfall, and he hit those on the way down like stairs. From the top, Tom waited for him to eat it, but much to his disappointment, Jason skied it perfectly and waited at the bottom.

Tom jumped off the lip and did the same, only near the bottom he scraped a rock, which slowed him down enough for him to lose his balance. He went headfirst downhill but rolled over to get his skis below him so he could slide for life if he needed to, and that gave him enough momentum to finish his roll and end up on his feet. He kept skiing without breaking stride. When he reached the bottom, he stopped next to Jason and shook his head.

Jason led the way back to the chair, and they whizzed up the line that was just for ski patrol, allowing them to cut in front of everyone and take the next chair.

"So how are the ladies at the Gold Pan these days?" Jason asked.

"I don't know," Tom replied.

Jason raised an eyebrow and studied him. "You hooked up with Lisa."

"Why do you say that?"

"It was inevitable. It made sense. And I noticed you didn't answer the charges."

"No, I didn't," Tom said.

"Oh, I get it. She swore you to secrecy. Julie did that to me, too. Yeah, you're going to have to propose."

"What?" Tom asked.

"Julie wouldn't go public with me until after I proposed. She said that given my reputation, people would think she was just another unfortunate floozy about to be left in my wake. I had to do something to distinguish her as different and worthy of more respect," Jason said.

"What?" Tom asked again.

"Yeah, dude, you're going to have to propose. But it's not all bad. I get lucky several times a week with a really hot chick who sometimes does my laundry."

"We didn't have this talk," Tom said.

"What talk?" Jason asked as if he already forgot.

"Exactly. Thanks."

"One more thing. When you propose, don't screw it up. You've waited a long time for her. Do it right."

Tom didn't reply. He just thought about it for a moment. Then something caught his eye. He pointed to it. "Check it. Rope duckers." He got on his radio to get another patroller to snowmobile out there, nab them, and take their tickets.

Jason rubbed his hands together excitedly. "We get to play dog hole! Game on!"

"Oh, how I hope they're season pass holders so they'll have to play to get them back!" he said to Jason. "Stout's avalanche rescue skills are surely getting rusty."

"Be sure to tell Scooter that we want him to dig economy dog holes—not super deluxe dog holes. These guys need the kind of epiphany that can only happen when they're running out of air in an economy-sized dog hole," Jason said.

As Tom dialed Scooter, one thought overrode his excitement about burying rule breakers in the little caves that Scooter would dig. It overrode his excitement about the resolution of a long-standing disagreement between Jason and him: whether avalanche dogs would dig out a person with pizza or jerky in their pocket first. The thought that overrode all else was simply whether Lisa would ever say yes.

Lisa answered the phone. "Hello?"

"Ragazzina?" Lisa's mom said on the other end of the phone. "I'm just calling to check up on you. It's been a while since you've called me. I said to your aunt just today, 'I haven't heard from my little Lisa in a while,' and do you know what she said? 'She must be in love.' "

Lisa laughed.

"Oh! So she was right! Tell me!"

"Yes, Mama, I think I am."

"Who is this boy?" her mother asked.

"My friend Tom," Lisa answered.

"Tom. Tom," her mother said again, sort of tasting his name. "He sounds pasty."

"Yes. Yes, he is," Lisa said. "He has blond hair and his legs glow in the dark."

"Good. Because let me tell you something. Italian men cannot be true. None of the Mediterranean men can. Their hearts are too passionate. They are too easily influenced by the tides of passion. They have high sex drives. They are like volcanoes. They are, what do you young people say? High maintenance. I say, yes, get yourself a nice pasty blond man. He won't be as nice to look at, but he won't break your heart either."

Lisa laughed. "Got it. Thanks, Mama."

"So, when are you getting married?"

"Oh, gosh . . . I don't know, Mama."

"Are you afraid to get married?"

"There are a lot of reasons not to get married, Mama."

"Reasons? What reasons? Wanting to go to hell?"

"Yes, Mama. That's exactly it."

"Don't get sassy with me, Lisa. You're not too old for a spanking." After an uncomfortable pause, which her mother seemed to take as a little victory, she asked, "Everything else is okay?"

"Everything else is great," Lisa said.

"Jill is eating?" her mother asked.

"It would warm your heart and make you proud to see how I am feeding Jill," Lisa said.

"What about your father's restaurant? Are the new chefs doing all right or are people in town saying the food is garbage now?"

Lisa wasn't sure what the right answer was. "My friends are all too poor to eat there. I haven't heard anything. What about you, Mama? Everything there is good?"

"Everything here is good. The weather's been sunny. I never have to shovel snow," she said.

Lisa laughed. "Well, enjoy the warm temperatures for me."

"Okay, my little Ragazzina," her mother said. "You make sure this Tom isn't milking the cow for free, okay? And don't wait so long to call your mother. I love you."

"I love you, too," Lisa said. "I'll call sooner next time."

"Okay, then. Good night, my Lisa."

"Good night, Mama."

Lisa hung up the phone and wondered whether Tom was really capable of a lasting relationship (there was that word again). She opened the door to the broom closet to look at the evidence on the game board, to look at all those women, but instead what she saw was that it was no longer there. Tom had taken it down.

And right then her phone lit up. "Message Received," it said out loud. She flipped it open and saw a text from Tom: "Mardi Gras Luge party now! Hurry! Wear beads."

"Luge," Jill said, out of breath when Mike answered the door.

"Luge?" Mike asked.

"Luge," Jill said again with a big smile.

"Cassie! Luge!" Mike called out. "Tarp?" he asked Jill.

"Optional," Jill said.

Cassie ran down the stairs. She and Mike threw on some clothes, snatched the tarp off the woodpile on their way out, and hurried up the hill with Jill.

The luge was approximately eighty yards of pure thrill. A string of Christmas lights ran along both sides of it, giving it a carnival feeling at night. Luge building worked only when the weather started to warm. On most days in the heart of winter, the snow was too cold to stick, but on this day warm winds had blown in from the south, making the snow just right. Eric and Hans had been waiting for this day, and using their groomers to plow the course behind employee housing where the suits wouldn't likely see it, they created what they called their finest masterpiece ever. Tom, Jason, and Scooter jumped in with shovels to polish it to perfection.

As Cassie, Mike, and Jill approached, Uncle Howard was just coming down the luge on his back, feet together, arms crossed across his front. He stood up and proclaimed, "This is their best luge track yet." To someone who didn't know him, it might have appeared as though he were not excited about it. He wasn't the most expressive person in the world by any means, but Jill knew him well enough to know he was thrilled.

He stepped aside just in time to avoid Coach Ernie, who had sped down behind him. "Woo-hoo! That track was . . . what's the word? Groovy? Rad? I don't know. It was *swell*!"

"Coach Ernie!" Jill shouted. "You're an inspiration!"

"Let me let you in on a little secret, Jilly," he said. "Skiing is the fountain of youth! High speeds keep a person young!" With that, he started up the path to the top again.

Jill and Mike looked at each other and shook their heads in amazement.

"Well then," Jill said, "I guess it's a good thing I moved back."

"I think it's a very good thing you moved back," Mike said.

Cassie raced ahead up the path to the start. When she was out of earshot, Mike said, "Thanks for getting us out here. She needed this."

"Thank me when she breaks some bones," Jill joked.

"At this point, it's all about maximizing the good times," he replied.

At the top were all Jill's friends. They had a bonfire roaring and were roasting hot dogs on sticks.

Tom was excited. "And I didn't think today could get any better! Jason, tell the people what you learned today."

"Pizza rules. Jerky drools," Jason said flatly.

"Meaning?" Tom prompted.

"Search dogs will dig out a person with pizza in their pocket before they dig out a person with jerky in their pocket," Jason relented.

"And whose contention was that from the start?" Tom asked.

"The almighty and all-knowing Tom," Jason said.

Jill and Mike said their hellos while Cassie hollered for them to hurry up from the top of the run. Mike and Cassie went first, disappearing down the chute like rockets, and then it was Jill's turn. She crossed her legs and arms and let gravity work its magic. The Christmas lights were a blur as she sped past them, through the curves, and finally slowed to a stop at the bottom.

She didn't see Mike or Cassie, and then *wham!* She was hit in the face with a snowball.

"Oh! You did not!" she shouted as she chased Cassie, who hid behind a tree, and then another. "You're going down, Cassie!"

Suddenly, Mike grabbed her from behind and held her. "Get her, Cassie! Get her!" For that split second before Cassie relentlessly threw snowball after snowball at her face, Jill liked how he felt behind her, liked how his arms felt around her.

"That's it!" Jill shouted. "You're both going to Arizona!"

"Do you give up?" Mike barked.

"Yes!" Jill screamed.

Mike let her go, and Cassie stopped throwing snowballs. They victoriously high-fived each other, and then Cassie started off toward the trail back up.

Jill shrieked and shook out the snow that had fallen down the front of her jacket. She reached under her coat, untucked her shirt, and held it open. Clumps of snow fell out.

Mike smiled and raised his eyebrows a couple times.

"Oh, you're into that, are you?" Jill joked quietly enough for Cassie not to hear.

Mike just smiled suggestively and shrugged.

"I will get revenge," Jill vowed loudly as she and Mike followed Cassie up the trail.

"I'm scared," Cassie said sarcastically. "Are you scared, Dad?"

"Oh yes. So scared," Mike replied.

When they hiked up the trail again and stopped at the top to pay homage to the luge makers, Jill took a little nip off Lisa's flask for warmth, or at least the illusion of it, and looked around at her circle of friends. She felt so lucky. So lucky and even grateful for some of the misfortune that had brought her back to Sparkle. Not the miscarriage. She wasn't grateful for that. But David's infidelity and the unraveling of the rest of her life felt neutralized. She was happy. Here in Sparkle, a person could be a playful kid forever—at least in some ways. Things like the luge didn't happen in Austin, and certainly not at the hospital there.

There were more trips down the luge, a few more snowballs, and some warm-up time near the campfire, and then finally Mike said it was time for Cassie to hit the hay. Jill was tired, too, so she said good night to her friends and followed Mike and Cassie back to town.

As they reached the Kennel, rather than say good night, Mike asked, "Want to come to our house for a cup of cocoa?" She looked up at his face and could tell he didn't want the night to end.

"Sure," she said.

And when they arrived back at the house, Mike heated the milk, poured Cassie a cup of cocoa, handed it to her, and said, "Off to a hot bath you go!"

She whined for a moment, but then trotted off obediently.

Mike poured the rest of the cocoa into mugs for Jill and him but added a little Baileys to theirs. "You know what they say. 'Candy is dandy, but liquor is quicker.' "

Was he flirting with her? Jill laughed and blushed.

He sat down across the table, looked right at her, took a deep, satisfied breath, and said, "This was a good night."

She smiled. "It was."

They drank their spiked cocoa, recalled funny moments from the evening, and laughed. His smile seemed sexier somehow, but she chalked up that perception to the Baileys. She was a lightweight. It didn't take much.

But then, as she was heading for the door, he rested a hand on her back for just a moment as he walked with her.

When they reached the door, she turned toward him and smiled.

He paused and then asked, "Do you ever think about you and me?"

"What do you mean?" she asked, avoiding his question.

He shrugged. "I have fun with you. Sometimes I think about you and me. It's probably wrong. It hasn't been that long. And you're going through your stuff. I'm going through mine. Cassie needs you. I'd never want to mess that up. But sometimes I think about it."

Jill waited a moment to see if he would say more, and when he didn't, she simply said, "Yeah, sometimes I think about it, too."

Then she reached up and gave him a hug, and he hugged her back. She glanced up at him before she stepped out the door, and what she saw was possibility.

chapter twenty-two

• • •

SNOW REPORT FOR MARCH 17

Current temperature: 16F, high of 21F at 3 P.M., low of 12F at 4 A.M.
Clear skies, winds out of the southwest at 30 mph with gusts of up to 40 mph.
109" mid-mountain, 119" at the summit. 0" new in the last 24 hours.
0" of new in the last 48.

Yesterday, Eric had led Jill to a shack behind the maintenance garage. Behind the shack was a water tank on skids, complete with a hose, presumably for fighting forest fires.

"I discovered this little gem in late October and I've had this dream ever since. You may be aware that tomorrow is Saint Patrick's Day. That tank now contains lime Kool-Aid. You and I are taking that baby up to Yellow Brick Road, turning on the pressure motor, and you're going to paint it green. I need someone to spray while I drive. Hans was going to do it, but he's passed out and I can't wake him. Lisa and Tom would not only be prime suspects, but would buckle under pressure when people start asking questions tomorrow. No one will suspect you."

"Because I'm no fun?" she asked.

He laughed. "No. Because you're a good girl. If this mountain was Gilligan's Island, you'd be Mary Ann. It will be good for you to be just a little naughty."

Jill smiled and didn't say no.

Now, after midnight, she found herself in Eric's old rain gear, a little drunk, sitting on top of the tank as if it were a horse, spraying the freshly groomed snow behind Eric's cat, and laughing hysterically. When the tank finally ran out of juice, she waved to Eric. He stopped so she could get back into the warmth of the snowcat, where he blasted the heat for her. She continued to laugh, and he joined her. Then he handed her another beer.

"You are a bad influence on me!" Jill laughed.

"Yeah? How does it feel?" he asked.

"So good," she said.

"If you let me, I could make you feel even better."

Jill laughed. In weak moments, she occasionally considered that. Eric was sweet. Just the other night, they had watched *The Breakfast Club* on some movie channel together. He had made her dinner and massaged her shoulders during the movie. They were friends—friends with chemistry. And as long as she was clear about what he was and what he wasn't, she could enjoy him for what he was. He was warm and gracious. But he wasn't boyfriend material. It was Mike she really had feelings for, of course, but Mike wasn't available. Eric kind of was. But thinking about Mike made Jill feel a little guilty just for being there with Eric, laughing, drinking, and having fun. Technically, it wasn't a betrayal, so why did it feel like one?

"Look at our work," he said. They turned around and looked at the green run behind them. In the dark, they couldn't see much. "We rule!"

"This is the naughtiest thing I've ever done," Jill said proudly.

"I could change that for you," Eric replied suggestively. "You'd have even more fun than this. . . ."

Jill's inner conflict roiled. Was it stupid to wait for Mike when who knew when, if ever, he might want that kind of relationship with her? Suddenly, it did seem stupid. Meanwhile, here was Eric with his sexy voice, who was fun and light, and who helped her lighten up and have more fun. It felt good to lighten up and have more fun. What would really be so wrong with capitalizing on all that he offered? Even drunk, she had enough sense to know that if it was a good idea tonight, it would be a good idea tomorrow, so she simply said, "Noted."

Eric headed back down to the maintenance garage. He got out to open Jill's door and help her down. Being a little drunk, she lost her balance, and he caught her. She started laughing again.

"Are you good?" he asked, and she laughed harder. He didn't let go, so Jill found herself in his embrace. "Good night, girl," he said, and gave her a little peck on the lips. "Go take a bath and soak the green out of your hands. Oh, and will you take these?" He handed Jill a bag of their beer bottles. "We're not supposed to drink and drive the mountain's three-hundred-and-twenty-five-thousand-dollar equipment. Go figure."

Jill took the bag.

"Hey . . ." He reached out his arm for another hug, so Jill gave him one. "I luv ya, Jilly," he said.

"Back at ya, babe," she replied.

Luv. Friend love. Happiness and warmth love. Not *"I'll give you a kidney if you need it"* love. Just luv. *Nothing wrong with luv,* she thought.

She threw the bag of beer bottles over her shoulder and walked back to the Kennel, clinking and laughing until she reached the point where she could see Mike and Cassie's house down the street. She sat on the curb across the street from the Kennel and looked back and forth from it to Mike and Cassie's house.

On the outside, the Kennel was a dump and Mike and Cassie's house was nice. On the inside, the Kennel was full of marijuana smoke and Mike and Cassie's house was full of grief.

The Kennel offered her the opportunity to live like Peter Pan and never grow up, to paint ski runs green, to play drinking games while watching *The Bachelor,* even to have sex with no obligations. And in Mike and Cassie's house, well, on the one hand, there appeared to be the opportunity to have a family, but it was likely just a dream. In her mind, she kept hearing Mike's voice say, *It's probably wrong*, and then listing all the reasons why it was impractical to consider the possibility of a different kind of relationship. She wondered if there would ever be enough room for her to be anything more than a babysitter. She could see herself wasting years of her life waiting and hoping for it like a carrot dangling in front of her. The house was so full of Kate. Their broken hearts were so full of Kate. There was no room for her there. She had absolutely been stupid for ever dreaming about it.

She stood, picked up the bag of bottles, and headed back into the place where there was room for her. But as she walked through the door, she wondered where she was headed and what exactly she was becoming.

As Mike pulled the laundry out of the dryer, he was thinking about how good it felt being with Cassie and Jill at the luge and on the day they had skied together. It felt so good to finally be happy again. It had felt good to hug Jill, too. And it all felt like moving forward. More and more, he realized that moving forward was the only path to happiness.

He carried the laundry basket up the stairs, and dumped it out on his bed. He pulled the towels out first and folded them, and then he folded all the clothes. This time, though, he put the pile of Kate's things away. As he was doing it, he realized it was time. He went out to the garage and brought in three large plastic storage bins, and slowly, carefully, he took Kate's things out of the closet that he thought Cassie might like one day. He reminisced for a long moment about the last time he'd seen Kate wearing each item: a wedding, her class reunion, a hot summer day, Cassie's school programs. He folded each one carefully and placed it in the bin. He couldn't figure out what Cassie might and might not want one day, so he ended up keeping all the things that had hung in the closet. He opened one of her drawers, pulled out pants and shirts, ran his hand over each one, remembered running his hand over her knee when she wore those pants, remembered running his hand over her shoulder when she wore that T-shirt. He put them in another bin.

Then he went downstairs and got a paper grocery bag. He put her socks and her underwear in it and her beat-up running shoes. No one else would want those things.

He carried the bag outside back behind the garage to the garbage can. He opened the lid. He lowered the bag into the can but could not make himself let go of the handles, so he lifted it back out. He couldn't pretend his wife's things were garbage. He wasn't ready to think about them sitting in the stinky can for days and then going to a landfill. He stood there for a long time, unsure of what to do with things that had no purpose, the things he should release. Eventually, he walked into the garage and put the bag high on a shelf next to some boxes full of other useless things he couldn't part with.

He took an empty cardboard box upstairs and filled it with her shoes. He wasn't sure what to do with those, either. On top, he put her purses that were a little worse for wear—her favorites. He sealed it with packing tape, and he put the lids on the bins.

And then he sat on the end of his bed, looking at her half of the closet empty, and he cried.

Mrs. Campbell stuck a green shamrock on the new kid's shirt as he stood awkwardly in front of the class. "This is Mauricio," she said. "I know it's Saint Patrick's Day, but do not pinch him because he wouldn't understand. Can you imagine being pinched by everyone on your first day of school in a foreign country? That would be cruel. Make sure no one from other classes bothers him either. Help him out."

Then she sat him right next to Cassie. Maybe by chance or maybe on purpose, Cassie wasn't sure. He didn't speak English, and this alone was reason for her to like him. With Mauricio, they wouldn't have to dance around the subject of her mother. They didn't have to discuss her at all. Cassie could tell he felt uncomfortable and probably missed his home, wherever it was, and that he was feeling his own kind of loss.

Since he didn't speak English, he was lost in class. She tried to model different tasks for him and help him however she could. Mrs. Campbell gave him an English-Spanish dictionary, and Cassie looked up words with him. When it was time to go somewhere, she poked him in the arm and gestured for him to follow her. Before long, he was stuck to her like glue.

She still jumped rope by herself at morning recess, but she noticed him sitting alone on a bench in the corner of the playground. At lunch recess, she took a basketball instead of a jump rope and got him to shoot baskets with her. He was awful. He mimed that he would rather play soccer.

At lunch, instead of worrying about being the last in line, she walked him through the line and showed him where to pick up all the things he needed. Together, they found a place to sit and eat, and she liked him enough not to leave him in the horrible, crowded, and largely uncivilized cafeteria by himself. Instead of going to the library for sanctuary, she stayed by Mauricio's side.

When he looked down to get the last bites of overcooked peas on his spoon, Cassie noticed a pendant on a chain around his neck. It was the Virgin Mary in a heart on a crucifix. Her new friend had a picture of the Madonna in a heart. A mother inside of a heart. Her mother had sent him to her. Mauricio looked up and smiled. Cassie looked at his pendant, pointed to her own neck, and nodded to tell him she liked it. He put his hands together in prayer and nodded back.

In addition to being St. Patrick's Day, it was Auger night, so the usual gang was at the Gold Pan. Tom still had the Auger, so he bought the patrollers who were there a round of flaming tequila shots. He proudly threw his down so fast that when he put the glass back on the bar, a tiny blue flame still burned.

"So, Jason," Tom shouted. "I understand you did something ridiculously stupid this pay period and have had the honor of writing about it in the Peter Book! Please do enjoy drinking the schwag off the serving tray before reading your latest excerpt for us!"

Instead of bringing the tray to his face and slurping the booze that had spilled, he sucked it up with a straw and then began to read: "My wife, Julie, and I were on our way to take a little trip across the border to Whistler. The Canadian border patrol, thinking I looked like someone who would have a backpack full of weed, asked to inspect it. As it turns out, I still had a bomb in there from the last time I did avalanche control work, and so naturally he thought I was a terrorist. Fortunately, I had my ski patrol ID in there, too, and so, four hours later, the guy simply took the bomb from me and let me drive on instead of sending me to jail."

The gathering shouted, jeered, and laughed at him, and then people settled down a bit and drank their green beers.

Lisa and Tom sat next to each other, trying not to be obvious, trying not to act differently from the way they had ever acted before. A couple of pretty young women walked by and flirtatiously said hi to Tom. He said hi back but under the table put his hand on Lisa's knee.

"Let's sneak out of here," he whispered to her.

"You first," she whispered back. "I'm going to pretend that I'm going to the restroom."

"Is that really necessary? Can't we just go?" he asked.

"If we leave together, people will talk," she said.

He didn't want it to hurt his feelings, but it did, and suddenly he didn't want to sneak out anymore. "Never mind," he said. "I think I'll have another beer."

Lisa watched him deflate, and she sat there for a moment, irritated, trying to choose her next words carefully.

Just then, Jason came over to the table. "Hey, here, have the rest of mine. Julie and I are getting out of here." He put down a little cocktail napkin in front of Tom and put his beer on it. Tom saw writing and picked up the beer so he could see if it had someone's name and number on it, but instead, in Jason's handwriting, it read, "You're being a dick. Don't screw it up. Either propose or sneak out the way she wants to." Tom slipped the napkin into his lap before Lisa could notice.

"Thanks," he called to them as they walked away. He took a drink and then, without looking at her, held his beer in front of his lips and whispered to Lisa, "I'm sorry. I know going public would cheapen this for you. Hiding it cheapens it for me. It's the greatest thing that ever happened to me and you're ashamed of it. But whatever. Let's just go. Any way you want to."

Lisa hung her head. "I'm sorry. I wish I had just walked out the door with you when you asked. We're friends and neighbors. No one would have thought anything about it. I don't know why I had to turn it into such a big deal. It wasn't worth hurting you over. It changed the energy between us, and I wished it hadn't because once milk begins to curdle, it rarely goes back to being milk." She put her arm around his middle and gave him a squeeze from behind.

He put his hand on her hand and melted a little. "Let's go," he said. He stood and wove his way through the crowd. She walked out behind him. Out on the street, she put her arm through his. She rested her head against his shoulder for a moment.

"I'm sorry," she said.

"It's okay," he replied. "We're both going to make mistakes. We're going to make a lot of mistakes. That just has to be okay."

"Yeah," she said. "I know. I just hate making them. I'd never mean to hurt you."

They walked in silence down Main Street. So many businesses, it struck Lisa, were about image—boutiques, galleries, home décor. They all had immaculate storefronts. Then there was the old hardware store that had been there forever. It was a fine store, but not pretentious. Of all the businesses downtown, it was her favorite. It was real. It was functional. It reminded her of Tom. Across the street, the Pioneer Saloon was packed with tourists and rich new arrivals. The Gold Pan was too much of a dive for them, which was why all the locals went there.

Weary of the downtown scene, she guided Tom up across the street into the residential area, past the homes of old friends and neighbors. She loved the charm of all the small historic homes. On one side of them Sparkle Mountain towered, and on the other, Big Daddy. Sometimes she felt a little squished between the two mountains, but not tonight. Tonight, she felt nestled by them.

She realized she felt more at home in her home. The town seemed warmer walking through it with her arm in Tom's. And as they approached her house, she understood what he meant when he said that being with her felt like coming home.

Finally she spoke. "Let's take a green bubble bath. You can have the good spot. We could drink green beer in the green bubble bath."

He pulled her into him with one arm and kissed the top of her head as they walked up her sidewalk.

chapter twenty-three

. . .

SNOW REPORT FOR MARCH 28

Current temperature: 23F, high of 36F at 3 P.M., low of 18F at 4 A.M.
Clear skies, winds out of the southwest at 10 mph.
109" mid-mountain, 119" at the summit. 0" new in the last 24 hours.
13" new in the last 48.

Jill stood next to Cassie and Mike in eager anticipation for the big moment. Cassie's dummy was the third to be launched. Ten dummies in all waited at the top, four of which belonged to Jill's housemates, who stood on the other side of her. Jill knew the Kennel guys had spent years mastering their craft and that Cassie's first attempt was likely no match, but she wanted so badly for Cassie to have some victory.

Tom's dummy was turned loose first. It was made of old mufflers welded together in human form. He had painted it red with a white cross and strapped a broken radio to it. Behind it, it pulled a doll strapped into a cheap plastic toboggan. Jill wasn't sure how to judge how well it did, since it was the first, but to her left Tom looked disappointed while Hans and Eric knuckle bunched, so Jill assumed it hadn't done well.

Hans turned to her and whispered, "Eric and Tom are going

to look so pretty." The Kennel guys had a bet: The winner of the Dummy Downhill got to pick out dresses for the other guys to wear to the Dirtbag Ball, and Hans had already chosen secondhand wedding dresses for them, confident that his dummy would win again.

The next dummy looked like a flying nun. It went substantially farther than Tom's.

Jill looked to her right and exchanged a hopeful glance with Mike. His expression changed to something more serious and contemplative, and Jill didn't know how to read it. Then he smiled just a little and looked back up the hill.

The fabric on the hang glider fluttered as the dummy slid down the slope. There was more drag than Jill anticipated. It launched and looked great with the doll sailing behind. Mike cheered. Then a gust of wind picked it up higher and blew it sideways. It still went an impressive distance, much farther than Tom's and a little beyond the flying nun, but Jill didn't know if it would be good enough to win in the end.

"Well, not too bad," Cassie said.

Jill patted her shoulder and said, "Well, I thought it did great. It looked great. We may need to revisit our design and refine it for next year. Hans puts six pounds of buckshot in the boots of his and then fills them with cement for more weight and momentum. It will be interesting to see how his does."

"I'm thinking that if we used Plexiglas for the kite instead of fabric, it would have had less drag. At the very least, we could stretch spandex on the frame instead of nylon." Cassie sounded so mature and serious for her age.

Jill turned to Mike. "She's going to be an engineer," she said proudly.

He smiled. "Yeah, she's pretty smart."

For a moment, Jill imagined the three of them were a family, and it felt good. Mike looked back over at her, in a way that made her suspect he was thinking the same thing.

Eric's dummy, which he had constructed out of a Mr. Wonderful doll, soared down the slope, up the ski jump, and sailed. While it was seemingly suspended in midair, a shot was heard and his dummy's head exploded. Jill jumped and looked at Eric, alarmed.

"Again?" Cassie asked.

Eric explained calmly, "I have an ex on the U.S. Women's Biathlon Team. She does this every year."

Jill looked at Scooter and Hans wide-eyed. They just shrugged.

Scooter's shark was next off the slope. It rolled midair, but there was no rule about a dummy having to land right side up. So far, it had sailed the farthest and was in the lead. Hans looked a little nervous.

Finally, after all the others, Hans's moment of truth came, and it was everything he'd anticipated it would be. His metal dog shot down the hill, off the jump, and into the air with the force of a cannon. Its velocity helped it defy gravity for much longer than Jill would have guessed. It landed about forty yards beyond Scooter's shark. He pumped a triumphant fist in the air and shouted, "Yes!" He shook Cassie's hand and then Scooter's. Then he whispered something to Scooter and they both turned to Cassie.

"You gave us a good run for our money, kid," Scooter said to her.

"You can have the season pass," Hans said. "Obviously, you know, the mountain gives us ours for free."

"Sweet! Thanks!" Cassie said, elated.

Mike shook their hands, too. "That's really nice of you."

"Our pleasure," Hans said.

Scooter turned to Eric and Tom. "I really have to wear a dress?"

"Welcome to the Kennel," Tom said.

Eric added, "Wearing a dress can be a real handicap when it comes to picking up girls. It makes us fine-tune our skills."

"You have to turn it around in your mind and think of it as the ultimate icebreaker," said Tom.

Scooter rubbed his pierced face and then nodded as he accepted his fate.

Then he said to Cassie, "Come on, kid, let's go to the platform and get our medals." Cassie hugged Jill's waist.

As the three winners worked their way through the crowd, Mike closed in for a sideways hug and then kept his arm there while they watched Cassie bend her head forward a little and receive a bronze medal.

"Are you going?" Jill asked Mike.

"Jill," Eric interjected, "you promised to be my date."

"I'm not dogging you, bro," she replied in her best Kennel lingo.

Mike took his hand off her shoulder and shook his head. "Cassie and I are laying low that night." He looked back and forth between Jill and Eric. "Well, see ya," he said coldly, and wandered off to the podium.

"Did you catch that *Wild Kingdom* moment?" Tom asked her quietly.

"What just happened?" Jill asked.

"They both think of you as their platonic wife," he answered.

chapter twenty-four

. . .

SNOW REPORT FOR MARCH 29

Current temperature: 28F, high of 36F at 3 P.M., low of 23F at 4 A.M.
Mostly clear skies, winds out of the southwest at 25 mph.
100" mid-mountain, 118" at the summit. 0" new in the last 24 hours.
0" of new in the last 48.

The day before, Cassie had looked up the words in the English-Spanish dictionary but didn't know how to conjugate verbs, so she just pointed at him and then at herself as she said, *"Por favor, enseñar cocinar."*

"Teach you food?" he had asked back.

Cassie nodded. "Mexican food," she answered.

"Tomorrow?" he asked.

"Sure," she answered. Even though she hadn't asked her father yet, she knew neither of them had plans. They never did.

"Write foods I get at store tonight," she said.

He looked confused.

She picked up the dictionary. "Um . . . *Escribe ingredientes,"* she said.

"Ah." He nodded and made a short list. Mike was a sport and took her shopping that night.

In keeping with her father's request, the next day Cassie did not bring Mauricio home before Jill got there. They did their homework at the public library first, and when the clock said five, they went to her house. Jill was already inside, just coming back down the stairs.

"Jill, this is Mauricio," Cassie said. "Mauricio, this is Jill."

"Mucho gusto, Mauricio," Jill said, and shook his hand.

"Mucho gusto," he replied. Then he turned to Cassie. "Mama?" he asked.

"No," Cassie replied.

"Tu papa," Mauricio said, placed his hands over his heart, and then pointed at Jill with a questioning look.

"No!" Cassie said with too much force. "Papa," she said, then put her hands over her heart and said, "Mama." She shook her head. "Jill. No. Mama."

Mauricio nodded that he understood.

Neither noticed the look on Jill's face. "So you're going to make something delicious?" Jill asked, clearly changing the subject.

"Mole," Mauricio replied.

Mauricio and Cassie went to the kitchen, where he showed her how to grind up chilies for mole and Cassie tried to teach him English words for what he was doing. He had a habit of talking to himself in Spanish. To Cassie's ears, his language was soft like feathers and lullabies. He mimed for her to be careful not to touch her eyes after handling chilies, which escalated in an unforgettable performance reminiscent of being pepper-sprayed. She laughed at his dramatic flair.

He pointed to things, and she got them for him, sometimes opening packages or cans. As she handed him the three different kinds of chilies, the tomatillos, and the bar of chocolate, she wondered how such exotic things would blend together.

They had been friends for a few weeks, and in that time he had not asked about her mother and she had not asked about his home. She liked this friendship based solely on kind gestures and companionship. It was simple and uncomplicated. That was the thing about pity. It complicated things.

Jill made a big deal about how delicious the chicken and mole was when Mauricio and Cassie proudly served it. Mauricio beamed, and this made Cassie's heart swell more.

She knew that one day he would learn English well enough to ask about her mother. But for now she savored the complexity of his mole sauce, with its three different kinds of chilies, the tomatillos, and the dark chocolate—such exquisite complexity. And it made her wonder if a boy who could create such a wonderfully complex dish might also turn out to be a friend who would stick with her.

"So, Magoo," Pete said as John, Ben, and Mike all sat together for dinner. "How's it going with the babysitter?" Tonight Pete had some mashed potatoes in his mustache.

"Wait," John said as he cut his meat. "I thought the plan was not to sleep with her. I thought he said it would be too hard to find a new babysitter."

"Word on the street is that he is in love with his babysitter," Pete said matter-of-factly.

"Really?" Mike said incredulously. "Who said that?"

Pete replied, "Barb. She saw you two at the Dummy Downhill and said something about the way you looked at her."

"Barb imagined that," Mike said.

"Barb's pretty astute," Pete replied.

"She knew I was in love with Becky before I did," John said. "Good call."

Mike shook his head and smiled.

"A woman like that isn't going to stay in the Kennel much longer. She was a nurse, for God's sake. She's probably just waiting for her divorce settlement before she moves out and buys something," Pete said.

"Wait, do we know for sure she's staying here? Soon the mountain will be closed. After that, what's keeping her here?" John asked.

"Exactly," Pete said. "That's what I was getting at."

"She hasn't said anything about leaving. Her uncle is here. So are her friends. I think she's attached to Cassie," Mike said.

"Yeah, you're going to want to secure that deal here pretty soon before she wakes up one day and realizes there's not enough to keep her here," Pete said. "I mean, I still think you should go to the bar and sleep around and whatnot because somebody's got to do it and it can't be me. But according to Barb, it's her that you want, so, you know, don't doddle too long."

"I just want a good babysitter for Cassie," Mike said.

"Yeah, whatever," said Pete.

"I'm going to call bullshit on this one," Ben said. "You haven't gotten laid in a year or more and you have no spankavision. You must be going out of your freakin' gourd by now. Of course you're thinking about nailing her."

"I'm not thinking about nailing her," Mike said.

"We're sorry," John said. "Making sweet love to her," he corrected.

Mike rubbed his brow and shook his head. "Are we done now? Are we done with this ridiculous conversation?"

Pete shrugged. "Ah, for now, maybe."

"Good," Mike said.

chapter twenty-five

• • •

SNOW REPORT FOR MARCH 30

Current temperature: 29F, high of 36F at 3 P.M., low of 24F at 4 A.M.
Mostly clear skies, winds out of the southwest at 20 mph.
107" mid-mountain, 118" at the summit. 0" new in the last 24 hours.
0" of new in the last 48.

The next morning, after Cassie left for school, Mike asked Jill, "Hey, what do you know about this Mauricio kid? Should I be concerned that my daughter is hanging out with a boy these days?"

He set two plates of pancakes on the counter, pulled up a stool, and sat across from her. He felt uncomfortable about how he had left things at the end of the Dummy Downhill. It was hardly appropriate. It wasn't like Jill was his girlfriend. He looked through the doorway to a family picture that hung on the dining room wall. No, Jill definitely wasn't his girlfriend.

"Nah," Jill replied. "She likes him because he doesn't speak English. They can hang out without talking. At least that's what she told me."

Mike looked away from the picture and back at Jill. Here was someone his daughter could talk to. Kate wasn't here anymore. Jill was. "I know that's supposed to make me feel better," he said, "but that my daughter wants to hang out with a boy and not talk is still a concern."

Jill laughed. "You've got nothing to worry about. Your daughter is solid," she said.

Pete's voice echoed in his head as he wondered aloud what was really going to keep Jill in Sparkle. The seed of doubt was sprouting and growing. He had to root it out. "Hey, Jill? When ski season is over, do you intend to stay here—in Sparkle?"

"I've been thinking about that lately," she said, and stopped.

She didn't say yes or no. He hadn't expected that. He had expected her to say yes and put his fears to rest. "And?" he asked.

"I came here to get my bearings after having my world turned upside down. I came here to heal. It's been, you know, like a vacation from real life in some ways, or maybe more like a trip back in time. But ultimately, I'm not eighteen anymore. It's been fun, but soon it will be time to get on with life. I'll be a single woman who needs my medical benefits and a middle-class salary. I haven't started looking for new jobs yet, though."

He nodded. "I understand." Well, her answer afforded him a little time, and he wasn't going to waste any of it. "Hey, do you have to work today?"

"It's my day off," she answered.

"Do you feel like taking a couple runs together or is that not really what you want to do on your days off anymore?" He was surprised to discover a tinge of anxiety as he waited for her answer.

"Oh, I like to ski on my days off. I just like to get off the beaten path a little more and ski something different."

"I'm up for that," he said, hiding his relief.

And so they found themselves trekking up the Southback, quiet and a little awkward. Occasionally they talked, but they kept it light.

The snow had warmed the day before and iced up overnight. Now the high-elevation sun was beginning to melt it into perfect corn snow. By afternoon, it would be heavy slush that grabbed skis and blew out knees. They neared the top, and their boots broke through the crust as they walked through a wind-varnished patch.

"So why did you live with Howard when you were a teenager?" Mike asked.

"I guess the short answer is that I was having a tough time in high school. Uncle Howard realized my parents' religion was doing a number on me, and so talked them into letting me stay with him."

Mike asked, "Your parents' religion?"

"They're Mormon. It's so hard to explain, really. It still makes me crazy. They believe I'm not going to be with them in the same level of heaven. It's a bit much. It's a bit much to have your soul called into question all the time, especially after a tragedy when you're already asking why—why me. You know."

"I'm pretty pragmatic about it. Like I just think we make choices, and then things happen, and then other things happen because those things happened. You know, we get in our cars, it snows, and then we slide on the ice. Someone decides to fry a turkey, the grease spills on the burner, and their trailer burns down. I get married and have a child, and my wife dies, and now I'm a single dad. It's kind of like karma only without this idea of deserving what you get."

"I hate that idea of deserving. It's a pointless idea. Very few people get what they deserve. And the whole idea of anyone looking at anyone else's misfortune and judging it as something they deserved is appalling to me," she said.

"And that's why I'm going to start the Church of the Stuff Happens."

"Stuff happens," Jill agreed.

"That it does. But it's not always bad. I say I need a nanny in the FAR, and you hear me say it, and now you're in our lives and you're my friend."

Jill smiled. "It's nice when good stuff happens, too."

Mike looked out over the snow-covered peaks for a moment, and then he said, "It's selfish, but I wish you would stay."

"Well, it's not entirely selfish. You're probably wishing that for Cassie," Cassie said.

"Partly," he said. "It's just that I realized recently that all of the moments where I could imagine my life being not just okay again, but actually happy again, were moments when you were with Cassie and me."

"It's only been eight months for you guys," Jill replied. "That's too soon. Especially for Cassie. Just yesterday, Mauricio asked if I was her mother, and you should have heard the tone of her voice when she corrected him." She shook her head. "I can't put my life on hold waiting for something that might never actually happen."

"I didn't mean that," Mike said. "I wasn't talking about a relationship or anything." Suddenly he felt guilty, as if he were betraying Kate and Jill had just called him on it. "I just meant I liked spending time with you."

Jill blushed and nodded. "Of course. I'm sorry. That was stupid of me to read too much into that." She stabbed the snow with her poles a couple times. "Ready?"

"Yeah."

He watched her push off and speed away from him. She

made a few quick turns and dropped out of sight. He pointed his skis down, but instead of following her, he took a slightly different route, expecting that their separate paths would meet up down the road.

chapter twenty-six

• • •

SNOW REPORT FOR MARCH 31

Current temperature: 29F, high of 36F at 3 P.M., low of 24F at 4 A.M. Mostly clear skies with occasional rain or snow flurries, winds out of the southwest at 20 mph.
103" mid-mountain, 117" at the summit. 1" new in the last 24 hours. 1" of new in the last 48.

Eric stumbled over to Jill. He had a few more stains on the front of his wedding gown. "May I have this dance?" he asked, and held out his hand. Even though the song was fast, he wanted a slow dance.

She obliged him. They moved to the dance floor and put their arms around each other. She was wearing a halter dress she had fashioned out of paper grocery bags completely covered in duct tape, so her back was bare where he placed his hand.

"You can rest your head on my fake boobs if you want," he said.

"That's really tempting," Jill said, not tempted at all.

"They're pretty cushy," he said.

"Hmm," Jill replied.

"And then maybe later, I can rest my head on your boobs," he said.

"Yeah, I don't think so," she said.

"Jilly, you're hot," he slurred.

"Why, thank you, Eric," she said.

"I've had a crush on you since the day we met," he said.

"Well, I am awfully cute," she replied, trying to keep the tone light.

"You're not just cute—you're hot," he said, and then he whispered in her ear, "I could make you feel so good."

Since he was drunk, Jill didn't bother to argue or try to bring him to his senses. She knew he likely wouldn't even remember this conversation tomorrow. "Yeah, I know, baby," she said. "But then I'd be spoiled for life because no other lover would ever measure up to you. Besides, I'm saving myself for marriage."

"Really?" he asked, captivated.

"Oh yes," Jill said with a straight face.

"Jilly, you're such a good girl. Jilly, what if we got married?"

"Oh, Eric, I don't think you're ready to get married," Jill replied.

He stood back and gestured at his wedding gown. "I think I am," he said. "I really think I am."

Eric dropped to one knee. "Jill, will you marry me?" he shouted. People within earshot turned to watch. Lisa took a picture.

"I'd love to, Eric, but I'm not divorced yet, honey. Ask me again in a few months," she said. He stood back up and Jill rested her cheek on his fake boobs so he wouldn't see her laugh, while Lisa snapped another picture. Jill laughed thinking about tomorrow, when he'd hear the news from someone else that he'd proposed to her.

Eric wrapped his arms around Jill tighter and said. "When I'm your husband, I'll never let anything bad happen to you."

And even though she knew he was very drunk, and even though she knew he wasn't the one, a little part of her heart melted. "Thanks, honey," she said. They really were the words she most wanted to hear.

He didn't let go when the song ended, so she said, "Please excuse me, darling. I have to go to the bathroom." Instead of going to the bathroom, she had every intention of slipping out, getting her boots and coat from her locker, and walking home.

Right before she walked out the door, she took one last look at the whole scene, at the drunken mass of people, at the guy dressed up in a giant foam penis costume, at Hans passed out on the bar in his wedding dress, and Scooter, also in a wedding dress, shaving a happy face into the hair on the back of Hans's head.

No, while it had been fun apparently going back in time to high school for a few months, it was definitely time to move on. If she stayed in Sparkle, she would wake up in another ten or fifteen years still at the Kennel with a dog named after beer, a marijuana habit, and a stranger in her bed.

At the Kennel, Bud Light and Ale were snuggled on the couch together and Stout was stretched out in front of the woodstove. Jill stopped to stroke the fur on each one's head. She wanted to fall asleep stretched out in front of the fire like Stout but had worked up a sweat dancing throughout the evening and now felt crusty, so instead she took a shower.

In front of the mirror, she stopped and studied her stretch marks. She stroked them and then looked up into her own eyes. All she could think was, *Wow, look what I've gone through.* It was almost a neutral observation this time. And she realized she simply felt proud of herself for the mere fact that she was still standing.

When she was done, she put on her long underwear and took an extra towel into the living room, put it on the floor in front of the woodstove, and sat there stroking Stout's fur as she waited for her hair to dry. She closed her eyes and savored the heat on her face.

Just then, Eric and Tom burst in, carrying Hans. Bud Light and Ale jumped off the couch right before Eric and Tom dropped Hans on it.

"That's it," Eric said. "That's the last time I carry him anywhere."

"Light beer isn't making him any lighter," Tom said. "Hey, Jill. Hans passed out on the bar and Scooter was about to shave off his eyebrows. We figured we'd better get him out of there before Scooter pierced him."

"That's friendship right there," Jill said.

"Jill." Eric's eyes lit up and then glazed over. "I'll be right back." He went into the bathroom and pissed loudly.

"I think he's breaking some kind of record in there," Jill said to Tom.

Tom waited. "Nah, Stout pissed longer than that just this morning. Hey, I think I forgot something at Lisa's. I'll be back later."

Jill laughed.

Eric came out and squatted next to Jill. He opened the door to the woodstove, put another log on, and shut it. Then he pulled two pillows out from under Hans and put them on the floor. He laid his head on one and curled up behind where Jill sat cross-legged. "Jilly," he said, "you're my girl."

Jill sat there in front of the woodstove and watched the fire through the glass pane in the door. Eric put an arm around her waist and either fell asleep or passed out, she wasn't sure which.

She thought about Mike, about that terribly embarrassing moment when he said he hadn't been talking about a relationship. How she wished she could go back and unsay all those things she had said, all those things that gave away just how much she had been thinking about him. Stupid, stupid, stupid. It was just as she thought. Nothing was going to happen there.

Nothing was going to happen here, either, which was why it felt safe to simply enjoy the feeling of warmth and fondness. She lay down on her side facing Eric, with her head propped up on an elbow. When he slept, she could see all the sweetness inside him. She wondered what it was that made a person's face change when they slept, what it was that revealed more of their spirit.

She rolled over and snuggled into Eric so that he was spooning her, and again she felt the warmth of the fire on her face. It wasn't time. She wasn't ready. And Mike had known it when he'd said a little while ago that she was working through her stuff. But tonight she felt grateful for this little glimpse of what loving another man might feel like if she were to do it again—simply watching him as he slept and seeing all the sweetness inside him. She wondered if men had thoughts like that, if somewhere there really was a man who would watch her sleep and see all the sweetness inside her. She wondered whether David ever had.

Sometime in the night when the fire died down and the cold was beginning to pull her out of sleep, she was aware of Eric carrying her to bed and crawling in beside her. She wasn't sure what to think about that. She was pretty sure it was platonic. She wasn't positive whether or not she should be concerned, but in the moment it simply felt warm, so she dozed right through it. He put his arms around her again and nuzzled his face into her neck. Then his breathing became very regular and rhythmic, and she figured maybe he just needed a little comfort. Maybe all of them, no matter how afraid they were of true intimacy, occasionally needed a little comfort like that. If the experience of intimacy was a rainbow, sleeping next to a dear friend would be the yellow part. It was a warm fragment of intimacy. It was something.

She woke five minutes before her alarm was set to go off and turned it off before it woke Eric. She didn't want to deal with a sober and hungover Eric in her bed in the morning. She didn't want to deal with all the things people said to each other after the alcohol wore off and they realized they'd gotten too close. She carefully unwound herself from his embrace and tiptoed out of her room.

chapter twenty-seven

• • •

SNOW REPORT FOR APRIL 1

Current temperature: 29F, high of 36F at 3 P.M., low of 24F at 4 A.M.
Mostly clear skies, winds out of the southwest at 10 mph.
99" mid-mountain, 113" at the summit. 0" new in the last 24 hours.
1" of new in the last 48.

At the end of the day, Jill swept some runs with Jason. At the bottom, he stopped to talk to some friends, so Jill was alone when Mike walked toward her on his way to somewhere else. She stepped out of her bindings and picked up her skis.

"Hey," he said a little awkwardly.

"Hi," she answered.

"I just wanted to congratulate you on your engagement," he said with a forced smile.

"Oh yes," she said, trying to keep it light. In fact, she did feel guilty for spending the night in Eric's arms the night before. There was no reason to, she knew. Mike had been clear about what he hadn't meant when he said he didn't want her to go. She hadn't done anything wrong, she told herself. "Thank you very much. When a man asks you if you want to rest your head on his fake boobs, it's hard to say no."

"I'm sure you'll both be very happy." There was an unmistakable edge. It heightened her sense that she had betrayed him somehow.

"Oh yes," she said, "I'm sure of it. I'm sure my super religious parents will love him."

"Grooms in drag generally are a big hit with super religious parents," he said, his tone softening, much to her relief.

"Did you tell Cassie yet?"

"No, I figured I'd just let you invite her to the wedding." The little edge was back. Did he really have feelings for her or was he simply a possessive person?

"Yeah . . . maybe we just won't talk about this with her. What do you think?"

"I trust your judgment."

"Hey, Mike? Is everything okay?"

"I'm sorry," he said. "I guess something's eating on me a bit."

"Yeah?" Jill asked, hoping he would talk. Maybe it was something else. Maybe it had nothing to do with her.

But he avoided further conversation. "All right, well, I better let you get back to your job. See you the morning after tomorrow."

"See you then," she said and watched him as he walked away.

As she walked into the FAR, she passed Tom. "Hey, your fiancé is pretty embarrassed today," he said.

"Oh," she said sympathetically. "It's not easy being my fiancé. There's so much you have to do. First of all, you have to remember you proposed. . . ." She laughed.

Tom laughed, too. "He was hoping you'd grab a pizza and join him for a cat ride tonight."

"He proposes and I have to buy? How is that fair?"

"Should I tell him you'll be there?" Tom asked.

"Yeah. Sure," she said.

When she got to the maintenance shed, Eric took the pizza from her, set it down on the track, and said, "Thanks for coming." She nodded and smiled awkwardly as he held her hand and helped her up on the track of the snowcat.

"What kind did you get?" he asked as he closed his door.

"Well, since I didn't know what your cholesterol was these days, I got veggie with half the cheese," she answered.

"You're already putting me on a diet and we're not even married yet?"

She laughed and opted not to comment.

"So yeah," he began. "I understand I proposed last night." He bit his lip.

"No worries, Eric. You were super drunk. You would have married Tom."

"Oh, I don't know about that," he said.

"Well, I *am* better looking," she replied.

"You are much better looking," he agreed. "I guess I just wanted you to know that, you know, while I wouldn't have proposed sober, I also wouldn't have fed you a bunch of shit just to get into your pants while I was drunk, either. I mean, you *are* the type of girl that a man wants to marry. You're beautiful, sweet, and smart. And most importantly, you can rip on skis."

Jill laughed.

"Don't laugh. Tom and I have given the ax to many a woman who could not rip on skis."

"Not before you slept with them, though," Jill said.

"Hey, just because I sleep with a woman doesn't mean I'm going to ski with her. I am much choosier about ski partners. So see, you should be honored," he said.

"I am honored," she said, humoring him.

"Good. You should be. If I was going to marry anyone, I'd want to marry you."

"Right," she said. "Yeah, Tom explained why you can't get married—the whole alpha male thing."

"Let me tell you something," he said. "Tom is full of shit. I don't buy that whole we-are-animals thing. It's just been his excuse to sleep with a lot of women. Don't let anyone try to convince you men aren't in control of themselves. Men are in control. It's all about values. My parents are the same age as my friends' grandparents, so I was raised with a different set of values."

Oh yes, it shows, she wanted to say sarcastically, but didn't.

"No, I just look at my life—part-time here, part-time there, making a little money but not a lot, and I don't think it would be fair to ask a woman to follow me. And I don't want to change my life. I like the little part here and the little part there."

"Eric, you don't have to explain, really. We're good. I never took your proposal seriously. Really."

"Well, I just wanted you to know that you are special to me," he said.

"You're special to me, too, sweet guy. Pizza?"

"Yes, please."

She handed him a slice. He pulled up to a big tree with a huge red lace bra stretched around the trunk, got out, and wrapped the cable around the tree. Then he got back in and explained, "I used to have the hardest time finding that tree, so I put a bra on it."

"Problem solved," Jill said, wondering if that ingenuity also reflected the values of his elderly Catholic parents, and laughed to herself.

chapter twenty-eight

• • •

SNOW REPORT FOR APRIL 4

Current temperature: 33F, high of 35F at 3 P.M., low of 32F at 4 A.M.
Mostly clear with occasional showers. Winds out of the south at 15 mph.
98" mid-mountain, 110" at the summit. 1" new in the last 24 hours.
3" of new in the last 48.

Mike came home before Cassie woke up. He wasn't sure if he would, so he had asked Jill to be the Easter Bunny this year. He wondered whether she had by chance chosen some of the same hiding places Kate used to and whether Cassie would notice the difference if she hadn't.

Jill waved from the kitchen and greeted him with a smile. "Hi!" she whispered loudly.

He waved from the door, took off his coat, set down his things, and met her in the kitchen.

"Thanks for letting me be the Easter Bunny," Jill said. "I had so much fun. It's one of those things I never thought I'd ever get to do."

He felt a pang in his heart just thinking about what that would be like—wanting to be the Easter Bunny and never getting to. "Hey, Jill?"

Jill sensed his trepidation. "Yeah?" she answered, concerned.

"I was a little bit of a jerk to you the other day," he said.

"I wouldn't say that," she said.

"I'm sorry. I just . . . you just feel like part of our family, and when I heard about Eric proposing, I don't know. You know, the Kennel guys are notorious—not necessarily in a bad way or anything, but you know, their lifestyle is different than mine, and when I heard about the proposal, even though it was ridiculous, I don't know, it just got me wondering if you'd rather have that—something with no demands, and whether any woman would ever want to deal with all the baggage I come with."

She didn't want to make the same mistake she'd made before by reading too much into something, so she kept it as light as she could. "While it *is* hard to compete with a man in a wedding dress, I don't think you have anything to worry about."

"Look, I don't want things between us to ever be weird or anything. Cassie needs you and I don't want to mess that up. I just wanted to say I'm sorry."

He slouched back in his chair, his head cocked to the side a little as he studied a spot on the table and then picked at it awkwardly. He looked so vulnerable to her.

She stood up and walked over to him. "No worries," she said. "We're good."

Thinking she was leaving, he stood up, too.

She put her arms around him and rested her cheek on his chest.

He put his arms around her, too, and held her, resting his cheek on the top of her head. It felt to him like laying down a burden. So many things had been in his arms. Just this week, a woman handed him her dead two-year-old child, who had choked on a piece of meat and died before they got there. He had put his arms around a distraught elderly woman when her husband died. He had pulled a seven-year-old boy alive, thank God, out of a frozen pond. And he had helped a battered wife off the floor, examined her face, and then guided her into the aid car so a doctor could check her for internal injuries. He had held so many people in his arms, but no one since Kate's service had held him in theirs. Not like this. Not for all the time that it took to soften. He felt his breath jerk and thought he might cry, so he pulled back and let go before he lost control.

She didn't look up at him. She just nodded as if she understood, and then she left. What was becoming clearer and clearer to him was that avoiding a romance didn't translate to avoiding disaster. This path was just as doomed.

Outside the Kennel, pieces of tennis balls the dogs had chewed up and buried over the winter were surfacing like buried treasure. The yard was littered with them. Scooter had set up a series of wooden pallets stolen from behind the grocery store from the sidewalk to his trailer like a bridge through the afternoon slush. In a few particularly sunny locations, the snow was gone, leaving large patches of mud and dead grass.

Jill took the sidewalk to Lisa's front door instead of cutting through the muddy yard. She knocked and let herself in.

"Hey!" she said.

"Hey!" Lisa answered back.

Jill could hear the shower upstairs and pointed to the ceiling. "Tom?"

A big smile spread across Lisa's face. "I don't kiss and tell."

An equally big smile spread across Jill's as she nodded her approval. "It's about time. Hey, mind if I check my e-mail for a sec?"

"Go for it."

Dear Family and Friends,

Happy Easter, everyone! We're so sorry to be missing Easter egg hunts with the kids! Holidays are an especially hard time to be away, but we're so grateful today to celebrate the resurrection of Christ, for His showing us and making possible the principle of eternal life. What faith! It gives us such comfort to know that this very principle is what will allow us all to be an eternal family and gives us reason to strive to live the best lives we can so we can be together forever. I just can't bear the thought of life ending at death and being separated from each other! We love you all so much and are so grateful for this hope.

Love,

Elder and Sister Anthony

Jill went to her settings and blocked her parents. It didn't mean she would never talk to them again. It didn't mean she would never go to another family gathering. It just meant she wasn't going to make herself read any more of this.

"I just blocked my parents," Jill said.

Lisa handed her a raspberry muffin, fresh from the oven. "Good."

"Why couldn't I have gotten parents who didn't think I was going to hell?"

"Well, you got Uncle Howard, and everyone in Sparkle envies you for that," Lisa said. "And you've got me." Lisa gave her a sideways hug, and Jill rested her head on Lisa's shoulder.

"True enough."

"Uncle Howard?" Jill called through the door of his library.

"Come in!"

She opened the door and hugged him. "It's been too long! I brought a picnic!"

"Oh, that's nice of you! Let's eat outside," he said.

They sat at a picnic table outside the Summit Lodge, and Jill unpacked her goods. She had brought Jarlsberg cheese, smoked wild salmon, and a baguette from Mari's bakery, the same thing he had brought her on her first day back in Sparkle.

"So how's life?" he asked.

"Change is in the air. I can feel it. I can't see it yet, but it's coming. I'm feeling a little uneasy," she replied.

"I know that feeling," he said. "I've been having it lately myself. Restless."

"Yeah?"

"Yeah. I've been thinking about going to Argentina for a couple months to climb with some old buddies of mine."

"Yeah? When would you go?" she asked.

"Next week," he answered with a big smile.

"I think you should do it."

"I think I will," he answered. "I'll leave things tidied up here in case you want to stay here instead of the Kennel. You could try to get unsuspecting passersby to borrow books."

Jill laughed. "That sounds perfect. I think I will," she said.

"You know, that would warm my heart."

"How many copies of *Siddhartha* do you have?"

"I used to have seven," he said, "but they're all over the mountain now. That's part of the job. You have to look for copies at the Barkin' Basement and other used-book stores. You can never have too many copies of *Siddhartha*."

"I'm on it, Uncle Howard," she said, looking forward to some solace up there. "Maybe I'll get a vision while I'm up here and know where to go next."

Uncle Howard looked confused. "Go next? What do you

mean? I hoped you were going to take care of the library one day when I leave this world."

Jill shook her head slowly. "I haven't announced it yet, but I'm leaving," she said regretfully. "I can't stay here."

Uncle Howard looked surprised. "Why?"

"Well, for starters, it seems that you are the only person whose growth hasn't been stunted by living here."

"You're confusing Sparkle with the Kennel. No disrespect to the Kennel boys, but I think if you got out of there, you'd see Sparkle differently. Look at Mike. Has Mike's development been stunted?"

"No," Jill said.

"There are a lot of ways to live in Sparkle. You don't have to work on the mountain. You could work in the clinic. You could be a life-flight nurse. You could work for the doctor that rebuilds or replaces everyone's knees. No one dies on his table. You could buy your own house after the settlement and live any way you want to."

"I just feel like I'm avoiding reality by living here."

"What's reality? Misery?" he said with a smile.

"Well, part of reality is that I'll need to support myself after the divorce. I couldn't support myself on what I'm making now."

"Well, you know I support you wherever your heart leads you. I just encourage you to be really clear between whether it's your heart leading you somewhere or whether it's just old patterns leading you back to something more familiar. Following old patterns isn't quite the recipe for happiness that following your heart is."

"Thanks, Uncle Howard," Jill replied. She rested her head on his shoulder.

They were quiet. She looked all around her, at the unlimited space and infinite peaks, and wondered where in this big world she really belonged.

From the top of the mountain, Jill could see the keg parties starting up in the parking lot. Lots of people were sitting in lawn chairs, a few even barbecuing. The last day of the season was unmistakable. Jill organized some things in the Pneumonia Shack and took a few runs on the easy cruisers where most of the drunk people were skiing. She was tired of drunk people.

At the end of the day, Tom found her in the Pneumonia Shack, packing up first-aid supplies for the season. "Hey, Jilly. Take the last sweep with me."

"Sure thing," she said.

"Hey, Coach Ernie was just in the FAR. Looked to me like he shattered his tibia. He had been skiing with Howard. Howard said he hucked off a little drop and ran into a tree just after he landed."

"Oh, no," Jill said. "At his age, that's not going to heal fast. Wait, I just went back to the part where Coach Ernie was hucking off a little drop. That's crazy. At his age? Good God."

"He asked if you would take care of his dog while he's in the hospital and getting back up on his feet again. She's a golden retriever. Nice dog," Tom said.

"Tom, I don't know. My plans are uncertain."

"What do you mean?" he asked.

"I mean . . . I don't know. I love Coach Ernie. I'd love to help him."

"Well, how about you take her and if your uncertain plans take you elsewhere, I'll be her foster dad until Coach Ernie can take her again."

"You would do that?" she asked.

"Oh sure. We could always use another dog in the Kennel. We need to get the dog–human ratio back to one to one. And dig this. Lisa's going to die when she hears this. The dog's name is Amber. Haha! Now you have a dog named after beer in the Kennel, too! Hahaha! She's going to freak. You're one of us now, Jill."

She laughed and said, "That which you fear the most will meet you halfway."

"You've been hanging with Howard," he said, and chuckled.

She smiled and collected her things. "All right, well, say good-bye to Roger."

Tom knocked on the wall and shouted, "Good-bye, Roger! See you next year!" Then he turned to Jill and said, "I'm going to miss that rat. Maybe we should get one at the Kennel just to make it feel homier."

"No," she said definitively.

They hiked across the top of the ridge above the Super Bowl. There were a few other skiers and snowboarders hanging out, not quite ready to go down and end their seasons. Jill and Tom were in no rush, either, so they planted their skis in the snow and sat back against them. Neither of them said much for the longest time.

The sun shone on them, but it was getting low in the sky and losing its heat. Soon the soft corn snow would be setting up again. Jill hoped the guests would go before the top of the snow hardened into crust.

When she was young, the end of the season always felt like so many things, but this year it felt like all those things times a hundred. It felt like the end, like dormancy or even death.

"I hate the end," Tom said.

"I know," Jill replied, not knowing what the future held for her, assuming this was the last time she'd sit at the summit in the sun.

Finally, the rest of the guests dropped for their last run. Jill and Tom watched them.

"Well, shall we?" Tom asked.

Jill took a big breath and savored the moment. "It's nice to be the last people up here," she said. Then she stood up and put on her skis.

"We'll go earn turns until July. I've got my own high-speed quads right here," Tom said as he slapped his thighs.

She only laughed and didn't tell him that she might be gone by then.

He stepped into his skis. "Ready, little sis?"

"Yeah. But wait," Jill said. "I want say thank you for everything this winter. Thank you from the bottom of my heart." Her eyes started to water.

Tom stared at her for a long moment and then just opened his arms. "Come here," he said as if he were humoring her, but she knew he understood.

She gave him a quick hug, the kind where you slap each other on the back, and then said, "Ready." She said good-bye to the mountaintops, dropped off the edge, and passed through her winter world one last time.

That night, Eric and Hans were getting wasted at the Gold Pan and Tom was at Lisa's, which left Jill at the Kennel by herself. She turned off the TV, and just as she crawled into bed, rain began to thunder on the roof. It was almost like Sparkle itself was sad to be closed. She peeked out her window at the dark ski hill and felt lonely like she hadn't felt in a long time.

She called the dogs. Amber had been nearby, just waiting for the chance to get up on her bed. Stout ran in and joined them. Bud Light, meanwhile, moved his old creaky bones at a much slower pace. Jill had to help him up onto her bed. Ale stayed in his own bed, where he felt comfortable.

Jill looked at herself in the mirror on the ceiling snuggling with the dogs and thought how funny it was that she had gone from thinking of dogs as stinky, shedding agents of fecal contamination to having them on her bed and simply finding them comforting. Bud Light liked a spot near her feet, but Stout snuggled right up against her belly. Amber stretched out on her other side so they were back to back. Jill liked how they sealed her in tight. When she used to sleep with David, it always felt as though there were a wind tunnel between them. She was always cold. Now, all sealed in and cozy, she began to see the wisdom of sleeping with dogs instead.

She took another look into the mirror above her bed—Travis's mirror. He would be back next fall. Things would return to normal. The Kennel would be all male again and she would be a nurse somewhere again.

She knew that she would likely receive a settlement after the divorce that would make her financial situation more comfortable, but it might be contingent on the sale of the house, which could take a while. Plus, whatever the settlement was, it wouldn't last forever. She needed to get her career back on track and prepare to support herself again. No matter how much she loved Cassie, she had to be pragmatic. Tomorrow, she would start her job search.

But until then, she gave herself permission to simply be in that moment with the warm dogs on her bed and the rain thundering on the roof. She remembered something Uncle

Howard said around the time she was graduating from high school—that she didn't need to worry about her future, that it would come, and that she would know what to do in any given moment.

chapter twenty-nine

• • •

SNOW REPORT FOR APRIL 5

Current temperature: 34F, high of 37F at 3 P.M., low of 33F at 4 A.M. Mostly clear with occasional showers. Winds out of the south at 10 mph.

96" mid-morning, 108" at the summit. 0" new in the last 24 hours. 0" of new in the last 48.

The next day, Eric threw a few last things into his suitcase. He stepped over Scooter's extension cord on his way to Tom's car. Tom put a ski patrol vest on Ale, complete with a photo ID tag, so that Eric could bring Ale on the airplane with him instead of putting him in a kennel, where the baggage handlers would put him below with the luggage. Tom walked out to the car with the dog.

Eric came back into the Kennel, looked around one last time, and then paused in front of Jill. "Well," he said.

"Well," she said.

"It's been quite a winter."

She nodded. "It has."

"Well, I love you," he said.

"I love you, too, sweet guy," Jill said, and kissed his cheek.

He gave her a big hug, and they stayed like that for a

moment. Finally, he took a deep breath and said, "Come out for a visit. My mom makes the best raspberry-rhubarb pie."

"I'll see what I can do," she said, and let him go.

He let go, too, but kissed her cheek. "I'm going to miss you, Jilly," he said before he walked out.

"I'll miss you, too," Jill said.

Mike stared at the ceiling of Sleep Country and wondered if this was a stupid idea. The memory foam was nice. It was undeniably better than the futon. The futon. He and Kate bought it in the late eighties. The day they upgraded was a good day. How he ever slept even one night on it, he was not sure now.

No, this was a good idea. Even if Jill left them, his parents could sleep in it. But he hoped Jill would not leave them. He hoped this would help Jill know how much they valued her. He hoped her own space would make her feel she belonged.

But he also worried that her own space might make her feel it was her only space. He didn't want that. Sometimes he imagined her in his bed, holding her, finding comfort in her, allowing her to find comfort in him. Would that really be a huge mistake? Or would it be one of the greatest things that could happen to him?

He shifted on the bed. It was even nicer than his. He wondered how this move would be seen by her, what she would make of it. He walked over to the counter and set down his credit card.

Back at the house, Ben helped him move the desk downstairs. They went back up for the drawers. Mike carried the one that held files. Files of purchases Kate had made. Files full of her medical bills. A file with her death certificate. All those files. He felt the heaviness of them in his arms. Would it be impossible to start a new chapter in his life with all of this weight in his arms?

Next, they moved the futon out to the curb with a FREE sign on it. His first bed with Kate. The bed where Cassie had been conceived. They had bought the new bed when Kate was pregnant. There was a lot of love in that old futon, and now it sat on the curb like worthless junk. "Someone will be glad to get this," Ben said as they set it down. Something about that helped. He wasn't throwing it away. He was sending it out into the world. Still, he felt his attachment to an era that the bed now represented. He knew the importance of not giving in to those feelings. He had been in the homes of people who kept everything because everything represented something. They were buried. They were stuck. They could not move forward. No, falling into that trap wasn't an option. He had to be strong enough to let go of things. Things were just things. He wouldn't forget the love just because he gave away the futon. He knew this.

So he turned his attention to the new bed, still in the back of his pickup. He and Ben untied the rope that held it in place and then carried pieces of the frame upstairs and assembled it. When they carried the new mattress into the house, Mike walked backward up the little stairs, glancing up at the futon on the side of the road, knowing it was the right thing to do but still feeling a bit as if he were betraying Kate, just leaving her on the side of the road with a FREE sign. As if the new bed were Jill, being brought into the house to replace Kate. And it was stupid, he knew. Stupid thinking. Untrue stupid thoughts.

He walked Ben out, thanked him, and sent him off with a six-pack of Alaskan Amber.

The futon seemed like such a personal item to have on his curb. Such a personal item to give to a stranger. He turned his back on it again and went upstairs to put sheets and blankets on the new bed.

She needed a dresser in here. The closet was cleaned out. That was something. But she needed a place to put her things. She needed a drawer in the bathroom. He moved the little reading table back, the lamp, and the alarm clock.

He found a paper and pen to write her a note since he would be at work when she arrived the next night, but he couldn't figure out what to say. Everything he could think to write made it sound either like a grand gesture for which she should be indebted enough to stay, or like a casual thing of no importance. Neither was true. What was true was simply that he liked her. Maybe loved her. And he wanted her to be comfortable. He wanted her to stay. But he couldn't write that, so he put the paper and pen away.

As Cassie stuck her head in the room that used to be the office, what struck her was change. A change had happened. A room that was one way when her mom was alive was now another way. The change involved making space for a new person. It seemed so permanent.

It was strange how all winter she had known her mother wasn't coming back, and she had appreciated how Jill was a nice babysitter, but now as she looked at this room, the permanency of the situation hit her again. Things had changed and they weren't changing back.

She had noticed how her dad looked at Jill. She had noticed how Jill looked back. And while it made her uncomfortable, she never really saw it as much of a threat—until now. Until this moment when her father had carved out a part of their home for Jill. What did it mean? Was she part of the family now?

Cassie felt angry but didn't know whom to feel angry at. Jill obviously was the outsider and an easy target. But her dad . . . Was he forgetting? Was he forgetting all about her mom? Was it happening? Was this how it happened—so slowly that it was easy not to notice, or at least in small amounts that were easier to swallow? She felt mad at him, too—mad at him for not freezing the moment in time when their family was together and happy, when everything was right in the world.

At the same time, she knew it was stupid to be mad at either of them. She knew Jill wasn't trying to be her mother. She knew her dad could never forget. She knew this was just how things were now.

Still, as she looked at the new bed and all the empty space, she shook her head. She did not like it. Sure, she wanted Jill to be comfortable here. She just didn't know if she wanted Jill to be *that* comfortable here. Cassie already had a family, and Jill wasn't it.

chapter thirty

• • •

SNOW REPORT FOR APRIL 6

Current temperature: 36F, high of 38F at 3 P.M., low of 34F at 4 A.M. Mostly clear with occasional showers. Winds out of the south at 10 mph.

94" mid-mountain, 106" at the summit. 0" new in the last 24 hours. 0" of new in the last 48.

Cassie had thought about the bedroom all day, so by the time she got home, she was ready to let Jill know where she stood. It wasn't going to be pretty. She walked into the house and found Jill sitting at the dining room table reading her father's paper. Coach Ernie's dog, Amber, lay at her feet.

"Hey! I found a couple things for you while I was searching secondhand stores for copies of *Siddhartha* for Uncle Howard. Come look!"

Cassie suspended the speech she had prepared long enough to look at two cookbooks—one Thai and the other Italian vegetarian. "Thank you," she said.

"How was your day?" Jill asked.

Cassie paused and bought herself some time by flipping through the cookbooks while she considered whether this might be an opening to say what she had wanted to say all day. Then she looked over at the paper Jill was reading and noticed it was the classifieds page. Jill had circled two ads. "What are you shopping for?"

Jill paused. "I'm not shopping for anything. Was your day okay?"

"Yeah, I guess it was okay," Cassie answered. She sounded agitated. "Why won't you tell me what you're looking for?"

"Why won't you tell me what's bugging you?" Jill answered.

"What's bugging me is how you and my dad look at each other, and how he took my mom's things out of the laundry, and now he's changed a whole room for you. Is he why you took this job? To position yourself to be his next wife?"

Jill was taken aback and paused to regroup. "I took this job because I needed the money. Over the last five months, though, I've grown to love you like family. . . ."

"But you're not my family," Cassie said. Finally, the words that had been building up pressure inside her all day exploded out like gas.

"You just made it so much easier to tell you what I need to tell you," Jill said.

"What," Cassie said, more like a demand than a question.

Jill set down the classifieds so Cassie could see. "This isn't how I wanted to talk to you about this. Look, Cassie, I won't be able to afford to keep this job much longer. Ski patrol season is over. Even with both jobs, it wasn't really enough to live on. When my divorce is final, I'll need the salary and insurance I had with my old job. I'll need to go back into nursing."

Cassie stared at her as if she had been betrayed. "Does Dad know about this?"

"I talked to him a little bit about it."

"He didn't tell me," Cassie said.

"I don't know why he changed up the room, Cassie. It's possible it's to make the job more appealing for the next person. I don't know. I do know he's not ready for a new woman in his life. He's a great man. Of course I notice that. But we've all been through a lot. And my hiatus here is about up." Jill put her hands up. "I'm no threat. You don't have to tell me I'm not family."

Cassie scowled at her and then marched off to her bedroom and slammed the door. She wished there had been a way to take the cookbooks with her without looking like a sellout, but there wasn't, so she left them behind. How soothing it would have been to look at pictures of food and lists of ingredients. What a welcome relief it would have been to step out of all the noise in her mind and think about something else. There was so much noise in her mind, she couldn't hear her own thoughts. So many conflicting things. So much confusion. So much raw emotion—abandonment, anger, guilt.

She opened her math book and began converting fractions to decimals. Part of her hoped that she would hear a knock on her door any second and that Jill would come in, sit on the edge of her bed, and somehow make everything okay. The other part of her hoped that Jill would knock on the door, open it, and then fall down when Cassie threw her math book and hit her in the head with it. But Jill didn't knock on the door.

Instead, she just left Cassie a plate of food in the refrigerator, brushed her teeth, and crawled into her new bed. Cassie had heard each step through the thin walls. For a moment, she considered knocking on Jill's door, but she didn't know what she would say. Maybe *I love you like family, too.* Or maybe *How could you leave me?*

chapter thirty-one

• • •

SNOW REPORT FOR APRIL 12

Current temperature: 38F, high of 40F at 3 P.M., low of 33F at 4 A.M. Mostly cloudy with occasional showers. Winds out of the south at 15 mph.

286" at the base, 454" at the summit. 0" new in the last 24 hours. 0" of new in the last 48.

It was Jill's second night at Cassie's since the "exchange." The first night may not have counted, since Cassie had stayed at the library until it closed, then come home, eaten leftovers out of the fridge, and gone straight to bed. They had avoided each other the next morning as well.

Cassie was gone when Jill first arrived on this late afternoon as well. She went to the kitchen and began to cut celery, broccoli, onion, zucchini, and carrot for a stir-fry. She cut the celery, zucchini, and carrot diagonally, the way Cassie liked.

She had been wondering how she might have handled that moment with Cassie better. She had felt backed into a corner. It was hard to tell someone you loved them like family only to have them remind you that you aren't their family—even if it was a hurting little kid. Still, she was the adult, Jill thought. Some damage had been done, and a ten-year-old was unlikely to have the skills to fix it. Fixing something was a difficult idea, though. Words can't be unsaid. Feelings can't be unhurt. *Sometimes,* Jill thought, *you just have to go on.*

So when Cassie came home, Jill served up dinner, and they sat together awkwardly at the dining table. Jill asked Cassie about her day, and Cassie answered. Cassie complimented Jill on dinner, and Jill said thank you.

And then Cassie said, "I wasn't really mad at you. It's just sometimes I want my mom back so bad."

"These are tough times," Jill replied, because the other replies weren't true. She couldn't say, *I understand.* She didn't understand. She understood a little, but no one really understands what it's like to be anyone else. And she couldn't say, *That's okay,* because it wasn't okay to be hurtful, even when you're hurting. "The best we can do is be more gentle with one another in the future."

"I don't want you to leave me, too," Cassie said.

It was the "too" at the end of that statement that made Jill's eyes well up. The conversation seemed to slow down. "I meant what I said, Cassie. I do love you like family. I don't want to leave you. Life is complicated. I'm on my own now. My choices are pretty limited."

"I know," Cassie said, as if she understood.

Things felt different. It was as if they were on different sides of a river. But at least now there was a bridge.

chapter thirty-two

. . .

SNOW REPORT FOR APRIL 23

Current temperature: 30F, high of 33F at 3 P.M., low of 26F at 4 A.M.
Cloudy, winds out of the southwest at 10 mph with gusts of up to 20 mph.
Lifts closed.

As Cassie and Mauricio walked out of the Sparkle Public Library, Cassie heard a woman call Mauricio from down the street.

He looked up, said to Cassie, "Come on," and started to walk toward the woman who had called him.

She was short—not much taller than Mauricio—and her long dark hair was pulled back into a tight ponytail. Her nose bent a little to the right, and her smile was big and generous.

"Mama," Mauricio said, *"se llama Cassie.* Cassie, this is my mother, Esmeralda."

Esmeralda shook Cassie's hand. *"Mucho gusto,"* she said.

"Mucho gusto," Cassie repeated back.

Mauricio and his mother began to converse in Spanish, and although Cassie didn't understand what they were saying, she picked up on a few things. She heard the word *casa* and saw

Mauricio point toward her house. She heard the word *padres* and saw Mauricio shrug. He gave a long explanation of something, and at the end, she heard, "*. . . no . . . mama.*"

Whatever he said elicited a huge sympathetic response from Esmeralda. Cassie realized he knew. Even though she had never told him, he knew.

"My mother says to have dinner with us," Mauricio said.

"Enchiladas," Esmeralda said enticingly. It was impossible not to like her instantly.

"I have to ask my father," Cassie answered.

Mauricio translated and then said to her, "I walk with you." He hugged and kissed his mother good-bye.

Esmeralda reached out for Cassie's hand again. *"Hasta luego,"* she said, and held Cassie's hand for a moment. Cassie nodded and smiled, and then they parted ways.

As Cassie and Mauricio walked toward her house, she said, "Your mother is nice."

"Yes," Mauricio said.

"My mother is in heaven," Cassie said plainly, figuring she wasn't telling him anything he hadn't figured out.

"Where?" he asked.

"My mother is with God," Cassie restated.

"I thought maybe," Mauricio said quietly. "I'm sorry."

Cassie thought she heard pity in his voice and was sad that their friendship would be ruined now. She always knew that one day Mauricio would learn enough English that the topic would come up and their friendship would run its course.

"My dad is with God," he said.

This Cassie did not expect. "I'm sorry," she said.

"He work at store. Men come . . ." He mimed a gun and shot it. Then he shook his head.

"I'm so sorry," Cassie said, and even though when you're

ten, you don't put your arm around your best friend if he's a boy, she did anyway, but just for a second.

Mauricio looked over at her. "We eat enchiladas tonight." The conversation was over, at least for the time being. And to Cassie it seemed they were still friends.

Mike called Jill, and when she answered he said, "Quick! Cassie's having dinner at Mauricio's. It's my big chance to have dinner with a grown-up who isn't a firefighter! Are you free? Would you be my dinner date?"

"Sure." She laughed.

In his fake ladies' man voice, he said, "I'll walk over and pick you up." Then he returned to speaking normally. "How much time do you need?"

"By the time you get here, I'll be ready," she said.

"Sweet," he replied, and hung up. He wrote Cassie a note, combed his hair, popped a breath mint, put on his coat, and left the house. Every second of this rare freedom counted.

As he knocked on her door, he realized he hadn't picked up a date in fourteen years. Should he have brought flowers? No, that would have been over the top. Regardless of where his thoughts sometimes went, they were just friends, right? Just friends.

She opened the door. She looked pretty. Should he tell her she looked pretty? Would that be nice, or would that be creepy because they still had a professional relationship? Instead, he simply asked, "What are you hungry for?"

"Food," she answered as she shut the door behind her. "Any kind."

"I've been craving Chinese," he said. "What do you think about that?"

"Perfect."

As they walked to the Golden Dragon, Mike noticed new buds on most of the trees. He noticed some crocus in Julie and Jason's yard, pushing their way out of the dirt. He noticed the chickadees singing. Everywhere, life was returning.

At the Golden Dragon, he and Jill slid into a booth together, and suddenly the date took on a whole new level of real for him. Sure, on one hand he was just having dinner with a friend. But on the other hand, he wouldn't have been doing this if Kate were alive, and that made it strange.

The restaurant was lit by red lanterns hanging above and candles on the table. It was uncomfortably dark, but fortunately not so dark that Tom and Lisa didn't spot Jill as they walked out of the lounge.

"Join us?" Jill asked.

"For just a sec," Lisa said, and slid into the booth next to her. "It's our last night together in a while."

"Lisa is a park ranger in the summer," Jill explained to Mike as Tom sat next to him.

"Can't pay the bills all year on a ski instructor's salary," Lisa said plainly.

Tom winced.

"Drinking at the Dragon tonight? What gives?" Jill asked.

"Lisa doesn't want anyone to know about our torrid affair," Tom said. "So we come here and drink covertly."

Lisa kicked him under the table.

"Are we crashing your party?" Tom asked. "Are you guys on a date?"

"Nah, you're not crashing our party," Mike answered, relieved at how Tom and Lisa took the pressure off. "Cassie's having dinner at a friend's house, so it's my rare night out."

"Nice," Lisa said, looking back and forth between them for any signs.

"Are you hungry?" Tom asked Lisa. He pointed to the menu. "Because we could have the Sizzling Happiness meal."

"We're really not intruding?" Lisa asked.

"Not at all," Mike reassured her.

"Sizzling Happiness, huh?" Jill asked.

"Oh yes," Tom said. "Trust me. You and Mike will be so glad you had the same Sizzling Happiness that Lisa and I are about to have."

"What do you think, Mike? Would you like some Sizzling Happiness?" Jill asked, laughing.

Mike smiled as he held her eyes for a moment, and then with mock seriousness he answered, "I think I desperately need some Sizzling Happiness." Jill blushed.

Lisa asked, "Jill, how long has it been since you've had some Sizzling Happiness?"

"I don't even know," Jill answered, looking down and smiling uncomfortably. Mike found it completely endearing.

"I think some Sizzling Happiness would be really good for you," Lisa said. "If you have the opportunity to have some Sizzling Happiness with Mike here, I think you should take it."

So Mike ordered it for them as well.

The Sizzling Happiness jokes got bolder and lewder as they each enjoyed a few drinks. Jill now would look him straight in the eye in an almost challenging way each time she said "Sizzling Happiness." It was sexy. It was sultry. Each time she said it like that, he had the impulse to jump over the table and take her.

The jokes and the smoldering stare-downs continued as they ate their spicy Szechuan pork and Kung Pao chicken. Mike chewed his food slowly, aware of all the sensations in his mouth, aware of his hunger to kiss Jill indefinitely. He watched her pick up some vegetable chow mein in her chopsticks and bring it to her mouth. Something about the way she watched her food to make sure she didn't drop it caused her to lower her eyes the same way she would if she was kissing. He could imagine it, his fingers in her hair behind her head, his lips on hers, their bodies pressed up against each other. She glanced up and caught him looking at her, smiled, and turned her attention back to picking up fried rice with her chopsticks.

Finally, Lisa rubbed her full belly and groaned, "Tom, I can't take any more Sizzling Happiness."

"So you're saying you're completely satisfied?" Tom asked.

"Yes, I'm completely satisfied," Lisa answered.

Tom replied, "Well, you know what they say about Chinese food—you're hungry for more of it in about an hour."

Which made Mike think about that kind of all-night sex, the kind where maybe you take a short nap or have a snack, but otherwise it's more or less a marathon. He imagined Jill's skin next to his, imagined touching her everywhere.

Just as the Sizzling Happiness jokes wound down, the fortune cookies arrived.

"You know the game, don't you?" Lisa asked Mike.

"The game?" Mike asked.

Lisa explained, "You read your fortune out loud and then add 'in bed' to the end. Observe." She cracked her fortune cookie and then read, "The last wish you made will come true . . . in bed." She gave Tom her naughtiest smile.

Mike picked one, cracked it, and read, "You will soon develop a new interest . . . in bed." He laughed and looked at Jill. "Excellent."

Tom was next. "You are the master of every situation . . . in bed. Remember that, Lisa."

"I'll look forward to that tonight," she replied.

Finally, Jill took her cookie. "Concern for another brings an unexpected reward . . . in bed."

Mike was glad to hear it.

"Hm," Lisa said, and made her eyebrows go up and down as she looked at Jill.

After dinner, Lisa and Tom said they needed something at the grocery store.

"So, wait," Jill said to Lisa. "Is this 'See you in October'?" She turned to Mike and explained, "Lisa hates good-byes. She does her best to sneak off before anyone knows she's leaving."

"And I would have if it hadn't been for you meddling kids," Lisa replied like every villain on *Scooby-Doo*.

"Okay, I'll pretend it's not happening," Jill said, and hugged her for a long enough time that Mike wished he were Lisa. "Thank you," Jill whispered in Lisa's ear. "Thank you for everything."

"Oh, quit that," Lisa whispered back. "Now let go of me so I can go get lucky."

Jill laughed and let go. As Lisa and Tom walked away, Lisa looked back and gave Jill a little smile. Jill waved and teared up. Mike took her hand.

"Hey, want to take the scenic route?" he asked.

"It would feel good to walk off some of that food," Jill answered.

"Is it okay if I hold your hand through town?"

"I don't know. Will it ruin my reputation?" she teased.

"Yes, but you'd be doing me a big favor. My boss, Pete, and his wife, Barb, keep wanting to fix me up with Barb's friends, and it's getting harder to dodge that bullet. If this hits the rumor mill, I'll be off the hook."

"So, you're just using me," she joked back as they walked down the street.

"Yes," he said with mock seriousness. "If you had the same suspicions about Barb's friends as I do, you would do the same thing."

"Okay," she said. "But you owe me."

"That's fine. I don't mind owing you." He gave her hand a little squeeze.

So they walked up Main Street, and then, instead of walking up a block toward their houses, they walked down a couple blocks to the riverfront park.

The moon had come out and reflected on the rushing water. He caressed her hand as he held it and they strolled along a sidewalk that ran beside the river through the park. He was well aware that every time he had tried to tell her something about what he felt for her, it had resulted in even greater confusion; so this time he didn't. He just put his hand on her face and kissed her long and slow. He hoped she could feel what he wanted to say but could find no words for.

And then he thought of Cassie coming home to an empty house. To a house without Kate. And to a house without him because he was making out with Jill—Jill, who wasn't Kate. Those thoughts broke the spell. "Cassie's probably home by now," he said.

Jill nodded.

He took her hand again, and she rested her head against his arm as they walked back up to town. It felt strange being with someone other than Kate. It felt both exciting and wrong all at once.

It was the time of year everyone in town dreaded—melt-off, where it seemed mud was everywhere, where basements flooded, where everything that had been buried by snow all winter resurfaced—leaves they hadn't raked, clutter they hadn't picked up. Melt-off was a transition, and transitions were messy and uncomfortable. He saw his grief like the snow that remained in patches in people's yards—very deep near the house, where a winter's accumulation of snow had slid off the roof into a pile so high that it had almost reached the eves. Still, in the glow of the streetlights, he could see other places in their yards where the snow had melted off and the new green tips of bulbs were breaking through the surface. It still felt too early and too cold for anything to grow, yet despite that, life had begun to return.

As they approached his house, he said, "Want to come in for a drink? After Cassie goes to bed, we could . . ." He let his proposal trail off.

Jill hesitated. "Part of me does, but at the same time, Cassie . . . I don't know where the line is between discretion and betrayal."

"It's all new territory to me," Mike said. They passed his sidewalk and continued on to the Kennel. When they reached it, he gave her a good-night kiss.

"I wonder what exactly your unexpected reward will be," he said.

She smiled. "Yeah, I wonder. And I wonder what your new interest will be."

"Hm . . . I have some ideas," he replied, and kissed her once more.

When Jill walked into the Kennel, Hans glanced up from an action movie he was watching, said hello, and then did a double take. His eyes narrowed. "I know that look," he said, and bolted for the window to see who might be out there. He put his hands on the windowsill and watched Mike walk back home. Hans raised his eyebrows and pointed back and forth between Mike and her.

"I don't know," she finally relented. "It's not that easy."

"You're a smitten kitten," he accused.

"It's just, you know, Kate hasn't been gone that long. And I'm still technically married. And I need to go back into nursing to make a living, and so I've got no business starting something I can't finish."

"Wait a minute. Are you saying you're *leaving*?"

"Eventually, yeah," she said apologetically. She didn't tell him that she had sent off two applications just this week—one to a podiatrist in Denver and the other to a dermatologist. She was rethinking the dermatology position, though. Some pretty young people got skin cancer at these high elevations, and she wasn't sure she could cope with that. No, they weren't babies, but still, if she could avoid any type of nursing where anyone died, that was the goal.

"But you have a dog named after beer. You belong here," he said.

Rather than argue with him that, no, she did not *belong* in the Kennel, she simply said, "Thanks," because it was nice to be welcome.

"Mike's a good man," Hans said. "No one in Sparkle needs a nurse?"

"I haven't seen any want ads," Jill replied.

"That's not how it works around here. It's all word of mouth." He paused and thought. "Okay, I just thought of one possibility. Kaitlyn. She works at the health department in Colorado Springs. Big commute, but doable. She's engaged to some rich dude. It's possible she'll quit. Okay, I thought of another. Heather. It's possible we had relations a couple years ago. She was a nurse for that knee doctor guy, you know, next door to the bike shop. She's married now and very pregnant. I mean she's out to here," he said, holding his hand two feet in front of his belly. Maybe she'll be taking some time off. Jaqueline. It's possible we had relations a few years ago. She's a school nurse at a few local schools, including this one. Rumor has it she met some rock climber dude from Utah and is spending her summer vacation with him to see where it leads."

"Good leads," she said. "Thanks." But she was thinking she wanted a real opportunity—not a temporary one and not one where she'd have to wait to see if it even came to pass. Next week, she decided, she would get on it and actually go to Denver to pick up applications and check out different places.

"Consider this. I was talking to Travis back in February and he was telling me how he was nailing the home care nurse when his mom walked in, but that's not the important part. The important part is that he had a home care nurse. What about that? Surely there are enough people having big wrecks up here that there's a need, right?"

"Probably," Jill replied.

"Or, how about this? When Travis and I were ice climbing in Yellowstone last year, we met a bunch of nurses. All but one was from Boise. They had come out to visit their friend who was spending the summer working as a nurse there in the national park. Apparently some of the bigger national parks have nurses. So you could do ski patrol in the winter and work national parks in the summer. Works for Lisa. Maybe you guys could even work at the same park."

"Fun," Jill said, but she didn't really like that idea. She wanted a home. "Well, hey, thanks for the brainstorming session."

"My pleasure." Hans turned his attention back to the TV, and Jill took off her coat and hung it up. And then, without looking back at her, he said, "Jill? Mike is the only guy I can think of that I'd let anywhere near you. Just sayin'."

"Yeah?" She was touched.

"True, that. This winter, I got wind that a few different guys wanted to tap that, meaning you, and I let it be known that if they did, they better have a good dentist."

"Really?"

"No busters messed with you, did they?"

"No, they did not," Jill said.

"Enough said. But I think about Mike, too. Do you know how many married women hit on me every year?"

"No," Jill answered.

"Lots. And I don't want Mike to end up with a woman like that—someone who is going to screw him over. He's been through enough, you know? I mean, I don't know the guy that well, but you know how it is here. We all know each other well enough."

"Yeah," Jill replied, and went to the bathroom to brush her teeth.

She looked at herself in the mirror as she let Hans's last words sink in. She hadn't considered that, really. She hadn't considered that if she didn't end up with Mike, he would end up with someone else. It had just seemed like the two options were her or no one. And she sure hadn't considered that the new woman might possibly be a person who lacked morals or character. Had Jill not been looking at herself in the mirror, she wouldn't have seen the glimmer of fear in her own eyes, and she might not have known just how deeply she did care.

chapter thirty-three

. . .

SNOW REPORT FOR APRIL 24

Current temperature: 38F, high of 50F at 3 P.M., low of 32F at 4 A.M.
Clear skies, winds out of the southwest at 10 mph.
Lifts closed.

Tom leaned into Lisa's window. They had already hugged and kissed good-bye. He knew she did not like good-byes. She had told him plainly that she preferred them to be quick, like tearing off a Band-Aid. But Tom wasn't ready to let go.

"Change your mind," he said. "Change your mind and stay."

"Come on, Tom. We've been through that. I've got to make a living. My five months a year as a park ranger pay for my winter as a ski instructor. You know I can't support myself on my ski instructor salary," she said. "And besides, this is what I went to college to be able to do. This is who I am. I'm Ranger Lisa."

"Is Ranger Dan going to be there?" he asked. He'd been dying to ask for weeks but hadn't wanted to seem insecure. Now, though, he couldn't help but ask.

"Is that what you're worried about?" Lisa asked.

He wasn't sure what the right answer was. "I'm worried about losing you any number of ways," he finally said.

"Don't be," she said.

Suddenly, he felt bold. He felt willing to risk everything. "What if we got married? What if we got married and combined incomes? Then could you stay?"

"Don't do that, Tom. Don't ask me out of fear. And as far as me staying, you've got to respect who I am enough to let me go for a few months."

He took a step back, hurt. "I'm sorry, I guess," he said, confused.

"I'll see you in just a few weeks, just like we planned," she said.

He bit his lip and nodded.

"I love you," she said.

"I love you so much," he replied. And then he watched her drive away. He raised his hand to wave right before she turned out of sight.

Lisa was remembering the morning Cody left, the morning she looked at her crucifix and pledged to have faith that she was born to experience a greater love than what she had experienced so far. As she drove away with Tom's proposal fresh in her mind, as lame as it was, she realized he must be the answer to her prayers and wondered what the repercussions of leaving the answer to her prayers would be. Did a person do that? Turn her back on the answer to her prayers? Was she making the biggest mistake of her life by leaving him? Did a love like this come around twice in a lifetime? After twenty-some years of dating and not finding it, it seemed unlikely she would again. She wondered if these things were fated, if they could not be derailed or if there were only detours to the same destination. She hoped so.

The sun had finally begun to melt the snow from cobbles along the river shore. Cassie and Jill had walked Amber down to let her play in the water.

Cassie had prepared a dinner picnic of grilled sandwiches like those she saw prepared on a cooking show, with melted Swiss, cranberry relish, and turkey, and she carried them proudly in her backpack.

As they walked together, Cassie kept her eyes low and hoped she'd hear her mother's voice.

Jill threw a stick into a little eddy behind a big rock in the middle of the swift river. Amber had to swim upstream to get it, but somehow she did, and once she had it in her mouth, she swam downstream very fast until she worked her way over to the shore and back up to Jill and Cassie. She dropped the stick next to their feet.

"I was a little worried she was going to end up in New Mexico," Jill joked. Then she noticed a change in Cassie's mood. "Hey, is everything okay?" she asked.

Cassie shrugged. "My mom and I used to come down here a lot. That's all."

"It's a beautiful spot," Jill said.

"Yeah," Cassie said. She pulled a rolled-up towel out of her backpack. Inside, the sandwiches, wrapped in foil, were still warm. She handed one to Jill, and they peeled back the foil and took their first bites.

"Mm!" Jill said. "Cassie, you are truly gifted. This tastes so good. I didn't realize how hungry I was."

They ate quietly for a few moments while Amber retrieved the stick a couple more times, and then Cassie said, "This is where my mom told me she was sick. I asked her if she was going to die and she said that everyone dies. I got really mad and started screaming, 'Not you!' at her, like that, over and over. 'Not you!' I cried and cried until all I wanted to do was sleep. She hugged me. And then we just sat here together. But when I remember it, I try to take the part out where I screamed at her for being sick. I wish I could just erase that part and never remember it."

"Oh, Cassie," Jill said, wiping away a few tears. "That breaks my heart." She reached over and smoothed Cassie's hair.

Amber picked up the stick and dropped it closer to Jill. Next to the stick, Jill noticed a white rock with rusty stripes that looked like a heart. "Look," she said to Cassie as she reached for it and handed it to her. "This rock is shaped like a heart."

Cassie looked at Jill questioningly. She took the stone and inspected it. Sure enough, one side of it was shaped like a heart. "May I keep this?" she asked.

"It's yours," Jill said.

"Did you know I collected these?"

"Nope," she answered.

"My mom and I collected them."

Cassie put the heart-shaped rock in her pocket and put an arm around Jill's waist. Jill put an arm around her shoulder, and they just stood there like that, eating their sandwiches with their free hands. Cassie watched the sparkles on the water and wondered things ten-year-olds generally didn't wonder about, like all the ways in which souls might be connected.

chapter thirty-four

. . .

MAY 3: NO SNOW REPORT AVAILABLE

Opening Day is October 31. Season passes available for purchase online.

Jill had her things by the back door ready to go. She had served Cassie granola this morning instead of making her usual muffins. As soon as Cassie left, Jill bolted out the back door. She didn't want to run into Mike. She had done the same thing the last two times she had seen Cassie off in the morning.

The first babysitting morning after the Golden Dragon and the kiss, Cassie had been running late. She'd grabbed the sandwich bag with two blueberry muffins in it that Jill had prepared for her and run out the door with a, "Thank you! Have a good day!"

Jill had taken her time cleaning up the kitchen. She had actually juiced oranges that morning, wanting Mike to have something better than what could be bought at the store. She had put orange zest in the blueberry muffins, making them a whole new level of delicious. She'd looked at the clock. Five to eight. Usually Mike had come home by this time.

She had plucked all the remaining muffins out of the tin with a knife and arranged them on a plate. Then, with a little brush, she'd leisurely scrubbed the muffin tin before putting it in the dishwasher. She had washed the mixing bowl by hand. Five after eight. He still wasn't there. Jill had taken out the garbage, returned, and washed her hands. Ten after eight. And that's when it hit her that he might be avoiding her.

Maybe he regretted the kiss. Maybe he realized that he was in over his head, that he wasn't ready.

Jill had guzzled the orange juice she had prepared for him with so much care. She hadn't wanted him to see that she had gone to any trouble. Then, almost in a panic, she'd thrust the glass in the dishwasher and dashed out the door.

Today, though, she made it out with five minutes to spare. She still went out the back door instead of the front, just in case he was walking down the street.

She found the extra key that Lisa kept above a window in the back of the house and let herself in to use the computer. The house felt so empty and cold without Lisa in it. It enhanced Jill's sense that something was wrong.

The kitchen was clean, except for a shot glass by the sink and a used tissue. *Lisa wouldn't have left that,* Jill thought, and then remembered how Tom often said he was going next door to water Lisa's plants. They had to be Tom's. Oh, poor thing.

She turned on Lisa's computer and waited for what seemed like forever while it powered up. Didn't the machine know she was in a hurry? She had stayed in Sparkle three weeks too long. Now it was uncomfortable. Just thinking about Mike avoiding her made her cheeks burn. She could not get out of Sparkle fast enough.

All but two of the positions listed for Denver on Monster.com were for hospice and long-term care facility work. Jill supposed if she had to, she could do that. Death was a natural part of life. It wasn't the same as when babies died. The other two ads were for nursing in the air force and for an HMO looking for a nurse-practitioner. She wasn't a nurse-practitioner. Colorado Springs had a lot of home care positions available. That might be the way to go. Still, it would involve getting to know people and their families intimately and getting attached to them. It was unreasonable, but deep inside, she simply didn't want to work with patients who were going to die. She knew, of course, that ultimately everyone dies, but she wanted as much space between her and death as possible. She wanted to work in a clinic where she weighed people, took their temperature and blood pressure, and then left them alone in a room with a gown. That was all she wanted to deal with day after day. Nothing more. She decided she would wait another month before pursuing any long-term care or home-nursing positions.

She looked for positions in Durango, Aspen, Vail, Telluride, and Breckenridge, and the only thing that came up was an ad to sell Avon. That wasn't hopeful. Maybe Hans was right. Maybe Monster.com and the classifieds were not how hiring was done in small ski towns. Maybe to get a job she really wanted, it was time to hit the pavement.

Back at the Kennel, Tom and Hans were eating breakfast and getting ready for a day of window washing—their off-season job.

"You're late," Hans said. "Did you and Mike have some quality time this morning?"

Jill made a face. "I was on the computer at Lisa's, trying to figure out what I'm going to do when my divorce is final and I no longer receive a thousand dollars a month from my ex."

"You could wash windows with us," Tom said.

"Good to have options," Jill replied, and went back to her room to search through boxes for job-hunting and interview clothes. She took a few pieces out of the box and laid them on her bed. Nothing seemed quite right.

"Knock knock." She knew that voice. Mike. He stood in her doorway. "Tom and Hans were leaving as I was walking up the path. They said to just go on in. I hope that was okay."

"Sure," she said, confused.

"Nice mirror," he said, pointing to the ceiling.

"Yes, I'm very kinky," she said dryly.

Mike just looked up and nodded. "I haven't seen you in a while."

"Well, that first morning after our, um, date, you were late, so I figured maybe you needed a little space," Jill said as she folded clothes and put them back in the boxes.

"I was on a call. Rollover on the highway. We were out there for a while."

"Oh," Jill said, feeling foolish for making assumptions.

"Cassie's birthday is the sixteenth. She wants to canoe or kayak on the reservoir to the waterfall. Did she ask you to join us already? She told me she was going to invite you and Mauricio."

"She didn't mention it. Maybe she changed her mind," Jill replied.

"No, she didn't change her mind. She was probably just distracted by homework or whatever."

"Hm."

"Well, please save the date. Sunday the sixteenth. I know it would mean a lot to her if you were there."

"Okay," Jill said.

"Hey, last night we took Heather down to Denver. Do you

know Heather? She works for Dr. Westin at the sports medicine clinic. She's eight months pregnant and was just put on bed rest until she delivers. She told me that she's taking maternity leave after that, but that she and her husband are trying to figure out a way for her not to have to come back to work at all. So, today Dr. Westin doesn't have a nurse. FYI."

"Thanks for the tip," she said.

"So . . . are we okay?" he asked.

"Yeah, we're okay," she replied even though she still felt awkward.

He looked back up at the ceiling. "I think I discovered my new interest," he joked.

She laughed. "You can see why I'm ready for a new era of my life."

He smiled and nodded. "I'm so glad I got to see the infamous Kennel."

"If anyone saw you walk in, your reputation is ruined," Jill teased.

"Worth it," Mike replied, reaching for her hand and pulling her into him. He kissed her tenderly and said, "Well, as much as I'd like to develop my new interest and give you your unexpected reward right now, I'm going to forgo immediate gratification in hopes that you'll find your way to Dr. Westin's and secure a position that will keep you here in Sparkle."

Jill laughed.

He kissed her once more, pointed to the ceiling, and said, "We can explore this later." Then he left Jill to dig her old nursing shoes out of the back corner of her closet.

Jill clasped her résumé and copy of her nursing certificate as she walked up the little sidewalk to the old blue mining house that Dr. Westin's office was in. On the porch sat a bicycle, and in the waiting room sat a very hairy man in a knee brace. Jill assumed the bicycle belonged to the doctor. She picked up a copy of *Skiing* magazine and had a seat. She had enough time to read an article on Kicking Horse mountain resort and look at some of next year's gear. Finally, a very athletic-looking woman with a weathered face hobbled out on crutches. Behind her walked the doctor in a white lab coat. He wore glasses with thick, dark frames. His salt-and-pepper mustache matched his bushy hair. She thought his face looked kind.

He patted the lady on the shoulder and said, "See you in two weeks," then pointed at the man in the knee brace and said, "Dennis. Good to see you." Then he pointed at Jill and said, "I don't know you yet." He scrambled behind the counter to look at his appointment book. "Who are you?"

"I'm your new nurse?" she replied.

He smiled, glanced down at her nursing shoes, and then looked up at the ceiling and said, "Thank you," as if she were the answer to his prayers.

chapter thirty-five

. . .

MAY 16: NO SNOW REPORT AVAILABLE

Opening Day is October 31. Season passes available for purchase online.

Thanks for coming today." Mike held his paddle in the water for an extra second to rudder, keeping the canoe on course.

"Oh, it's my pleasure!" Jill, in the front, turned around and smiled. "I mean, how many eleven-year-olds want to do something this cool for their birthday?"

Cassie and Mauricio were ahead of them quite a ways in Mike and Kate's kayaks. Cassie was eager to get to the waterfall at the other end of the seven-mile lake.

"Well, last year's birthday was a pretty bad one. Kate was in a lot of pain and on a lot of morphine. I don't know how much she was with us, but we brought a cake into her room and Cassie blew out her candles there. After she blew them out, she started crying. It was awful. And this year, you know, it's the first birthday without her mom, and I think she was feeling really fragile about it."

Jill turned around to look at him. Amber was sleeping on a blanket in the middle, between them. "She hides her feelings pretty well sometimes, but I figured this had to be an uncomfortable day in those ways."

"You're really important to her. So, thanks."

"She's important to me, too," Jill said, and continued to paddle.

"Look. There's a redtail over there," he said. They paused to watch the hawk circle for a moment. "Well, should we catch up with them?"

Jill nodded and dug her paddle in.

Mike found himself staring at her hair, her neck and shoulders, her back, her hips. "What was your favorite birthday?" he asked.

"Oh, easy. When I was six, I woke up with a new bicycle in my room. Does it get any better than that?" she answered. Her heart ached a little when she thought of her parents, how much they really did love her, and of all the things they ever did right.

"I'd still love to wake up with a new bike in my room," Mike said.

"What about you?" she asked.

"When I turned twelve, my dad, uncle, and a couple guys from the station—my dad was a fireman, too—took some of my friends and me camping. They let us tell dirty jokes and swear as long as we promised not to breathe a word of it once we got home."

Jill laughed. "That's so manly!"

"Yeah, well, when you're twelve, you pretty much think that's what being a man is all about."

She laughed a little more.

"A lot of my birthdays were at the fire station because my dad was working, and that was always pretty cool. I mean, it seemed normal to me, but my friends were always stoked to be at the fire station. Dad would let us have target practice with the hose and try to knock over cones."

"Aw, that sounds fun!" she said.

"If you really think so, you can have your next birthday party at the fire station, too. I think the guys would like that. Bring your friends," he joked.

Jill laughed even more. "I think I've been living at the Kennel too long, because about fourteen rude jokes just popped into my mind," she said.

"Oh, it's all right," he said with a big smile. "We've heard all of them."

"What would be your dream birthday now?" Jill asked.

Mike was quiet, so Jill turned around and looked at him. His smile gave his answer away.

She exploded with laughter again. "I'm sorry," she said. "After living at the Kennel for six months now, I really should have known the answer to that."

"Men are not complicated," he said with a big smile and a shrug.

Later, when they reached the waterfall, they tied their boats together, and Jill carefully turned around so that her body was facing Mike. They sang "Happy Birthday" to Cassie in English and Spanish, and she blew out her candles.

They ate cake, taught Mauricio some new words, and asked him about Mexican birthday traditions. When they were done eating cake, they went a little closer to the waterfall, enough to feel some spray, enough to see rainbows above them everywhere. Amber sat up and tried to bite the mist, and Cassie laughed and then led the way back with Mauricio right beside her. It wasn't long before they were quite a ways out in front.

"So when's your birthday?" Jill asked Mike as they paddled.

"Early June," he answered with a big, hopeful smile.

She turned around and smiled back. "Hm," she said, and held his gaze a couple seconds too long. "I'll keep my eye out for a good birthday dream girl for you."

"Don't you think you should know what I'm looking for?" he asked.

"I thought you were not complicated."

He laughed. "She should be really kind, understanding—just beautiful inside and out. Of course, she needs to get along with Cassie really well and help her win a season's pass in the Dummy Downhill because it saves me money. She needs to have good luge and canoe skills, but doesn't need to be able to do both at the same time. Also, she needs medical experience so that she can understand the things I usually don't talk about with anyone. And something about her will just make my world okay—not because she tries, but just because that's the effect she has on me."

Her big smile turned into something tender as she looked back at him and then gingerly spun around in her seat. She kept her hands on the gunnels as she worked her way over the dog and toward him. He met her halfway for a kiss that he hoped Cassie wouldn't see.

And then they were quiet for a while as something new settled into them both, something like peace, something like knowing their place in the universe.

After they dropped Mauricio off and got home, Jill helped Mike unload the boats and carry them into the garage while Cassie took the leftover food into the house.

The moment they set down the canoe, he took her in his

arms and kissed her passionately. "I've been thinking about that all day," he murmured, and kissed her again, this time more tenderly. He opened his eyes and noticed that while Jill's were still closed, she was smiling. As he pulled back, her eyes opened, warm and affectionate—perhaps even loving, so green and clear and true. He couldn't help himself and kissed her once more.

He still had Cassie's birthday dinner to prepare. It took all his will to say, "Let's go inside before I get all caveman on you. I'll unload the kayaks later."

Jill started laughing.

"What?" he said as if he didn't know why she was laughing. "I think I deserve a medal for rallying the self-control it took to stop just now. I don't think I could do it two more times, and I don't want our first time to be on my garage floor."

Jill continued to laugh and shook her head. "No, that sounds awful."

He put his arm around her shoulders, and she leaned into him and rested her head on his chest as they walked toward the door. Then he let his hand slide to her low back and then back into his own pocket as she walked out before him.

At Timber Creek Campground in Rocky Mountain National Park, Tom set up a big white canvas wall tent, which was no small effort. He pumped up a double air mattress, put two egg-shell pads on top of it, and made the bed. He draped tulle from the wedding veil that he'd worn to the Dirtbag Ball over the bed from the top of the tent pole to make a partial canopy. He'd also prepared a special stick studded with nails from which to hang candle lanterns and suspended it from the ceiling of the tent. He brought in a cooler with champagne, berries, and chocolate, put it in the far corner near the bed, and placed two plastic champagne flutes on top. He stood back and nervously admired his efforts. It looked good.

He forced himself to take a few deep breaths, then looked at his watch and set off for the amphitheater, where Lisa would be giving a talk tonight on greenback trout, which were once thought to be extinct. He lingered nearby but didn't go into the area and sit down until after Lisa had started talking.

Truthfully, he didn't hear a word of Lisa's presentation. He tried to think of the words he would say later. He imagined the words she might say. He watched her talking in her park ranger uniform and imagined taking it off her. He imagined the sex they were going to have tonight. He fingered the ring in his pocket and imagined it on her hand. His breathing suddenly became nervous and jittery. It was forty minutes of pure torture.

At the end, Lisa asked, "Any questions?"

Should he raise his hand and say, *Yes, I have a question,* and then drop to his knee right there? Would that be romantic? Would that be awkward? *Should I?* he asked himself. *Should I do it now?* But he decided to stick with his original plan.

Lisa thanked everyone for coming, and the audience dispersed. As she was putting the pictures and charts from her presentation back into her canvas bag, an older gentleman approached to tell her fishing tales from his youth. Tom sat back down and wished him away, but he was going nowhere. Lisa caught Tom's eye and smiled. Eventually, the older man's wife dragged him away, and Tom approached Lisa.

Breathe, breathe, breathe, he told himself.

"What's wrong?" she asked him.

"Nothing's wrong," he said.

"I can tell something's wrong," she said.

He suppressed a laugh and shook his head.

"Why are you laughing?" she asked. "Why is that funny?"

He took her in his arms and kissed her. "Do you have everything?"

She looked around. "Yes."

He followed her to her car, where she dropped off her presentation materials and exchanged that bag for a little pack in which she had packed a few things for the night. Tom took it from her and threw it over his shoulder. Then he took her hand and led her to the tent.

"Wait right here a sec," he said to her.

He went inside, lit the candles, and opened the cooler. Then he went back to where Lisa waited, took her hand, and led her inside.

About seven different wisecracks crossed her mind, but miraculously, she kept them to herself.

He took her hands and began, "Lisa, you're my best friend. You make me laugh. You make me grow. You make me want to be a better person. I love being with you. When I'm not with you, I wish I was." And here Tom forgot the rest of what he had planned to say and just started spilling his heart. "I want to wake up with you every morning, wrestle a little, and then make you oatmeal. I want to chop your wood for you and shovel your sidewalk and scrub your back. I want to make your life easier. I want to massage your legs when they're sore from too much skiing. And at the end of every day, I want to crawl back in bed with you, and fall asleep with my arms around you. I love you so much and want to love you just as much as you'll let me."

He dropped to his knee, held out the ring, looked up at Lisa, and waited.

She sat on his knee, kissed him, and whispered in his ear, "Yes."

chapter thirty-six

. . .

JUNE 1:NO SNOW REPORT AVAILABLE

Opening Day is October 31. Season passes available for purchase online.

Wes Heusser had earned his money. When all was said and done, the judge ruled all assets be liquidated and split 60–40 in favor of Jill. In addition, she was entitled to five years of spousal support.

As Jill was walking out of the courtroom, David caught up to her.

"Jill," he said.

She turned around.

"Jill, I just want to say I'm so sorry. I'm so sorry for all the pain. All of it."

She looked at him and caught a glimpse of the man she had once married. "Thanks."

"I hope one day we can have a cup of coffee and catch up and be friends," he said.

She didn't know what to think of that, so she shrugged.

He handed her an envelope. "Maybe read this later."

"Okay."

"I can't believe this might be the last time I ever see you," he said.

She paused and studied him. *Yes, it might,* she realized.

"Well, good-bye, then, Jill. I wish nothing but the best for you."

"Good-bye, David. It's been significant." It was all she could think of to say.

He didn't try to hug her or kiss her on the cheek, and for that she was grateful. He didn't take her hand and squeeze it the way people do after someone dies. She was grateful for that, too. She followed him out of the courthouse, and this time no woman picked him up. This time, he got into his own BMW alone and drove away.

She caught a taxi back to the airport. In the backseat, she opened his envelope and read his card.

Dear Jill,

I want to thank you for all the good times, for marrying me in the first place, for the Bahamas and Mexico, for the ways you made holidays special, for the ways you made me feel loved. I want to apologize for failing you. I think I will live with that regret for the rest of my life. I hope you can find it in your heart to forgive me one day. I guess I just wasn't strong enough to weather our loss. I love you, Jill, and I always will.

Love, David

She wondered whether his mistress had dumped him, but she appreciated his gesture nonetheless.

On her flight back to Denver, she thought about her options. She could buy her own little home now. She could.

Her mind drifted back to David, imagining what it might be like to have a cup of coffee with him one day. And it wasn't that she didn't forgive him. It wasn't even that she had strong negative feelings about it anymore. It was more that she would rather spend that time having a cup of coffee with Mike.

She thought about Mike's dimples and the sparkle in his eyes and realized she couldn't wait to see him again.

She hadn't expected to feel any more unburdening, but she did feel it—the past lifting off her chest, off her shoulders, off her heart. She felt the next chapter in her life beginning and felt ready for whatever it might hold.

chapter thirty-seven

• • •

JUNE 3: NO SNOW REPORT AVAILABLE

Mike poured some blueberry batter onto the waffle iron. "Hey, there's something I want to talk to you about," he said to Cassie.

"Yeah?" she asked. She wondered if she was in trouble.

"Yeah," Mike said, and turned to look at her. He wasn't sure how to begin, so he took a big breath and then just said it. "I'm falling in love with Jill."

"I kind of thought so," Cassie said.

"It's confusing for me because I loved your mother and I still do, and sometimes that makes me feel like what I'm feeling is wrong. I mean, I know she would want me to have a good life . . . a good life with love in it."

"She wrote about that."

"What did she say?" he asked.

"She said to keep living."

"Your mom was incredible. She was strong and beautiful and smart and no one could ever replace her. I will love her always." He paused. "And now Jill is in our lives and she is a gift, too. She's kind and funny and it feels good to be around her. I think we're happier when she's around."

Cassie thought for a moment and then nodded.

"And she loves you." He turned back to the waffle iron for a moment and put the waffle on Cassie's plate. Then he poured a little more batter onto the griddle. "It's kind of awkward, because I want to date her but I also know that you two have a special relationship and I don't want you to feel like I'm taking her away from you. I wouldn't be. And I don't want you to feel like I'm betraying your mother, either. Or like I'm going to forget about her, because I couldn't. I'll always love her."

"Yeah, I know," Cassie said.

"We've been through a lot of changes this year and I didn't really want any more of them. But then Jill showed up and I don't want her to leave us or for some other guy to get her. She belongs with us."

"Well then, I think you should go get her," Cassie said.

Mike smiled. "Thanks."

Jill put extra clothes, dog food, a toothbrush, water, oatmeal, and some ramen into her backpack, and then she and Amber hiked all the way up to Uncle Howard's place. He was still in Argentina.

It took half the day to get there, and once she did, she spent the other half reading *Snowboarding to Nirvana*. As the sun began to set, she noticed someone walking to the summit, and as he neared, she realized it was Mike.

"It's my birthday," he said. "I thought you'd be interested to know."

"Oh, is it?" Jill replied.

"I wanted to spend it on a mountaintop with you. Is that okay? Hans said you were up here."

"It's more than okay," Jill said, jumping into his arms. "Happy birthday. Can I offer you anything?"

A mischievous smile crossed Mike's face before he said, "Definitely," and kissed her. "But I'm going to need to eat first." He smiled as if he were joking, but she suspected he was not. "I brought some things to eat and drink."

Jill smiled. "What did you bring?"

Mike unpacked a bottle of Syrah, his camp stove, and a Tupperware container full of tortellini with marinara sauce that just needed to be heated up. "Cassie made it, so you know it's good," he said.

"Mm!" Jill replied.

Then he pulled out a chocolate torte.

"Oh . . ." she sighed.

He stuck a birthday candle into the torte. "So I can wish," he said, and gave her a desirous look.

She blushed.

He opened the wine and passed the bottle to Jill. Then he poured the pasta into the pan, fired up his stove, and put the food on.

"This smells so much better than the ramen I was going to eat tonight," Jill said, grinning.

"Ramen is nasty," Mike agreed. He stirred the pasta for a few minutes and then handed Jill a fork. They ate it right out of the pan, their faces close. From time to time, the magnetism was too much, and they kissed between bites.

"Cassie is a culinary genius," Jill said.

"Yeah, I'm so lucky."

"Who's with her now?"

"Barb," he said. "Pete's on duty. Barb knew it was my birthday and volunteered."

"That's sweet," Jill said.

"That's Barb."

She set down her fork and reached for the wine.

Mike set down his fork, too, so Jill passed him the bottle. He took a few drinks and then pretended to yawn and dropped his arm behind Jill.

She turned to him and laughed.

"What?" he asked innocently.

She managed to put on a straight face to play along.

He passed the bottle back to her. "Here," he said. "Drink some more."

"Candy is dandy, but liquor is quicker?"

He laughed. "Oh, I see your plan now," he said.

She took a generous drink and handed the bottle back to him. They passed it back and forth while watching the sun drop behind endless peaks until at last they were left sitting in the dark.

He set the stove on the ground and put the dirty pan and forks in a plastic bag to wash later. Then he climbed up on the picnic table and lay on his back to look at the stars.

"Join me," he said.

Jill lay down next to him. He reached for her hand and laced his fingers in hers. He gently ran his thumb back and forth across her palm. She breathed in his smell—warm, spicy, and a little salty from his sweaty hike up. She found it insanely sexy. She fought her sense of urgency, though, aware that Mike might be having conflicting feelings about being with someone other than Kate. That was big. She wanted to let him set the pace.

"It's been a long time since I just stared at stars," he said.

"There are so many tonight," Jill said. "They're almost blinding."

After a long pause, Mike said, "This is a really nice moment."

"I was wondering what you were thinking," she said.

"Oh, that's not what I was thinking. I was wondering when you were going to crawl on top of me and kiss me."

Jill laughed. "Oh, I was very close. That thing you were doing to my hand was totally working."

"You liked that, huh?" he asked.

"Mm," she said with a big smile and a nervous giggle.

Mike rolled over on his side and kissed her for a long while. She caressed the nape of his neck. He paused and gently touched her face. "So, I can hike back down tonight, or I can stay with you."

"You're welcome to stay with me," she said.

He wrapped his arm around her, and they looked at the stars a little longer, taking time to get used to lying next to each other, taking time to absorb what was happening. And when the temperature dropped to the point where Jill began to get chilly, she sat up, took his hand, and led him inside.

Cassie looked at her notes and transcribed to the best of her memory the things Coach Ernie had shared with her over the winter.

My mother was the fastest ski racer here in Sparkle from 1988 to 1991. Racing against her challenged other people to be their best. She had good sportsmanship when she won. The people who raced against her were shooting for silver. Coach Ernie said she had what it took to be an Olympic champion.

She put her own memory book away and brought out the book her mother had written for her. She randomly opened a page near the end and read:

God, wherever you are and whatever you are, this prayer is for my family. When I go, there will be a hole left behind in their lives. When it's time, and a good person comes along, help my family welcome her. If Mike never loved again, I would think it was because being married to me had been such a horrible experience. It would be a tribute to me if he wanted more of what we had. Similarly, I hope Cassie's experience with me as a mother made her more loving to all women and able to see maternal energy in all the places it's found—teachers, neighbors, friends . . . all the kind people we come in contact with every day. May there be enough maternal energy floating around this world to fill that hole until the right person completes this family again. And when that person comes along, may she see all the beauty in my Cassie that I do. And may she see that Mike's heart is bigger than the sky and treat it like the precious thing it is. May she have strengths that were my weaknesses. I am humble enough to know I wasn't perfect. No one is. But maybe this new woman and I together will have created something more whole than one person ever could have. My prayer is that my family doesn't shut down, but that they go on and continue to love. I don't want them to be broken. I want them to be whole. I don't want them to be lonely. I want them to be loved. So please, God, whatever you are, please send them a deeply kind and deeply loving person when it's time, and please let them embrace her.

Cassie shut the book, picked up the heart-shaped rock Jill had found, and held both to her heart.